The Legend of the Lightscale

Book Two of The Scale Seekers

By A.R. Cook

Also from Author A.R. Cook

The Scholar and the Sphinx Series

The Scholar, the Sphinx and the Shades of Nyx
The Scholar, the Sphinx and the Fang of Fenrir
The Scholar, the Sphinx and the Threads of Fate

The Scale Seekers Series

The Secrets of the Moonstone Heir
The Legend of the Lightscale

Short Stories

"The Lady in the Moon & her Lantern" in *Willow Weep No More*
"The Man Who Called Death's Wind" in *Shadows of the Oak*
"The Saintly Stew" in *The Kress Project*
"Demons in the Pages" and "The Last Quest of the Drunken
Wizard" in *Chronicles of Mirstone*

Cover Artwork by Trisha Stadel
www.miraculux.de

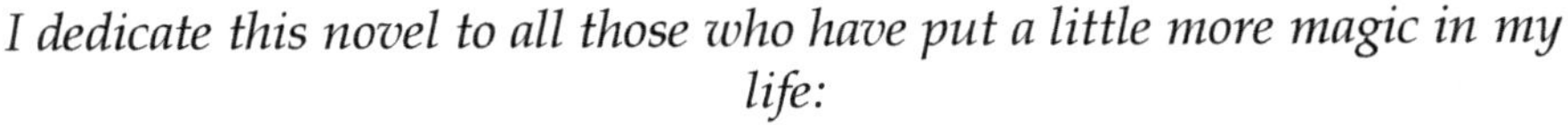

I dedicate this novel to all those who have put a little more magic in my life:
my husband David, my family, my friends, and the readers who truly bring stories to life.

Ah, so you've returned. Or are you new? I can never remember, when there are so many pressing matters to attend to, like stirring up a little fun...

I'm Gothart Grandwitt, of the infamous House of Grandwitts. A pleasure for you to meet me, I'm sure. I see that curious look on your face, so let's acknowledge the goat in the room. Yes, I'm a goat. As to why a goat is six feet tall, walking on two legs and wearing a suit, that's quite a magnificent story, nearly as magnificent as I. But it's also a secret.

That's not what drew you here, though, is it? No, you are more interested in my dear friend, Desert Rain. Poor girl, sequestered away in the desert for all those years, to suddenly be responsible for restoring lost memories to a Distortionist, and unleashing who-knows-what twisted horrors on all of Luuva Gros. That's quite a turn for a hermit – quiet, lonely serenity, to unbridled chaos where everyone wants your head.

Oh, wait, I'm supposed to present this in song, aren't I? That's how these things typically begin, with a bard singing a soul-stirring melody about heroes and history and all that nonsense. Let's see then, I know I have a mandolin here somewhere... ahem...

The Sages, great dragons,
Knew that each life one day passes,
So they bestowed their Ancient Magic
To twelve lads and lasses

To maintain the balance in the land,
And to protect us from the Wretched siege,
And the "dragon blessed," they are called,
The council of the Hijn.

But there was one Hijn who hid away,
Too scared to reveal her powers,
Deep in the sands of the desert lands
She idled away the hours
Skin golden as the sun, ears long as the day,
One eye brown, one green, laced with pain,
And a moonstone mark shine from her face
The curse of Desert Ra-a-a-a-a-a-a-a-a-a-ain.

Excuse me. I have a slight vowel elongation habit with my "a's" when I sing. Stop snickering.

Then one day, into her solitude,
There came a Wretched of terrifying fra-a-a-a-ame
Upon her doorstep he did lie, half-dead,
Touched with compassion was Desert Ra-a-a-…hmm. Rain.

Now don't look at me like that. Yes, I led Katawa to her front door, left him there unconscious and memory-stripped for her to deal with, but it's just business. One must make a living, you know. The Darkscale Clan pays handsomely to be rid of their…pests. And a Distortionist is no laughing matter.
But I digress. Where was I?

When his memories returned to him,
The Wretched gave a horrid shriek
Remembering the injustice done to him,

I suppose it doesn't help matters that Katawa kidnapped the Hijn council. Talk about adding insult to injury – or death, in Skyhan's case. All we have now is Desert Rain, and the tree-lover. Leave the future of all Luuva Gros in the hands of a Hijn that won't use her magic, and another Hijn who grows flowers. There's a comforting thought.

It would have really helped for her to have Skyhan's sword Silverheart, before he, you know, blew up. Now that was a sight! And you should have seen the look on Desert Rain's face, watching as the man she's adored for years just vanishes in a blinding blaze right in front of her…

Oooh, I really shouldn't laugh at that. But if you can't laugh, then you'd cry, and what good is that?

Drat. My mandolin string broke. And I know how much you were enjoying that.

Dez must be dreadfully bored with her current company. I may just have to pay her a visit…

CHAPTER ONE
A Demon Storm Brewing

Flying upon the back of a Roc with the merciless rain thrumming over her shivering body, it took all the will Desert Rain had to keep from getting air sick. She tried to turn her mind to other things, but all she could think about were what troubles were ahead of her. She opted to deal with the present problem of controlling the queasiness of her stomach. She tugged her blanket tighter around herself, although it did little to keep her dry or warm. The rain would only continue the closer they came to the rainforest Flyr Mi Oraellyn, which in the Mutual Language meant the Forest Overlooking the Sea. Wiping the rain from her forehead and eyes, she glanced around at her fellow passengers to see how they were faring.

Mac Zarr was rather at ease, not at all bothered by the altitude despite being a person more comfortable in earthen surroundings — although if he were in his true reptilian form instead of his shifted human guise, he may have not been so relaxed. Even as the rain soaked his ruddy red hair, he nestled himself into his blanket and the Roc's back feathers, while he curled his long red tail to shelter his face. The Quetzalin Chiriku constantly fidgeted, pecked absentmindedly at her blue feathers with her blunt beak, sighed, and moaned in boredom. Unlike those of pure Quetzalin blood, her traces of humanity were evident in her slouched posture and her toned arms crossed over her chest. A warhammer was strapped to her back, although it was of lighter make than the typical sort, crafted for a female warrior. Clova Flor was unusually quiet, being a verbally abundant Hijn by nature, and she glanced back over her shoulder occasionally to check on the others of their party. Her emerald-green hair, normally done up in a styled nest atop her head, blew freely in the wind. She had to keep tucking tresses behind her ears, which tapered to a soft point, a feature of her elven heritage. A deep green moss, Ahshibana, trailed across her skin in swirls and patterns, rendering her skin a pale green to match.

Night washed over Luuva Gros in a film of cool hues, accompanied by an even cooler wind and the easing of the hammering rain. The silver smile of the moon *la Ternaut* peeked out between the retreating clouds. Desert Rain looked away from it. What had once given her courage now reminded her of her weaknesses.

The Roc, Gust, glided along steadily, its wings slicing through the wind. It could fly in its sleep, using the air currents to keep it aloft, but the flight and cold were taking a toll on the others. Clova beckoned it to find a spot to land. They had been flying over mountain chain for days, but now it had become substantially thinner, and lush greenery decorated the land below. This was the overlap, where the Azokind Mountains and the Forest Overlooking the Sea collided. Gust gently glided downwards, scanning for a suitable landing spot, and selected a clearing near the foot of the mountains. Great trees encircled the clearing, and the earth was cushioned by tall wild grasses. Clova was clearly more comfortable in these green surroundings than in the stark mountains. Her skin, which had been fairly pale a few days ago, was already returning to its healthy jade tone.

It did not take very long to set up a modest camp. They didn't have many supplies – four passengers tested the limits of what Gust was able to carry. All they had were waterskins, travel pouches with tinderboxes, stale herb-cakes and basic pocket tools, and the blankets that they had picked up from a small trading post they had passed by shortly after leaving Vaes Galahar. They managed to get a small campfire going, with everyone gathering any bits of wood they could find, and Chiriku sparked a decent flame with the flint from her tinderbox. Clova sent Gust to search for food, and in a short time the bird returned with a beak full of berries, wild beans and mushrooms to complement their herb-cake rations. It then flew off to hunt for its own meal.

Mac's nose wrinkled at the vegetation before him. He scratched the fluffy mop of hair on his head. "More brush sc-c-cruff. That bird doesn't-tkk know how to hunt meat-tkk?" he asked.

The Quetzalin smirked. "I'll go hunt something. I haven't had a chance to use my hammer in a while."

Clova made a sharp frown. "If you wish to find sustenance through slaughter, you may do so on your own." She turned up her nose, as she did by habit when it came to the topic of hunting animals. Chiriku did the same, although she turned up her beak at almost anything.

Mac could not help but grin a little. *Bird girl knows the quickest way to start an argument,* he thought. But Chiriku did not go off to hunt, weariness affecting all of her muscles. She nibbled on an herb-cake, silently grousing. Mac shoved the food into his mouth so quickly that he nearly choked. Meat or no meat, he would make do.

Desert Rain, meanwhile, never looked more miserable in her life. She sat near the fire, rubbing her arms and long, spindly fingers for warmth. Her ears, fringed around the edges and hanging down with rabbit-like floppiness to her shoulders, shivered in the chilly air. Goosebumps blossomed on her golden-ochre hued skin, and she had to wrap the ponytail of her long, dark hair around her neck as a mock scarf. Nights in her desert home were cold sometimes, but she would have been snug inside her underground home with a cup of warm cactus milk or tea. The chill that gripped her now lingered, and even the campfire could not chase it away.

Clova had become disturbingly quiet, staring blankly at the sky. Desert Rain had never seen her so pensive, although it was no wonder why.

"Do you think Kidran and Woasim have found out what happened yet?" Desert Rain inquired after a time.

Clova Flor shook her head. "I doubt that they've arrived at Vaes Galahar, but both can hear the voices of the winds. They already may have felt the dark vibrations of that demon's storm. I can't say if they'll come to meet us, or make their own plans. They can be so unpredictable. I hope they come to us." She paused, glancing over at Desert Rain. "You should eat something, Dezzy. You haven't had anything since breakfast this morning."

Desert Rain did not feel hungry. Most of this forest food was too sweet for her tastes, being so much richer in flavor from the food she scrounged up in the desert. She went to put a few mushrooms in her pocket, but her fingers brushed against another item already in there. She felt the velvety texture of the black pouch, the one that the cloaked thief in Syphurius had dropped during the battle between Katawa and…Desert Rain swallowed the pain of Sir Skyhan's demise and let it settle like a glacier in her stomach. She drew out the pouch, holding it in both hands. She wanted to find that thief, to get back at whoever had the audacity to steal the legendary sword of the Swordmaster. That seemed to be a task she could handle better than the one she was on now, although she had as much an idea about where to find the thief as where to find Katawa.

"What've you got there, Donkey Ears?" Chiriku chimed in.

Desert Rain jerked her head up, startled by Chiriku's voice. "Oh, this…it's…something that was left behind."

"I remember that-tkk," Mac said. "That fell off that no-good crook-kk that gave us the slip in Syphurius-ssck. That was right before you showed up, Miss-ssck Clova."

"A crook? Did he steal something from you?" Clova scooted closer to Desert Rain. "Is there anything in that pouch that would tell us who or what it belongs to?"

It had not occurred to Desert Rain to examine the pouch before, as she had been preoccupied until now. She loosened the leather string on the pouch and peeked inside. She reached in and pulled out a wind-up toy that sat comfortable in the palm of her hand. A large gold key was in the toy's back. The toy was the shape of a white goat.

"Funny looking thing," Mac interjected. "What's-ssck that little note on it-tkk say?"

Tied to the key was a paper note. Desert Rain held it before the fire light, making out the phrase, "Wind me up." After a moment's deliberation, she slowly turned the key in the toy's back. The toy jerked to life, and twitched about in a sort of dance in the palm of her hand. Gradually, the toy's movements became more fluid, until it barely seemed mechanical at all. Suddenly, it stopped dead. Everyone leaned in, staring expectantly at the little toy goat. With no warning, the toy sprang out of Desert Rain's hand and flew high into the air. It seemed to vanish for a second, but then they saw it falling towards them, except now it had inflated in size. When the toy came back down to the earth and landed lightly on its feet, it was no longer a toy. It was the tall, lanky form of Gothart Grandwitt.

"Ta da-a-achoo!" Gothart sneezed in the middle of his trumpeting. "I was wondering when you were going to look in the bag. It was rather dusty in there."

Mac, Chiriku, and Clova stared at Gothart, jaws gaped open. Desert Rain stood up, marched right over to him and got right in his face. "I should pop off your horns and knock you in the head with them!"

"Hello to you, too," the goat replied. "Is this always how you begin with old friends?"

"We are not friends," Desert Rain retorted. "This whole mess is your fault!"

"Really? How do you figure that?"

Desert Rain stared at him unbelievingly, finding it impudent that he should even ask that question. "You're the one that stole Katawa's memories! You left him in my house. And would you kindly tell me how Katawa's memories happened to end up in the memory shop? What happened, your client went back on his deal and you wanted to get a few coins for all your trouble?"

Gothart tapped a finger on his chin, a ponderous look on his face. "And somehow, by combining all those accusations, that makes me responsible for the fact that your Wretched went on a rampage?"

Desert Rain paused. She did not need anyone besides herself to heap blame on her. "If you're that same thief from Syphurius, you need to return what you stole from me." She held the pouch up to him. "Where is Silverheart? Is it in here?"

"Why don't you reach in and find out?" he asked in a daring tone.

"Oh, no. I'm not falling for any more tricks or surprises. If I reach in, I'll probably pull out a snake or something."

"If that's what you'd expect to pull out, you probably would then." He took the pouch from her hand, turned it inside out to expose it as empty. Returning the pouch right side out, he slipped in his hand in a presentational manner, like a party magician, and began to feel about inside. He reached in farther, and farther, until the pouch was up above his elbow. He proceeded to extract a series of random objects from the bag: colored handkerchiefs, silverware, juggling balls, a mandolin with a broken string, extra pairs of white gloves, bells, horse shoes, a broom, a vase, boots (none of which matched), and he would have continued to pull more articles out but Chiriku quickly tired of the magic show.

"Cut it out already!" she cawed. "Who's this rubbish-eater anyway? Between this guy and Donkey Ears, I feel like I'm on a farm."

"I don't-tkk suppose you have a chunk-kk of beef in that bag," Mac said, more as a thought to himself than as a question to Gothart.

"I don't know what's going on here, but the last thing we need is starting another spat," Clova said, directing the last part of her statement towards Chiriku. She turned with her classic smile to

Gothart. "Now then, Mister…?"

"Gothart Grandwitt, of the infamous House of Grandwitts." Gothart bowed deeply towards Clova.

"Mister Grandwitt." Clova nodded her head towards him. "From your sleight-of-hand display, I take it you are some sort of spellcaster?"

"He's a Trickster," Desert Rain corrected her. "And even less trustworthy than other Tricksters, I can assure you of that."

"Now be nice," Gothart chided teasingly. He suddenly realized he was chewing on the drawstring of the pouch, so he spat it out and tossed the bag back to Desert Rain. "Besides, how many Tricksters do you know, honestly? How can you claim I'm less trustworthy if you haven't met any others to make a comparison?"

"That's not the point, and I really don't want anything more to do with you. Go find someone else's life to ruin." Desert Rain walked to the opposite side of the campfire.

"Well, if I'm going to be treated so rudely," Gothart said, "Then I won't give you the help I was willing to offer."

Desert Rain rolled her eyes. Clova, however, continued her attempts to be cordial. "Mister Grandwitt, did Dezzy say something about you were able to steal that demon's memories?"

Gothart beamed. "Something not many can claim to do."

"I don't suppose you could do that again, with this…Katawa, I believe he's called? You know, make him forget what he's doing so we could stop him?"

Gothart sighed, putting his hands behind his head. "I doubt he'd let me come within twenty yards of him ever again without detaching my head from my shoulders. Besides, stealing the same person's memories twice would be ridiculously redundant. I really wouldn't want to waste my time on something I've already done before. This is so much more interesting, wouldn't you say?"

Clova's forehead wrinkled. "Interesting?"

Gothart's eyes brightened with excitement. "Why, yes! I mean, Luuva Gros was so dull before all this. Okay, yes, there are the occasional scraps between the Knights of Luuva and the Wretched, but we all know how those turn out. Frankly, the monotony was getting to me. And then, here comes along an opportunity to stir things up. My reputation's must be more wide-spread than I thought, for the Darkscale hire *me,* me of all people, to dispose of the Distortionist! He's so feared that even his own clan wants to eliminate him. I knew right away that this was someone who could liven things up a bit. This was an excellent challenge, something I haven't had in a long time."

Desert Rain turned to stare at him. Her voice was a harsh, thin whisper. "You think this is some kind of game?"

Gothart smiled with a shrug. "I could never be quite sure how it would play out, but not knowing is half the fun, isn't it?"

Desert Rain stormed over to him. "And now Katawa is raising chaos because you think it's funny?!"

A wry grin peeked out from the corner of Gothart's lips. "You see this as disruptive, but it's less stressful to see it as entertaining."

Desert Rain dealt a slap across Gothart's nose. The Trickster blinked as her in surprise, and then smirked. "Now *that* was funny," he laughed.

Desert Rain heaved a growl of exasperation. Clova took her by the shoulders and pulled her away gently, whispering delicate words of calming. The Forest Hijn turned back to Gothart. "It seems to me that since you had a hand in this catastrophe, it's fair that you should help us to right your wrong."

"Let me take a swing at him," Chiriku offered, cracking her knuckles. "I'll make sure he doesn't find it funny."

Mac plucked a small feather from the top of Chiriku's head. She instantly dropped her fists and spat a furious caw at the lizard. He chuckled, and turned to Gothart. "Ladies-ssck…never as dainty as you would think-kk, right?"

Gothart wrinkled his nose at Mac, scanning him with a critical eye. Mac did not let this sort of scrutiny faze him. He was used to it; the Lejenous class got it all the time outside the Bayou. "So, Mister…what-ever-your-name-is-ssck, I reckon that you let the cat-tkk — or should I say, the goat-tkk — out of the bag for a reason, other than to grace-ssck us all with your presence, and enlighten us-ssck to what a morbid individual you are."

Gothart gave the lizard a smug grin. "I was thinking of bestowing a peace offering on Dezzy — I like that, 'Dezzy' — but I have the feeling she's not in the mood to accept it."

"I don't want anything from you," Desert Rain said.

Gothart folded his ears down and stuck out his lower lip in a sad puppy-face expression. "Would it help to say I'm sorry?" he asked in a pitiful tone.

Everyone glowered at him.

"You're right. I don't really mean that anyway," he admitted. "Well, I'm losing beauty sleep as we speak, and so are all of you, who desperately need it more than I do. It's been a lovely chat. Let's do it again sometime when you're not quite so hostile." With that, Gothart Grandwitt poofed into a cloud of white smoke and glittering gold flecks, which hung in the air for a moment before being sucked into the black pouch like an inhaled breath. The random items Gothart had pulled from the pouch had also, inexplicably, vanished. Desert Rain tugged at the drawstring on the pouch, but the bag refused to open.

"Blast you, Gothart!" she screamed at the bag.

Chiriku came over and snatched the pouch from Desert Rain's hand. She tossed it into the campfire without a pause of consideration. Desert Rain made a slight gasp and quickly retrieved the pouch from the fire, searing her fingertips in the process. Oddly enough—or maybe not so oddly, being Gothart's bag—the pouch had not burned at all, although the tip of the drawstring flickered with a tiny flame. Desert Rain pinched the flame out between her already hot fingertips. "What in Luuva did you do that for?" she snapped at Chiriku.

"That obnoxious goat deserves to get his butt fried!" the Quetzalin retorted. "Why don't you ditch that stupid bag?"

Desert Rain was quiet for a minute. She tucked the pouch into her pocket. "I may not like him, but we might need him. He was able to subdue Katawa, after all."

Chiriku put her hammer back in its sheath, and she threw her hands up in the air. "This is why your life is such a wreck, you know that? You're too nice to everybody. You make excuses to justify letting idiots walk all over you. I don't get how people like you survive in this world."

"We all can't-tkk be eye-peckers like you, Chi," Mac noted. He settled down in a patch of grass by the fire, hands folded under his head. His scaled tail flicked back and forth. "Now if you all don't-tkk mind, I'm ready to settle down for the night-tkk. I'm exhausted."

"You're right," Clova agreed. "We can continue to talk about these matters tomorrow."

Chiriku snorted softly, a weary grimace on her beak. She didn't argue, as she staked out a place a little way off from the group and curled up for a deep sleep.

"Should someone stay awake to keep watch?" Desert Rain suggested. Not having wandered far from the desert for quite some time, she had no idea how safe a place the rainforest was. Images of wolves and wild cats and rogue Wretched prowled in her mind.

"Gust will return soon and keep an eye on things," Clova said. "Rocs can go for days without sleep and still keep up plenty of energy. I'll stay awake until he gets back."

Desert Rain gave Clova a tired smile. A yawn rolled out of her, every physical and mental thing about her being worn out. She lied back on the grass, pulling her blanket up to her shoulders, and sighed as sleep began its ritual of clouding her mind with the liquor of bliss.

Yet even in that intoxicating fall into slumber, there was a pinprick of anxiety in her heart, as if some far-off voice was shrieking to her just out of ear's reach, yet the terror carried like a white-hot arrow over the vast distance.

***

Something about this storm doesn't feel right, thought Dormilir. *Not right at all.*

Storms birthed from the Malaise Cloud that hung over the Inbetween found their way to the Tower of Thordayne sometimes. As Dormilir Drakewing sniffed the air at his shop window, he sighed, noting that the rain didn't have the acidic smell of Malaise Cloud residue. Yet this storm bore the same ill-will as any of the more poisonous downpours that brought the touch of decay.

That was the problem of situating a guard tower so close to

the Inbetween – aside from those Wretched they were ordered to keep at bay. Thordayne's Knights of Luuva were vital to guarding this stretch of land, otherwise the Bloodburn and Darkscale clans could beat a direct war-path to Syphurius, the center of trade among all the Noble Races. That would be like planting a dagger straight into the heart of the Noble Cities.

Dormilir shook his scraggly black hair, rubbing his forehead near his right horn. Curiosity was rarely a bedfellow of his, yet the murmurs circulating through Thordayne in the past few days had put him on edge. All he could gather – from what some of the younger knights had gossiped within earshot – was that the tower had received a dispatch a few days ago by hawk. Everyone had been ordered to be on high alert, particularly from anything coming from the south, where Syphurius lay. That was unusual, since most of the threats to the tower were from the north, three or four leagues from the border of the Inbetween.

It was even more unusual for a knight to go into hysterics. The day before, when he took a break from smithing, Dormilir had ducked into the mess hall for a quick drink. He spotted two knights, a tawny Falcolin fledgling that must have recently been promoted from squire, and the other a more seasoned human warrior, sitting nearby. The older knight was quietly consoling the other, who appeared so shaken, he might as well have seen a Bloodburn quake-raiser face to face. They kept their voices low, but Dormilir heard the Falcolin say, "But how? The Swordmaster? If he's really…what chance do we have if even *he* fell to that Wretched?"

Those words, Dormilir could scarcely believe. Swordmaster Skyhan was known to defeat whole armies of Bloodburn single-handedly, and yet one Wretched had taken him down? The

Falcolin boy must have misunderstood the facts, or maybe the dispatch had been misleading. He had scratched his mass of ebony beard in thought, and simply returned to his duties.

The thing was, it wasn't Dormilir's concern, since he was merely the tower's blacksmith. Also, being a Stonebreaker dwarf made him reclusive by nature, and he spoke little to the humans and Falcolin stationed there outside of dealing with their armor and weapon needs. Stonebreakers nearly never left the mountain city of Vaes Galahar, but Dormilir had been recruited years ago by the Knights of Luuva for his exceptional smithing skills, and they paid more than well. One had to go where the jobs, and money, took them.

What was his primary concern, at that moment, was the sudden appearance of a stranger standing at the door of his shop.

Dormilir froze in mid-walk when he noticed the shadow standing in the doorway. Normally, anyone living at Thordayne would just let themselves in, not hover at the door, and the Stonebreaker could sense this was someone with which he wasn't familiar. It must be some wandering traveler that the gate patrol allowed in; it was common in Thordayne for lost travelers to be let in for a night's stay, and they were normally gone by morning. Although one had to be careful about people traveling this close to the Inbetween – they could either be lost, or dangerous.

"Sorry, I'm closing up shop for the night," Dormilir said gruffly.

Even though the man was masked by the night's shadows, the dwarf could see a crooked grin on his face. "That's all right," the stranger said with a silky, too-inviting tone. "This won't take long."

Dormilir cocked an eyebrow, and pinched his lips together

as the man entered his shop. The dwarf's breath stuck in his throat as six more figures trailed in, and Dormilir didn't need introductions to know who those six were. He could instantly make out the bulky earthen form of Rukna the Mountain Hijn, a dragon-blessed who he had met before, and judging from the clothing and unique features of the others, the rest were all Hijn as well. Half of the Hijn council was standing in his shop, which made Dormilir wonder what in Luuva this stranger was doing speaking on their behalf.

"It's an honor," Dormilir said, bowing his head towards the six Hijn.

"I'm sure it is," the stranger said curtly. He was an odd-looking fellow, with skin tinted a light amethyst and steel-blue hair slicked and tied back in a pony tail. His ears were long and tapered at the ends to points, but unlike elven ears that pointed upwards, his arced down towards his shoulders. His outfit was as equally unusual, burgundy and violet but of a style and cut unlike anything Dormilir had seen. It looked misshapen, like a deranged seamstress had been possessed by abstract visions. But it was easy to overlook all of that, once Dormilir locked eyes with the man – *by Earthbelly's jaws!* Those eyes were yellow topazes, glistening with an alluring wile.

"What would you have of me?" the Stonebreaker asked, his eyes darting between the stranger and the six Hijn. Uneasiness seeped into his bones, as the Hijn made no greeting, no words at all. They barely even moved. They looked transfixed, but not by horror or awe. Perhaps it was the shadows being cast by his hanging lanterns, but the Hijn appeared to have some strange dark stains around their eye sockets and mouths.

"My servant informed me of this place," the stranger

replied, gesturing flippantly towards Rukna. He slowly paced around the shop, eying the various products of Dormilir's work. "I came to see if you have some parts to spare."

Did he just call the Mountain Hijn his servant? What lunacy is this? The dwarf held his ground as the stranger advanced closer to him, although for the first time since he could remember, a voice inside of Dormilir screamed for escape. "This is all for the Knights of Luuva," he said. "I have nothing to sell to *you.*"

The stranger flashed his eyes at Dormilir, his pupils tightening to cat-eye slits. But the same wry smirk lingered on his lips. "I'm not interested in anything of high quality. Your disposable pieces will do. Your…mistakes."

"I don't make mistakes."

"Oh, don't be so boastful. We all make mistakes. In fact, we all *are* mistakes." The stranger was close now, within touching range of Dormilir. "But where others cast mistakes aside, I embrace them. I nurture them. Such marvelous creations can evolve from what others scorn and deride."

Dormilir said nothing, but his glower spoke volumes. The stranger plucked a metal gauntlet from a rack of finished armor pieces near the wall. It was simple metalwork, overlapping scales of steel along the fingers and polished plates to cover the back of the hand and forearm. It had no cosmetic adornments, such as gemstones or engravings – it was born solely for battle. The stranger slid his hand into the gauntlet, and what happened next made Dormilir question his own sanity.

The gauntlet changed. It…*moved.* It rippled and flinched with involuntary life, stretching and pulling itself into a new form. The fingers extended into talons, the plating adopted a bruised, purplish color, and it lengthened to wind up the man's arm like tree roots, clinging to its new master. The spot on the back of the hand blinked open to reveal a pulsating fleshy orb, like an eye or a spherical heart, glowing like a fire-lit ruby. It had become part of the man, and yet even as an inanimate item, the gauntlet shuddered as if in pain.

"What dark magic is this?" Dormilir wheezed.

"It's Distortion." the stranger replied casually. "I need base materials to work with. Most anything will do, as you see. I have a pressing engagement coming up of the…violent sort, so my servants and I are collecting armor, weapons, men…"

"Men?" Dormilir kept his gaze steady on the stranger, while slowly reaching his hand around towards the back of his belt.

"I'm recruiting, so to speak. I'm afraid I made a bad impression on the Knights of Luuva with all that business in Syphurius. I don't want us to be at odds. I'd much rather we all get along, that we're all on the same side." The stranger walked back towards the Hijn, who hadn't budged an inch. One of the Hijn, a woman with long raven hair, bluebell skin and tear-shaped pearls under each eye, had a clouded glaze in her stare. The stranger patted her cheek. "And with pretty Miss V'Tanna giving us such an easy mode of transport with her tempests, we can pull in recruits from all over Luuva Gros in a short time." He paused, and snickered. "Forgive me, sometimes I get so enthralled with my aspirations, I prattle on. It's not like you'll remember any of this, but I miss having pleasant conversation. These six are rather useless for that."

Dormilir allowed him to chatter away, hoping the man would be so caught up in his talk that he wouldn't notice that the blacksmith was gradually withdrawing an iron hatchet tucked in his belt behind his back.

"However, they are useful for some things." The Distortionist snapped his fingers, and one of the male Hijn, a hulking mass of ash-gray muscle and a topknot of dark hair atop his head, extended his hand out and murmured a strange language. In half a second, Dormilir felt the hatchet in his hand burning, searing his skin, and with a yell he flung it onto the floor. The hatchet melted into a smoking puddle.

"What have you done to them?" Dormilir spat, clutching his scorched hand.

"Distorted their minds," the Distortionist sighed irritably. "I've explained what I do. I hate it when people don't listen."

"You…you must be what they've been talking about! That thing that fought the Swordmaster." Dormilir glanced behind him, at all the swords, shields, and armor he had forged. If he tried to use any of them, they would suffer the same fate as his hatchet. Praying he would be fast enough, he lunged for a bronze bell that was hanging next to the shop window – a warning bell, one of many throughout Thordayne that was intended to warn anyone in the tower of danger. Before he could touch it, he snapped back his hand as the bell flared orange with a magma heat, and melted into splatters at his feet.

"You won't get out of here," the dwarf bellowed, hoping his voice would be heard outside. "This tower is full of knights! Even with the Hijn Council manipulated, you can't fight all of them!"

The Distortionist scratched his chin. "Truth is, I could…I *have*. But I'd really rather not. What a waste of good material." He walked towards Dormilir, who dashed to climb out the window. The stranger's newly formed gauntlet lashed out like a whip and snagged Dormilir by the leg, and with a swift snap, it yanked the Stonebreaker back into the room and flat onto the floor.

"You need to set an example," the stranger cooed, as he approached the prone blacksmith. "None of my servants have seen how I work my abilities on people from start to finish. I want them to see how this is done. I want them to see what creatures they'll be commanding to do my will."

A strangled noise came from one of the Hijn, the only female other than V'Tanna. She was ethereally beautiful, despite her face and robes being dirty and her snow-pale hair mussed up in tangles. While she still didn't speak, there was a slight glint of recognition in her eyes, a tremble in her eyelids. Her breathing was rapid, and her lips quivered.

The Distortionist looked at her, and he shook his head. "Mage Skyhan, what did I tell you? You can't heal yourself of my Distortion. Do I need to make sure you remember that?"

He curled one of his fingers into a hook, and beckoned at her once with it. Her whole body spasmed as she blurt forth a stream of dark viscous oil from her mouth, and trails of the ooze trickled down from her nostrils and the inner corners of her eyes. She didn't cough or gag, but her face scrunched in helpless suffering.

"Monstrous bastard!" Dormilir roared, mortified at the sight of Mage Skyhan being tortured. He began to rise, but the Distortionist slammed one of his boots down on the dwarf's back. Dormilir growled in pain, feeling like his spine had been bludgeoned by a mace.

The stranger didn't even look down at him. His yellow eyes were still on Mage Skyhan, whose spasms had subsided. "Be a good girl now. I'd prefer to keep you intact than rip you apart.

Don't be a fool like your brother."

The female Hijn's breathing slowed, but her eyes narrowed, and the edges of her mouth tilted downwards.

Her attempt at a grimace didn't elicit any anger from the stranger. He donned a long, wicked smile. "If you hated that, then you're *really* going to hate this."

He hoisted Dormilir up by the neck, gripping him with a crushing strength. He dangled the dwarf off the ground, as he hissed, "Don't be too proud to scream. Let the music of my art ring through this tower, and bring more material to me. Before this night is over, we shall have a symphony of raw, incredible agony!"

CHAPTER TWO
Welcome to Juka Basin

The group was up early the next day. After scouting the surrounding forest for a while, Chiriku found a clean stream winding between the trees. They all took long drinks before refilling their waterskins, and the Quetzalin managed to catch a few fish by nimble hand. Mac welcomed the fish meat heartily, while Clova remained dedicated to gathering berries and mushrooms. Desert Rain attempted to catch some fish herself, reaching out over the stream, using her long index finger and claw as a hook. This proved to be painful, as she ended up getting bitten by fish but could never quite get one out of the water. Chiriku snickered at Desert Rain's efforts as she gutted her catches with a sharp stone she found in the stream, and then took them back to the campfire for cooking.

Desert Rain wondered how it was that Chiriku was so well adapted to surviving in the wild, and why someone with such skills had ended up cooped up in a merchant's memory shop. She also pondered about the issue that Chiriku was a half-breed. Falcolin and Quetzalin may not have been on good terms, but they both strongly supported keeping their race pure-bred. Apparently, either a Quetzalin or a Falcolin had fallen so deeply in love with a human that they overlooked that unwritten rule of pedigree. She wondered what had become of Chiriku's parents, if they had been in Syphurius when Katawa struck, and if they had gotten out all right. These were all questions that Desert Rain would like answered in time, but she doubted that Chiriku would answer any of them at present. Even if their minds had not been preoccupied by what they were going to do next, the memory-seller's granddaughter was not an open person.

After finishing breakfast, the group was once again on Gust's back and soaring off into the morning sky. Desert Rain had made sure not to eat too much before take-off, since she did not want to risk losing her breakfast in mid-air. Mac let out the occasional belch, adding, "There's-ssck no better compliment to give a cook-clk then to let her know your stomach's-ssck happy."

Chiriku snorted. "Spare me any 'compliments,' Mac. I'm downwind of you."

Mile after mile of forest canopy rushed by beneath them for hours. The treetops blended together so smoothly that they seemed to be one vast ocean of swaying green, being occasionally broken by the splotches of some small villages along the way. Desert Rain was rather relieved to see that nothing seemed to have become distorted or destroyed in any way, hopefully meaning that Katawa had not passed through here — yet. There was nothing out this way that would have held interest for Katawa, but then again, she could not say what was going on in that twisted mind of his. Those words he had uttered in the storm, the ones that perhaps indicated where he might be going, meant absolutely nothing to her.

Juka Basin was considered one of the Noble Cities, although it was not a city in the traditional sense. It was a collection of towns that were designed to accent the beauty of the rainforest surrounding them, rather than dismantling it. All these modest towns were nestled within a deep basin, which legend had it was created by the dragon Earthbelly pressing his underside into the earth. If you knew how massive Earthbelly was, according to the Ahshi elves, you could imagine how wide and deep Juka Basin was—it could have made a sufficient sea if it had been filled with salt water instead of forests and lagoons. This was the home of many of the eldest trees and plants in Luuva, and they covered the elven towns from above with protective hands of leaf.

The traveling companions knew they were flying over Juka Basin when the land took a sudden dip down, as if this portion of earth had deflated. This made it tricky for Gust to find a landing spot, but he found an open gap in the trees in which to descend. Unfortunately, what Gust had thought was a dry clearing was actually an algae-coated pond, and he cawed in panic as he landed smack in cold water. After some calm coaxing from Clova, the Roc ceased splashing the water with his massive wings and settled down, extending a wing to shore so his riders could dismount. He hobbled out of the water gradually, flapping his wings to dry off.

"I know this pond," Clova commented. "It's a short walk from here to Kapokis."

"Great, I gotta do what the flower lady says," Chiriku huffed as she shook off, having gotten wet from Gust's tantrum. "And what's in this Kapokis place anyway?"

Clova did not respond. She immediately set off down some unseen trail that the others hastily followed. Clova had even forgotten about Gust, and it took Desert Rain to remind her for the Forest Hijn to whistle the command for the Roc's dismissal.

As they walked along, the mass of trees grew even thicker until barely any light could penetrate through the overhead foliage. Desert Rain could not even find the tops of the trees, for the lowest limbs and branches of the trees—even being the lowest, they were still about a forty foot distance from the ground—wove tightly into each other, creating a ceiling. The shade of perpetual twilight hung around them, and it was a wonder Clova could find her way through the ferns that blanketed the forest floor. The ferns, oddly enough, may have been the guides, for they seemed to slightly lean away to allow the travelers to pass through their green maze. It was most likely Clova they parted for, respecting the female heir of the earth dragon, but she was oblivious to this courtesy of nature. The trees must have noticed that she was troubled, for the seemed to whisper a sad song as the wind rippled through the leaves. Mac glanced around at the whispering trees.

"I must-tkk be losing it, if I'm getting the spine-tingles-ssck from trees-ssck," he murmured to himself.

"It's not just the trees," Chiriku pointed out. She was right. There were quick movements of faint light darting in and out of the trees, but the foursome caught them out of the corners of their eyes. There were tiny murmurings, unlike the whisperings of the trees.

"Are we being followed?" Desert Rain inquired in a low voice.

"Twiights," Clova explained. "They're moth fairies. They mostly come out at night, but some live around here since it's not so bright under the canopy. They're very curious, but they won't harm us."

"Fairies-ssck, eh?" Mac smirked. "Li'l bug people, you mean. We call them 'rare commodities-ssck' in the merchant circle. You'd be set-ttk for life if you got your hands-ssck on one." At that moment, he was hit from above by an acorn—which was odd, since there were no oak trees nearby. A light twitter of laughter came from somewhere overhead.

"Harmless-ssck, sure," Mac huffed as he rubbed his head.

Chiriku snickered, and Desert Rain muffled a giggle behind her hand. This made Clova smiled for a second, but the smile dropped once her mind went back to her current business.

It was a shorter walk than Desert Rain expected, when Clova halted before a huge moss-covered tree. It was not a distinctively special tree, other than it was rather bulbous in shape. It was about fifteen feet wide and the moss on it was different from the usual kind—rather than growing in clumps, it spiraled up the tree in a swirl of exotic patterns. It was Ahshibana, and it was a marker for an elven town. What was missing was the town.

It had been quite some time since Desert Rain had visited Juka Basin, but she was pretty sure that she was supposed to see something—anything—indicating that there was a town in the immediate area. Maybe an Ahshi walking by, maybe the elk that the Ahshi tamed for transport, maybe the trees starting to thin out. Oddly, she thought she heard the sweet sound of Ahshi music trickling through the trees, the light airy singing of reed flutes. Yet there was quite literally—except for a plethora of these massive trees surrounding them like sentinels—nothing.

"Uh, Miss-ssck Clova," Mac spoke up after a minute of silence, "I don't-tkk know what kind of cities-ssck elves live in, but all I see is a funny-looking tree."

Clova approached the tree in front of her, searching for something. She traced her finger along a particular swirl of Ahshibana, and it shimmered a vibrant green. The glow pulsated for a moment before dissolving into the bark.

"A sort of…door chime?" Desert Rain wondered, to which

Clova nodded.

It took a while before there was a response to Clova's action. Slowly, the Ahshibana began to swirl about, like a thin layer of foam on top of a warm drink. Spots on the bark bubbled, and ballooned into broad flat mushrooms, ginger-colored on top with spotted gills on the undersides. The mushrooms wound in a spiral staircase up the tree, up into the tangle of branches above.

"Come," Clova said, as she started to ascend the mushroom stairs. The others followed, Chiriku being extra wary, glancing about to make sure they weren't being followed. Desert Rain couldn't imagine how these mushrooms could support a person's weight, but as they ascended the stairs, the mushrooms handled them with ease. She was beginning to think about how she was getting quite tired of stairs—first the stairs leading down and up in the tunnels under Syphurius, then the narrow stairway on the Ascendence of Glo'rath, and now this—when they came to the top, slipping up through a gap in the canopy. When all four had come up through the gap, the desert hermit, the lizard, and the Quetzalin were surprised to find themselves standing in Kapokis.

Kapokis was actually situated between two canopies: the lower one which the foursome had traveled under, and that they now stood upon; and a second higher one comprised of the trees' highest branches and limbs. The space between the canopies was about eleven feet high, and the light that shimmered through the upper canopy cast a tropical green light on everything. Hanging from the upper canopy's branches were various offerings to the trees: garlands of exotic flowers, mobiles of silver coins and bells, and small baskets of pungent herbs. The residents of Kapokis were everywhere, walking carefully along the twisting tree limbs, or sitting on woven mats colored with flower dyes. There were no houses to speak of, for each Ahshi family's "home" was indicated by their mats, the wicker baskets of collected spices and fruits surrounding them, and whatever offerings they hung above them. Each family also had a hanging lantern, filled with bioluminescent grasshoppers radiating a pinkish glow. These were not so much lanterns as insect houses, for the grasshoppers could come and go from the little grass-woven huts as they pleased, but most preferred to nibble on their grassy homes. Chiriku, who did not deal with insects on a regular basis, nearly crushed one that hopped onto her shoulder.

There were two Ahshi waiting for the foursome, an elven man and woman dressed in earthenly-colored garments, trimmed with bright exotic flowers and leafy patterns. Both of them had intricate swirl designs of Ahshibana all across their skin and faces. They smiled and bowed politely to Clova.

"*Artei miu,*" Clova said to the elves in greeting. The Ahshi were happy to see her, and after a brief exchange of pleasantries turned to lead the travelers through the winding paths of Kapokis.

Desert Rain looked down at the interlocked mass of tree limbs and branches she walked on. She had never seen trees grow this way, especially to make a sturdy walkway. Because of her prehensile feet, with the same elongated toes as her fingers, she found walking on the entangled tree limbs was not so difficult, and she kept a good grip. "Did you make the trees grow like this, Clova?"

"Kapokis was like this long before I became a Hijn. It is through the will and blessings of the trees that they adjusted themselves so the Ahshi could live here."

Chiriku laughed. "What, like the trees can think and move or something? They're wood."

"These elder ones can, if they truly wish to. Some say these ancient trees were affected by the Great Manifestation, and are now more than—" Clova gave Chiriku a discerning look, "wood."

"These folk-kk don't mind having no walls-ssck?" Mac wondered as he received some curious looks from the various Ahshi households. "There's-ssck no thieving or—" he raised an eyebrow to punctuate the meaning of his next word—"*privacy* issues-ssck?"

"The Ahshi believe in sharing whatever they have with their neighbors," Clova explained, "and thievery has never been a problem here. As for privacy, if one should really need it, there are always places in the forest to sneak off to. Otherwise, there is nothing that the Ahshi need to hide."

This was evident by the fact that some Ahshi decided to wear a minimal amount of clothing—some just accurately placed flowers and loin cloths—and Desert Rain found herself averting her eyes on more than one occasion.

"Clova," Desert Rain cut in, "as far as I knew, most towns in Juka Basin are easily accessible. I thought the Ahshi were open to travelers. Why is Kapokis so out of the way?"

Clova looked at Desert Rain over her shoulder. "This is a very special place, Dezzy. Don't be mistaken. Kapokis is open to everyone with peaceful intentions to visit. But it is a quiet, uninterrupted place of meditation, for this is the home of the Great Philosopher, the patriarch of the Ahshi."

Desert Rain felt a pang of uneasiness. "A king?"

"No, no," Clova replied with a smile. "He handles any problems that arise in Juka Basin, but he never makes anyone serve him. He is also the one who can speak with the Elfë Tiagas, which is why we must see him in order to ask for their help."

Desert Rain bit her lip. "So he's a wizard?"

"He would never call himself as such. He doesn't have the power that the Elfë Tiagas have, and he relies more on his intelligence and prudence than any magic to deal with important matters. I wish everyone were as patient as he." She leaned in close and whispered to Desert Rain. "Although he likes to ramble on about his personal philosophies, so smile and nod if he starts one of his lectures."

"Wait, *I'm* not going to see him, am I?"

Clova blinked in surprise. "Of course you are. Why would you think otherwise?"

Desert Rain swallowed hard. "I thought, since *you*'re the Forest Hijn and all, and I don't really belong here…"

Clova put her arm around Desert Rain in a hug. "You *do* belong, Dezzy. I don't know as much about the Wretched Katawa as you do. You need to explain to the Philosopher how calamitous this situation is. It's hard enough to get him to talk to his northern cousins as it is. I need you to do this, Dezzy. We need you to help us."

"I told you everything I know already. I don't want to tell it again." Desert Rain slipped out of Clova's embrace. Clova halted, shocked by her friend's coldness. Their elven guides turned back when they noticed that their entourage had stopped. They asked Clova something in Ahshi, to which Clova replied with a reassuring word.

"Dezzy, I don't understand," the Forest Hijn said. "Don't you want to help us? To help me?"

"No! I mean, yes, I want to." Desert Rain rubbed the moonstone on her forehead in frustration. "But the way I should be able to help you, I can't. After being bounced around to more places in the last week than I've ever been, I'm..." She sighed heavily to finish her point.

"You're exhausted, I know. I'm so…anxious, I guess." Clova held Desert Rain close for a moment. "You're absolutely right. You need a little time to yourself." She turned to the two elves, had a brief exchange with them, to which the elves nodded. "Paki and Tyla will let you stay with them a little while. I should go see if the Philosopher can meet with us later, so he isn't caught too off guard." She smiled at her friend. "I'm very happy to have you here with me, Dez. I wish the circumstances were different."

***

"This is embarrassing," Chiriku huffed as she shuffled uncomfortably on her mat. She glanced warily at the elves walking by, who smiled welcomingly at her. She scowled back. She threw the hood of her cloak over her head.

"Relax, Chi. Nobody's-ssck gonna hoodwink-clk you here." Mac stretched out on his mat. Due to the pleasant atmosphere, his lizard side was peeking through. He was getting a bit scalier, a bit redder, but he still had his grinning human face. "I must say, this-ssck is a nice place. No thieves-ssck, no back-stabbers-ssck, no swindlers-ssck. Makes me a bit homesick-kk."

Desert Rain sat quietly, watching as their two elven hosts went about their daily tasks. The Ahshi woman, Tyla, tended to her cooking, although her method of cooking was strange since she did not use a cooking fire—a fire on top of a tree would not be the best idea. She instead used a special red powder that she would toss into a clay pot full of water, causing the water to start boiling without the assistance of heat. This would have made a fine broth by itself, but she also tossed in a few edible roots and nuts. Paki was cutting some reeds he had gathered, using a sharp stone to trim off the leafy fringes along the reeds' sides. They were quiet, making Desert Rain wonder if they spoke the Mutual Language as those who lived in the other Noble Cities.

"Do you guys talk normal?" Chiriku asked Tyla, as if she had been thinking what Desert Rain had.

Tyla did not look up from her work, but answered politely. "Yes, we speak the Mutual Language."

"Good. Then you can tell me where around here I can find the Syphurians."

Tyla looked at Chiriku curiously.

"You know, the Syphurians who fled into the forest." Chiriku snorted irritably. "Most of them came this way when Syphurius was attacked. So where are they? What town are they in?"

"They are most likely in the towns on the western rim of Juka Basin," Paki replied. "Those would be the first Ahshi towns they would come upon. Those who could make the journey, that is."

"That's all I need to know." Chiriku stood up. "I'm assuming I can get down from here the same way I came up, right?"

Paki glanced up at Chiriku. "People who don't know the forests here can get lost easily. I wouldn't recommend walking around Juka Basin without a guide."

"Thanks," Chiriku said, "but I'll be fine."

Desert Rain got up urgently. "You're not leaving right now, are you?"

Chiriku grimaced. "You got a problem with that?"

Mac yawned. "Come on, Chi. Don't act-tkk like a toad in the frying pan, hopping away so fast-tkk. It's gonna be dark-kk soon anyway."

"Like I'm afraid of the dark. I'll climb down one of these stupid trees if I have to, but I'm going."

Desert Rain suddenly felt worried about Chiriku. The Quetzalin could take care of herself, she knew that, but the girl was also reckless at times. What would she do if she got hurt, all alone in those woods? "Wait until tomorrow, Chiriku. That way, we can go with you," Desert Rain suggested.

Chiriku pulled the hood off her head, not in compliance to Desert Rain's request, but so she could ruffle up the feathers on top of her head in irritation. "Look, Donkey Ears, maybe you got the wrong impression, but I'm not really 'with' you people. I needed a ride here. So, you want me to say 'thanks' or something? Fine, thanks or something. But I'm going now. I don't need anybody's help."

Desert Rain looked over at Mac imploringly.

"Don't ask me to butt-tkk in," Mac said. "Let the eye-pecker do what she wants-ssck. She always does anyway."

Chiriku curled the edge of her beak at Mac. She put the hood up over her head again, and turned to walk away. She paused, seeming a bit lost for a second, but then continued on, whether or not she knew her way around. After a moment, she heard someone following, and glanced back. She scowled at her follower, who was Desert Rain. "What in the Eternal Deep do you think you're doing?" the Quetzalin asked.

"If you really can't wait until tomorrow, I should at least go with you to the next town."

"I don't like travel buddies," Chiriku snapped. She kept on

walking, thinking she had ended the matter. She rolled her eyes when she felt that Desert Rain was still following her. "What is your problem??" she asked without stopping.

"You," was the reply.

That made Chiriku stop to turn around and look at her.

"Well, not my *problem*, so to speak," Desert Rain corrected herself. "More like my…" She hunted for the right word as Chiriku stared at her angrily. "My responsibility."

Chiriku gawked unbelievingly at her. She noticed that several Ahshi had stopped what they were doing and were eyeing them. She wrinkled her brow into a furious glare.

"Leave me alone, freak!" she seethed. She took one step back and abruptly slipped and fell through the lower canopy.

"Chiriku!" Desert Rain rushed over to where Chiriku had vanished. Peering down through a hole in the canopy, she saw Chiriku dangling upside down from a thick branch that had somehow snaked around her ankle and held her like a rabbit caught in a noose trap. The Quetzalin squawked in anger and fright, barely managing to catch her warhammer before it slipped out of its sheath.

"What happened?" Desert Rain called down. By this time, a group of Ahshi huddled around her, staring down at the hanging Quetzalin.

"What's it look like?" Chiriku screamed up at her. "The stupid tree gave out from under me!"

The Ahshi began to laugh. Desert Rain looked at the branch that snagged Chiriku. The way it was wrapped around the girl's ankle, like a rope, made it evident that it wasn't mere luck that kept Chiriku from plummeting to the forest floor below.

"The old elm doesn't like your attitude," one of the Ahshi

remarked as he laughed.

Desert Rain couldn't help but smile. "Clova told you they were more than trees. I think you should apologize."

"Apologize? This thing almost killed me!" Chiriku tried to reach up to grab the branch with one hand, since her other hand was keeping hold of her warhammer. "Tell it to put me down!"

"I don't think you want that, seeing as how 'down' is a pretty far drop," Desert Rain noted. She reached her hand down between the branches. "If you can extend your warhammer to me, I can pull you up."

"I don't need your help," Chriku huffed, and she struggled to catch the branch that held her. The weight of her warhammer and cloak, however, made it hard for her to reach.

Desert Rain watched patiently as Chiriku exerted effort after effort to pull herself up, to no avail. She had to admit, the Quetzalin was persistant. At some point, Mac came over to watch, and he chuckled at the spectacle. Finally, Chiriku grasped the branch at her ankle, pulling herself up into a crouched position— and found herself stuck.

"Having fun?" Mac asked. "I find it a tad sad when a tree has you beat-tkk, Chi."

"Shut up!" Chiriku cawed. She pulled out her warhammer and extended the butt end of it up to them. "Well? You gonna pull me up or what?"

Desert Rain and Mac grabbed the warhammer and pulled on it. Chiriku came up through the canopy with ease, the branch apparently having released her. Once settled, Chiriku brushed herself off, and slid her warhammer back into its sheath.

"You still want to go walking around alone in this forest?" Desert Rain asked her.

Chiriku clicked the teeth in her beak, glancing suspiciously at the trees around her. "Well, it wouldn't hurt to have a guide tag along…"

CHAPTER THREE
The Great Philosopher

Paki offered to guide Chiriku to the next town, but evening was quickly descending upon Kapokis, and he convinced the Quetzalin to wait until the following morning. Even though Chiriku muttered a sharp comment about elves being scared of the dark, she did not argue when it came to Tyla serving dinner, even if it was a meatless meal.

Clova had returned shortly after Chiriku's ordeal with the elm, and joined the group for dinner. She reported that she had gained permission to meet with the Great Philosopher, after he had his "evening meal," which she explained meant his two hours of solitary study.

"His biggest priority is to feed his mind, even moreso than his body," she further explained. "It worries me sometimes, that he'll waste away until he's nothing but a talking brain." She made a light laugh, but her melancholy demeanor was still evident.

"Is he a nice man?" Desert Rain inquired, watching one of the pink glowing grasshoppers crawling on a branch above her. Being used to acquiring insects for food, she wondered what such an exotic bug would taste like. The Ahshi respected all forms of life with profound respect, however, and to even squash a bug was a sign of discourtesy to the lifestream of the forest. She turned her gaze back to Clova.

"One of the nicest people I know," Clova replied. "He tends to get a bit distracted at times, though, he has so many thoughts racing around in his head. But he'll pay close attention at the prospect of someone telling him something new. That's how I convinced him to postpone his night teachings with his students so he could see us immediately — I said that I knew something of great importance that he didn't know."

Desert Rain grinned. "Was that some sort of bribe then?"

Clova sipped innocently from her clay cup of herbal tea. "More like… an exchange of information."

Mac lied across his mat on his back, passing an apple back and forth between his hands. "If words-ssck were a good bribe where I come from, then I'd be the richest-tkk man in Luuva Grosssck." He lingered on that thought, smiling to himself as he envisioned wearing the finest threads, and owning the grandest house floating smoothly on the swamp waters back home. His eyes brightened, as an idea hit him. "Say, how much do you think-kk I could get if I caught-tkk one of them li'l bug people?"

Desert Rain noticed that Paki and Tyla frowned at Mac's question, but they were too polite to say anything. "I don't think the Ahshi would like you harassing the wildlife," she pointed out.

"And the Twiights would like it even less," Clova added. "Not that they'd give you the chance to catch them."

Mac bit into his apple, chewing thoughtfully. "Thing is, one of them red token toads-ssck in the Bayou can get you fifty gold bits-ssck, and heck-kk, you can find those pretty easy if you know where to look-kk. One of them bug people's-ssck gotta be worth triple one of them toads-ssck." He apparently had not heard Desert Rain or Clova, as his entrepreneurial side was in full swing. Desert

Rain shook her head, knowing that if Mac really tried to go fairy-hunting, he'd probably come back empty-handed and very sore from being pelted by acorns.

***

The Philosopher was a pale, wirey elf, as to be expected from people who read more than eat. He was immediately distinguishable from the other Ahshi from the lack of Ahshibana on his body. There was a tiny bit of the special moss underlining each of his eyes, and this was to strengthen his eyesight so he could continue his studies at night in the dim light of his glowing bug lantern. Otherwise, he had no desire to wear the Ahshibana as much as the others, for he believed that subjecting the body to any kind of medical or herbal alteration (even a beneficial one) was to make oneself less "pure." Combining his life energy with that of another organism was to taint himself and that of the organism. He had expressed this belief to the Ahshi before, but he never pressed it upon them to change their lifestyle. While a very few agreed with him, most did not want to give up tradition.

He lived in perhaps what was the closest structure to a "house" in Kapokis, but it was nothing elaborate or boastful. It was a large knothole in one of the elder trees, a perfectly round space about ten feet in diameter. This was another accommodation of the tree, for there was no indication that the room had been carved out by hand. The Philosopher sat in the middle of this knothole, surrounded by his hand-made books, the paper made from pressed reeds and bound with strings of some sort of braided plant fibers. The ink he used to write in his books was made from a dark flower dye, and he had fashioned his pen from the hollow stem of some small woody plant. The make-shift books overwhelmed the room, leaving the elf little space to move at all, let alone lie down or stretch out. Outside his knothole was a large welcome mat, and his offerings to the trees hung from the branches above. These consisted mostly of scrolls with white wax seals, possessing the words of what he considered to be his most important discoveries and philosophies. Since he believed that knowledge was the most valuable gift, to give the trees his most beloved secrets was the greatest offering he could give.

He was in the midst of writing when one of his apprentices led Clova and Desert Rain up to his front entryway. He did not look up at the two Hijn, but he slightly sped up his writing so as to finish his final thoughts. Clova waited patiently, while Desert Rain unconsciously fidgeted as she took in the studious elf. He was not especially handsome, but one could argue that he had a boyish cuteness about him, even though he was probably older than he looked, as most elves were. His strawberry-blonde hair was pulled back from his face in a short pony tail, although one strand hung down over his face, and he periodically used the end of his pen to brush it back. He wore a hunter-green robe, cut in a similar style to those of spellcasters, but it had no embroidery or classy patterns as those of the students of New Magic.

"Artei miu, Lorihalynir Athro-kos," Clova said as she bowed her head in greeting. She said this as the Philosopher was dotting his last period.

"Artei miu, Hijn Clova Flor," the elf returned, still not looking up at the two women. He placed his book back into its appropriate place, and then checked to make sure all his volumes were still in order, as they always were.

"Sikay filana dosa, Desert Rain," Clova said, gesturing to her

companion.

The Philosopher looked up at them with bright azure eyes. Desert Rain smiled sheepishly, bowing her head. The elf seemed startled at first, gazing at Desert Rain for some time. The desert Hijn began to feel uneasy, as she managed to squeak out a hesitant, "Ar-tei mi-u."

A glint of fascination sparked in the Philosopher's eye. He slipped out of the knothole and stood silently for a full minute, looking Desert Rain over. Desert Rain felt like ducking behind Clova to escape the elf's scanning eyes.

"*Desert Rain sikay Hijn, padana lwi Ulomin,*" Clova explained to the elf.

The Philosopher made a small nod of understanding. He walked up to Desert Rain, gazing intently at her eyes. Desert Rain was uncomfortable, especially since she was beginning to think the Philosopher didn't speak the Mutual Language, and she was not very fluent in Ahshi. But finally, after a bit of scrutinizing, he asked, "Your right eye…It has dragon sight, yes?"

Desert Rain paused, and shrugged. "I can see in the dark with it, if that's what you mean—Great Philosopher, sir," she added quickly.

"Please, call me Anthron," the elf replied.

At this, Clova made a big smile at Desert Rain. It was not common for the Philosopher to warm up to an outsider so quickly. Anthron began to inspect Desert Rain's other features, using the tip of his pen to lift up one of her long ears to get a better look at it, and dared to lightly touch her moonstone marking. Desert Rain was going to ask him to stop, but he must have noticed the look of unease in her face, for he ceased his examination.

"Forgive me, Hijn Desert Rain," Anthron apologized, "but,

if I may say so, you are quite a unique specimen. Of all the Hijn I have met, you have the most…fascinating features. Were you born elven?"

"Human," Desert Rain corrected him. She could understand why he thought she may have been elven, since the tips of her ears tapered to points.

"Ah. Would you excuse me?" He returned to his piles of books, selecting one and quickly scribbling something down in it. He glaced periodically up at her as he wrote. Desert Rain looked quizzically at Clova. Clova gave her a reassuring smile.

"We appreciate you seeing us on such short notice, Athrokos," the Forest Hijn said, while the elf continued scribbling. "But we are in dire need of your service. We need to get in touch with your cousins in the far north."

Anthron paused a brief second, but did not look up. He kept on writing. "Explain," he finally said.

"I believe Desert Rain could explain it best, since she has suffered the most of this ordeal." Clova touched Desert Rain's shoulder comfortingly, seeing the panic in the hermit's eyes. Desert Rain gulped, cleared her throat several times, and opened her mouth to speak. At first, the words ducked back into her throat, rendering her speechless. When Anthron glanced up at her, raising his eyebrows in expectation, Desert Rain tried to explain again.

"Well, there's a Wretched who's been…uh…causing chaos, in some of the Noble Cities. He's been driving the people out of their homes, and he's hurt so many —"

"Yes, I know," Anthron replied casually.

Desert Rain froze. "You do?" she asked, astounded.

"I have visited with the Syphurians who came to us,

seeking refuge. I have gathered as much information from them as they were willing to give." He picked up one of his books off the pile, apparently the proof of his claim. He set it back down, and began rummaging for something. "Please continue."

"So…when we escaped him in Syphurius, he followed us to Vaes Galahar, where he attacked the Hijn council and kidnapped Mage Skyhan, and Rukna, and Merros and V'Tanna--"

"I am aware of that," the elf answered coolly, as he found a clay plate and a clean piece of paper in his clutter.

Desert Rain and Clova exchanged a baffled look. "How could you possibly know that already?" Desert Rain asked.

Anthron took up a little jar of ink, pouring it onto the plate. "You must understand the delicate linkage of magic in this world, Hijn Desert Rain. It is much like a spider's web. When you pluck a thread in one spot, it ripples through the entire web. When magic, particularly the powerful vibrations of Ancient Magic, is disrupted, it can be felt by all those who have the acute sensitivity to the worldly energies around them, as do elves. Could you press your hand in this, please?" He held out the plate of ink to her. Desert Rain stared at it in confusion, but did what he requested. He set the plate down, and then held out a piece of paper to her, pressing her hand down onto the sheet. He took her handprint and placed it into the book in which he had been writing.

"Now I may not possess the deep understanding of magic like spellcasters, or the Hijn," he continued, "but I could still feel a surge of darkness come over me, and I knew that a great calamity had occurred. Combined with what I had heard about this Wretched — quite a horrible brute, so I've heard — I surmised that it had something to do with him. Having been such an intense feeling of darkness upsetting the balance, it must have been an upset of Ancient Magic, which there are not many other than the Hijn that know that power. I deduced that the Hijn council and that Wretched had confronted one another, and since you have come to me for help, I can see that the Hijn lost."

Desert Rain blinked in astonishment, and wiped her ink-stained hand on her pants. "That's a very impressive deduction," she said. "Although, I am ashamed to say, I have never felt this…*web* of magic that you mentioned."

Anthron was writing again, eyes glued to the paper. "It's not that you don't, Hijn Desert Rain. It's that you have chosen to ignore it." He quickly observed her feet. "Prehensile toes. I really should take a print of those as well."

Desert Rain flared her nostrils and pinched her lips tight before speaking. "I don't mean to be rude, Sir Anthron, but you don't look like you care about anything I'm saying."

Anhtron wrinkled a corner of his nose in puzzlement. "Is it necessary for me to 'look' like I'm paying attention?"

"It would make me feel better if you did, yes. And maybe you could look at me like a person instead of some animal on display."

Anthron became thoughtful, tapping his chin with the tip of his pen. "Interesting." He jotted something down.

"Nevertheless," Clova cut in as Desert Rain was about to protest, "you must see what a drastic situation we're in. We think it's necessary that the Elfë Tiagas help us to stop this demon. Surely, they must have some secret knowledge of the elven power that could protect us from the dark power of that Wretched. Maybe they've imparted such secrets to you?"

Anthron made a brief laugh. "No, even I am not worthy of such information in their eyes. We Ahshi are too 'open-armed,' as they say. They think we are too willing to share what we know with other races. Most Ahshi don't even know how to find an Elfë Tiagas city anymore, let alone know how to connect with their psychic abilities. We have severed our ties with them. Let them live in their ice castles if they wish…it suits them and their cold hearts well."

"But if you told them about the danger Luuva Gros is in — they must see that eventually this terror could find them!"

Anthron knit his eyebrows at Clova. "To give away their most precious secrets because of one Wretched? They will never agree unless they saw the destruction themselves, and by then it would be too late. I take this plight very seriously, but I doubt they would even grace your request with a response."

Desert Rain's fingers curled, although her face remained calm. "So that's it? It's not even worth trying to talk to them?"

"You do not understand, Hijn Desert Rain, because you are not elven. Clova Flor should explain it to you sometime. Now, seeing as how I have postponed my night class for much longer than I intended, I will have to end this discussion. I bid you both a pleasant night." He abruptly turned around and went back to his place in the knothole room.

Clova Flor paused but then took a deep breath. "Athro-kos, I know how you detest speaking with your brethren, but—"

Anthron sharply held up a hand for silence. He opened one of his books and began writing again.

Clova sighed. She leaned in close to Desert Rain and whispered. "We should go, Dezzy. He doesn't like upsetting his schedule. Perhaps tomorrow we can try again, when he has more time to give us."

Desert Rain didn't move, even when Clova took her arm.

She walked up to the knothole, planting both feet firmly on the welcome mat. "Great Philosopher Anthron, I don't accept that."

"Dez!" Clova whispered warningly.

Anthron continued writing without glancing up. "You are dedicated to your request, Hijn Desert Rain, and I respect that. But you must understand, for me to waste so much of my limited energy for a plea that will go unheard—"

"I understand, Sir Anthron, that because you don't like talking to your cousins that you're willing to let more people suffer."

Anthron lifted his eyes to give her a penetrating glare, but then shifted his gaze back down to his paper.

"I'm a hypocrite," Desert Rain admitted. "There are people I don't like talking to either. I haven't attended a Hijn meeting since Dragons know when, because I wanted to be left alone. And now I need to take some reponsibilty for what's going on, because I have a hand in all this. It would be very easy for me to crawl back into my burrow and shut everything and everyone out again. I could let every Noble City go to the Eternal Deep, and not feel guilty about it at all. But I've traveled half-way across Luuva Gros for this, and for you to say that you're not even going to try to help because you and the Elfë Tiagas have some bad blood between you is the most selfish and stupid thing I've ever heard."

Anthron ceased writing. He slowly put his pen down, and slowly closed his book. He raised his head, his face set like marble. "Did you say *stupid*?"

Desert Rain didn't reply. She stared back into his azure eyes, her green eye radiating a fierce glow. It made Anthron soften his glare, even lean away ever so slightly. He opened his mouth, and found himself, for the first time since he could remember, unable to counter the argument.

"Dez, that's enough," Clova said, coming forth and taking her by the shoulder. "I think we're all tired from the long day. We can talk about this more tomorrow, when we've all gotten some rest." She firmly started to guide Desert Rain away. Desert Rain's intent gaze lingered on the speechless elf a moment longer, and then she turned to leave.

"Hijn Desert Rain—"

The two Hijn turned back to the elf, who looked at the desert hermit questioningly.

"You say you need to take responsibility for this, even though it may not be your battle to fight?" he asked.

"But it *is* my battle."

"Why?"

Desert Rain saw in Anthron's eyes that he was not looking so much for her answer, but for his own. "Because whether I like it or not, I'm a Hijn. Somewhere in me, I have the power to fight back. It's not easy. It's completely frightening. But it's what I have to do."

"No one would punish you if you let others fight, those who were more willing and stronger," Anthron said.

"But then I may as well join the snow elves in their frozen mountains, right?" Desert Rain gave him a small smile.

"Tomorrow," Anthron said after a pause. "I will send the Flightspeak to the northern elves tomorrow."

Clova was astounded, but then a relieved smile brightened her face. "You will?"

Desert Rain was familiar with the term *Flightspeak*. Grandma Luna had once explained to her that it was the psychic link all elves had, how they could talk to one another over vast distances. Elves dabbled in certain magics, mostly guard illusions to place around their cities, but they were naturally born with mental powers unlike any other race in Luuva Gros. They were taught not to abuse their psychic abilities, to the point where many elves only used them in dire circumstances.

"It will take some time," Anthron admitted, his voice unable to hide the tiny hint of nervousness. "I will need to concentrate on it for the whole day, without disruption. I cannot guarantee an immediate reply. The Flightspeak will tire me greatly, you see. It may take days until I receive any word from them, but I will…try." He took in a deep breath. "I will try," he repeated, brushing back that one strand of loose hair.

"We are very grateful to you, Athro-kos," Clova said, bowing to him. She was restraining her joy as much as she could, but she couldn't help but smile with a sunbeam's warmth. "We should let you get back to your class now. May Nature always look kindly on you."

"Thank you, Anthron," Desert Rain said evenly as she bowed. "I am glad to have met such a wise elf." She thought she could see, with the help of the vision in her green eye, Anthron blush a little.

"This is wonderful!" Clova clapped her hands as she sat cross-legged on her mat. The others staying with Paki and Tyla had already gone to sleep, but she and Desert Rain still talked in hushed tones. "I thought it would take more coaxing than that, and even then I couldn't say if he would really do it. But he's going to do it! Finally, a sprout of hope that can grow for us."

Desert Rain lied back on her mat, wondering if she was going to get any sleep that night—or if Clova would allow her to.

"Is Anthron truly that adverse to the snow elves?"

"You have no idea," Clova said. "The Elfë Tiagas have never forgiven those elves who chose to live among the other Noble Races, and the Ahshi think the northern elves are too stuck in the past with wishing to remain isolated. The Ahshi are so opposed to the old way of life that most have sacrificed their mental powers in order to begin anew. Even *I* can't remember how it's done…" She paused, as if trying to remember how to do Flightspeak, but then she shook her head and shrugged. "It's difficult to get Anthron to talk to the northern elves, as you saw back there. But you, you knew how to play him pretty well."

"What do you mean?"

"He's the Philosopher, Dezzy. You tested him, you called him 'stupid'! No one does that! I was a bit worried for you for a second."

"But you said he was a nice man—"

"He is, but he also has the authority to send away an outsider who doesn't pay him proper respect. I told you I couldn't do this without you, Dezzy."

Desert Rain grinned, even though she didn't believe that last thing Clova had said was true. "It's too bad Anthron didn't get what he was hoping for."

"What was that?"

"Well, you told him that we were going to tell him something he didn't know, but he already knew everthing we had to tell him. He was cheated out of the deal."

Clova was silent, which made Desert Rain curious. She saw the Forest Hijn look away, as if watching some invisible thing floating about. "Clova?"

Clova looked back at her innocently. "Hmm?"

"Is there something you're not telling me?"

"No, no," Clova replied, curling a lock of hair around her finger. "Well…maybe a little something."

Desert Rain turned over onto her side. "What?"

"Anthron didn't really get cheated."

Desert Rain knitted her eyebrows, grinning in curiosity. "I'm not following."

"It wasn't so much I said that I was going to tell him something he didn't know. I said I was going to show him something he'd never seen."

Desert Rain didn't react, not immediately. She felt a hot pinch in her temples. She dropped the grin. She sat up on her mat. "Some…*thing?*"

"Well obviously I didn't mean *thing*. I knew that he would have never seen a Hijn like you before, and I thought you and he would get along so well—"

"A Hijn like *me*?" She didn't really know why, but Desert Rain suddenly felt a burn that was welling-up inside her.

Clova saw the twinge of anger in her friend's eyes. "Dezzy, I didn't mean it like that."

"No, I *do* know what you mean. I know I was never like the rest of you. You got dragon markings, but you still look elven. Even I don't know what I'm supposed to look like." She gritted her teeth, and her skin flushed crimson. "I can imagine what you said. 'Tell Anthron I have this freak I could show him. Maybe he'd like to gawk at it for a little while.'"

"You know I would never—"

"When did I become a bargaining chip, Clova? When did I stop being a person and become a means to an end?" Desert Rain stood up. "He treated me like I'm some foreign animal to be studied! And you knew he would, didn't you? But you didn't care. You didn't care at all how I'd feel." She tugged down on her ears so hard, Clova winced at the notion she might rip them off.

"How can you say that? Sweetie, I'm your friend. I had no idea this would upset you so much."

"I'm tired of being used, Clova. I'm tired of being told one thing when it's really another. I'm sick of being lied to." Desert Rain turned to walk away from her, but Clova got up and tried to catch hold of her hand.

"Dezzy, I'm sorry. Please don't act like—"

"I don't want to talk to you." Desert Rain said this so sharply that Clova instantly released her. Desert Rain left her, walking quickly along the winding tree limbs, not really caring where she was going. She stepped swiftly around the sleeping families of Ahshi, until she stopped and leaned against a tree trunk. She stood there in silence, dwelling on the angry thoughts in her head, staring up through the upper canopy into a dark, mirthless night sky. She was in thought when a voice snuck up on her.

"Gila Gul?" Mac let out a lazy yawn and scratched his sides. "What's-ssck the matter? I woke up and you were raisin' your voice to Miss-ssck Clova. Poor lady's upset-tkk now. What happened?"

Desert Rain sighed. "I don't want to talk about it, Mac. You should go back to sleep."

"Can't-tkk, not if I know you're troubled. Now you can tell ol' Mac anything. Why's Miss-ssck Clova crying? You two have a squabble?"

Desert Rain looked down at her feet. "Something like that."

"That's-ssck a shame. But it's nothing that can't-tkk be

patched up, I'm sure."

"I don't know, Mac. I don't know."

Mac scratched his head. "You two are friends-ssck, ain't you?"

Desert Rain sighed. "I thought we were."

"Did Miss Clova do something to hurt-tkk you on purpose?"

Desert Rain lifted her head. "No, not on purpose."

Mac grinned his yellowish teeth. "Then it must-tkk have been an accident, and you can forgive her for an accident, can't-ttk you?"

Desert Rain looked at Mac, and smiled back. "Yes," she replied.

"Good. Then we should be getting back-kk so you can patch things-ssck up and get some shut-eye. Like-kk the ol' Bayou saying goes, 'It's easier going when the swamp is cool than when it's boiling.' At least, I think that's-ssck how the sayin' goes."

CHAPTER FOUR
The Return of Silverheart

When morning came, Desert Rain still hadn't quite gotten over her anger at Clova, although she had apologized for her rash reaction. She figured perhaps a good walk might help clear her head and dissipate her remaining ire, and since the Great Philosopher had said he needed the whole day to concentrate on his Flightspeak, there wasn't much for her to do in Kapokis anyway. Therefore, she decided to accompany Chiriku and Paki on their trek to the next town, even though the Quetzalin made some comment under her breath involving the word "clingy."

Mac, too, followed them down the spiral stairway of mushrooms that Paki summoned from one of the old trees. He was not planning on joining them on their short journey, for he had another plan for the day.

"Thought-tkk I'd take a look-clk around here, enjoy the scenery," he cryptically said. Desert Rain couldn't help but notice that he had brought with him an empty bug lantern, a line of string, and a piece of silver that had, supposedly, "fallen off" one of Tyla's tree offerings. The Hijn smirked and shook her head, knowing Mac's real intention for sneaking around this part of the forest with a small trap and a silver piece as bait. She noted Paki's expression, and it was clear that the Ahshi knew the intention as well. She hoped the Twiights would not be too hard on Mac.

The next town would be Palms' Dance, according to Paki, and would be an hour walk to get there. The elf, Quetzalin and Hijn traveled in silence for most of it, although Desert Rain asked Paki occasional questions about certain plants or sounds in the woods. Chiriku was less than impressed with anything Paki had to say. Her face was set in its typical grimace, and she cast suspicious glances towards any rustle that came frme the surrounding brush.

Desert Rain felt that if she was going to understand her feathered companion any better, now would be a good time to attempt a conversation. Not that she planned on being very successful in getting Chiriku to talk much, but Desert Rain knew who the Quetzalin was looking for, and imagined what inner turmoil the bird girl was going through.

"You're searching for your grandfather, aren't you?" Desert Rain asked eventually, after the silence had gotten too overwhelming.

Chiriku rolled her eyes. "You Hijn really *do* know everything."

"I ask because, he could be in any of the Ahshi towns on the western rim, if he even made it this far. He could have stopped in any of the villages between Syphurius and Juka Basin."

"What's your point?"

"That this search is not going to be as easy as you think, Chiriku. I know you get very determined when you set your mind on something, but he may not have come all the way to Juka Basin."

"Look, the old man never trusted any squatters from those woodland villages, and no way would he bunk with those dirty Lejenous. He's not a big fan of elves, but he'd stay with the crowd, and I know most of Syphurius feel the same way he does. They would hold out until they made it here."

"But like I said, he could be staying anywhere along the western rim."

"Then I'll look through every town if I have to."

Desert Rain nodded. She remembered when she had been Chiriku's age—at least, she thought she remembered—full of determination, or stubbornness, depending on how one viewed it. She imagined she loved Grandma Luna as much as Chiriku loved her grandfather, and she too would've traveled hundreds of miles for the sake of a beloved elder.

"I wish I could make the search easier for you," she commented.

"Cut out the bleeding heart crap, will you, Donkey Ears? You didn't even have to come."

Desert Rain narrowed her eyes, but then grinned. "Forgive me, Lady Legs."

Suddenly, Chiriku's beak was in Desert Rain's face. The bird girl's eyes blazed, and the feathers on her head were standing on end in fury. Her voice was soft but malicious. *"Never call me that."*

"If you're going to keep calling me Donkey Ears—"

"I can call you whatever I feel like. But you never say anything about my legs, my arms, my beak, my anything. You call me that again, and I will rearrange your face, I swear it." She whipped back around and stormed down the path, passing up her elven guide. Paki looked at Desert Rain, shaking his head with a knowing glance.

Desert Rain sighed. Talk about getting off on the wrong foot.

The canopy of the forest thinned after a while, allowing bright sunlight to ripple down, causing shadows of the leaves above to dance upon the forest floor. The path they traveled was one traveled many times by the Ahshi, through masses of ferns, around small waterfalls, along rock formations that were home to a variety of mosses and flowers. They traveled downhill and uphill, on soft dirt or rocky trail. Eventually they descended down into a small valley, where there was a lagoon sheltered by great palm trees from the gleaming sun.

These trees provided the homes of Palms' Dance, each household within the palms' stilt-like roots, which formed the foundations of tents that the elves could drape layers of leafy fronds over. Like Kapokis, there were few man-made furnishings within the homes - woven mats, wicker baskets, bug lanterns and tree offerings. In the waters of the lagoon floated large lily pads, upon which many Ahshi sat, playing music or merely enjoying the cool waters. There were guests staying in Palm's Dance, a few Falcolin, Quetzalin, and humans, most in their worn, dusty clothing that they had been wearing when they fled Syphurius. Some had opted for the earthy Ahshi attire, finding it freeing and comfortable. The sight of the Syphurians made Chiriku run faster to reach the copse of palms.

"I'm surprised to find Syphurians here. I thought we'd have to go farther west," Desert Rain said to Paki.

"There were many Syphurians, and the towns in Juka Basin are small. The people were divided between towns to provide enough resources to everyone. Without breaking up families, of course." Paki walked along calmly, and was greeted warmly by the residents of Palms' Dance. He spoke to them in elven, and he introduced Desert Rain. She frowned when he added the label "Hijn" to her name. At this, the other elves bowed to her and offered her flowers from their hair and necklaces, making Desert Rain blush in embarrassment. They began to speak rapidly to her in a mixture of elvish and the Mutual Language, and Desert Rain smiled and nodded dumbfoundedly.

Then she felt something move in her pocket.

Desert Rain had forgotten that she still had Gothart's black pouch with her. She put her hand on her pocket, making sure she had not imagined the movement. She felt it again. She politely excused herself from the elves, making a quick excuse of having to go "relieve herself." She hurried off back into the thick of the forest, and when she felt she was far enough away from any listening ears, she pulled the pouch out. She tried the drawstring, and the pouch opened easily. Peering into it, she saw Gothart, the size of his wind-up toy self, but the form was quite clearly him. He stood within a black space, looking up at her.

"Finally! I thought I was going to have to make this bag explode to get your attention," Gothart remarked.

"Of all times for you to…" Desert Rain checked herself, not wanting to get angry over nothing. "Now's not a good time, Gothart."

"Why, Desert Rain, you look dreadful. You could use a good trip to a salon, if you ask me."

"No one did ask you."

"Now don't get all moody. That doesn't get anybody anywhere. Believe me, I should know." He cocked a white eyebrow at her. "Why don't you and I chat for a bit? It's good to talk out the stress."

"I have nothing to discuss with you."

"You know, that little peace offering I told you about is still on the table."

"I already told you, I don't want anything from you."

"Really? Because I don't have much need for this." He snapped his fingers, and before him materialized a brilliant silver sword — it was unmistakable what sword it was. "But maybe you'll want it after you snap out of this grouchy mood you're in, eh?" Before Desert Rain could say anything, the sword vanished in a puff of smoke.

"You…you thief!" Desert Rain was ready to plunge her fist into the pouch to hit Gothart, but managed to restrain herself. "Silverheart does not belong to you!"

"No, I suppose it doesn't. Naturally I would have let you have it, but if I had allowed you to wield it on that Wretched back in Syphurius, as I felt you were planning to do, do you really think you would have slayed him?"

Desert Rain glared at him. No, of course she wouldn't have. Katawa would rip her apart before she had the chance to raise any weapon to hurt him — if she could bring herself to strike him down. Gothart knew that, but she wasn't going to give him the opportunity to say that he had in fact saved her skin by stealing Silverheart.

"What I do is none of your concern," she finally answered.

"Oh, you'd like to think that, wouldn't you? Why don't you pop on in here, and we can have this talk on an equal level. I feel like I'm shouting up at a giant with no self-esteem."

Desert Rain was, naturally, puzzled. "Pop on in? What, you mean come into the bag? I can't do that."

"Why not? I fit in here comfortably."

"Yeah, but you're…you're *you*. Whatever you are."

"Hey, it's a fancy trick, isn't it? Reach your hand down and I'll give you a tug."

Desert Rain sighed, figuring he would probably turn her hand a funny color or something. She reluctantly slipped a hand into the pouch, and a force pulled on her so abruptly that she barely comprehended it when she was sucked into the pouch, headfirst, and was tumbling down along a neverending stretch of black velvet. She landed on something soft, but all she could do was lie there, bewildered beyond words.

She was staring up at a white ceiling. After taking a moment to collect herself, she realized she was lying on a white couch. Upon looking around the room, she found that everything in it was white, from ivory tables to feather-stuffed cushions to the carpet that could have been made from clouds. There was a fireplace with an elaborate mantle, displaying an array of ceramic vases, candlesticks, porcelain animals, and ornaments. Sitting in an armchair by the fireplace was Gothart, dressed in a white bed robe, reading a white book, smoking an ivory pipe. The vast amount of whiteness was nearly blinding, especially after having tumbled through black velvet. Desert Rain blinked, squinting her eyes until they adjusted.

"Explain to me how this is a trick," she said, getting up from the couch.

"You're the one who thinks it's a trick," Gothart replied, still reading his book. "Like they say, 'Everything's an illusion unless you think it's true'…or something along those lines, whatever it is."

Desert Rain observed that there was a portrait over the mantle—of Gothart, of course. "You certainly like white," she commented.

"I like things clean," the goat said. "There was a time when I lived in much more…squalid conditions." He put down the book, but not before tearing out a couple of pages and eating them. He puffed on his pipe, which made Desert Rain smile a little, for it was rather funny to see a goat smoking a pipe.

"But I digress." Gothart put the pipe down on a side table. "As spellbinding as my history is—and I'll make a note to tell it sometime—we're here to talk about you. All is going well, I take it?"

"NO, it is not going well! How can you even ask me that?"

"Last I heard, you got that bookworm Philosopher to talk to his friends up north. I thought that was a good thing."

"How do you know that?"

"I've been in your pocket this whole time. Just because you forgot about me, doesn't mean I haven't been keeping an ear open. Not much else to do when you're in a pocket."

Desert Rain scratched her head. "Why have you been hanging out in my pocket this whole time? It can't be very fun for someone like you."

Gothart drummed the tips of his fingers together. "It crossed my mind that I might want to lie low for a while. That Wretched friend of yours might still be a smidge angry at me. You know, for taking his memories and all." He smiled in mock guilt at Desert Rain. "Besides, this situation could be very entertaining, if you would stop taking your sweet time."

Desert Rain narrowed her eyes at him. "Excuse me?"

"You're gonna wait for the northern elves to come to the rescue? Please. Once they find out how dangerous that Wretched is, they're going to put extra locks on their doors."

"We have to try, Gothart. And I'm sure the Knighthood is

looking for Katawa right now."

Gothart leaned forward. "Where would they be looking for him, pray tell?"

Desert Rain didn't respond right away. She sat back down on the couch, pulling anxiously on her long fingers. "I don't know."

Gothart's eyes brightened with interest. "You don't, eh?"

"No, I don't! Katawa said he was going after the Darkscale, but I wouldn't know where to find them." She paused, thinking. "Although…"

"Yeeeeessss?"

"He said something to me, in that storm at Vaes Galahar…a strange word. Probably a demon curse, or something. I can't even remember it." She sat back, crossing her arms.

Gothart mimicked her action, in irritation. "Oh, come on, you can do better than that. You're going to make this very dull if you can't remember anything you're told."

"It was something like…T'Lesh…L'Ten…"

"L'Teth Zurên," Gothart corrected her with a huff. "Secret bastion of the Darkscale. Guarded by about ten impenetrable gates of dark magic. Not even the other two Courts of the Wretched know how to get into it."

Desert Rain stared at him, her jaw agape. "How in Luuva do you know that?"

"Because I've been there."

"Wait a second — if that place is so secret and impenetrable, how did you get into it?"

Gothart grinned. "I'm special."

Desert Rain twisted the corner of her mouth, not finding his answer amusing.

"All right, I got in on an invite. The Darkscale weren't going to discuss their plans for hiring me at my pen...house. Penthouse." Gothart bit his lip and scrunched up his nose.

Desert Rain was, in a way, relieved to see that Gothart was susceptible to making a mistake—he must have had a slip of the tongue to make that reaction.

Gothart continued quickly to draw attention away from his slip. "At any rate, it's not the most pleasant of places. Much too dank for my tastes. Not that I could go back. Those demons made it quite clear to me that I wouldn't ever find my way back there on my own, and even if I did luck out in finding it, they'd—how did they phrase it—'rip me open and use my blood for wine.' Eloquent, aren't they?"

"What do you mean, 'if you lucked out in finding it'? You've already been there."

"The entrance to L'Teth Zurên is hardly, if ever, in the same place twice. That would be the effect of one of those 'magical gates' I mentioned. It jumps here and there throughout the Inbetween. You locate it with an amulet of sorts—at least, that's what they used when they brought me there."

Desert Rain pondered, biting her thumbnail. "That, actually, is good news. Katawa doesn't have any sort of magical devices, as far as I know, so it will take him some time to find that place. Until he does, he'll keep the other Hijn alive...hopefully." She glanced up at Gothart suspiciously. "Why are you telling me all this?"

"To give you peace of mind. Or not. Anyway, getting back to my initial reason for pulling you in here..." He started feeling his robe pockets, and checking his sleeves. When Desert Rain was about to ask him to skip the act, he reached into the back of his robe and withdrew Silverheart. The blade was as radiant as ever, the sapphire-studded hilt a wonder of craftsmanship.

"Ah, there it is." Gothart presented the sword to Desert Rain. "I believe you wanted this."

Desert Rain gazed at the wonderous sword in awe, and believed she could see an ethereal glow of power eminate from it. She was drawn to it, and the next thing she knew, she was standing before it, delicately placing the tips of her fingers on the hilt. It was cool to the touch. She broke away from the trance, and drew away her hand. "I can't use this," she said.

Gothart lifted the sword a little closer to her. "You were so eager to get your hands on this before. You don't want it now?"

"Of course I…but I'm not a fighter. I couldn't…" She looked at her hands, at her lengthy fingers. "I can't wield it. I can't wield any weapon." Then a thought brightened her countenance. "But I could find someone who *can* use it. There must be a knight who could use it against Katawa. When the Ahshi knights return…" The bright glint in her smile dropped. "*Whenever* they return. That could be weeks, not assuming they didn't go straight off into a wild goose chase after Katawa." She walked back and plopped on the couch, holding her head in her hands. "I don't know what to do…I just don't know!"

Gothart sighed. "All I asked is if you wanted this sword. Then you go into a tangent about, whatever it was you were saying. It's a simple yes or no kind of question. Come on—legendary sword of the Swordmaster, one time offer, no strings attached. Do you want it or not?"

Desert Rain raised her head, looking at the sword in Gothart's hands. In her mind, she could see the hand of the knight who should be wielding Silverheart, the one to whom it truly belonged. She could see his warm gray-blue eyes, his silvery hair, his pearly armor. She saw that it was not the weapon that held power; it was the one who fought with it.

"Without Skyhan, it's no more than a normal sword," she said sadly.

Gothart lowered the sword, leaning it against the side of his armchair. "I'll take that as a 'no,' then. That's too bad. But I'm sure there's some shop that would pay me a few gold for it."

Desert Rain snapped her eyes to him, her face flushing in anger. "You would sell it like it's some piece of junk?"

"I told you, I have no need for it. I thought you might want it as a keepsake. But if you really don't care about it—"

Desert Rain got up, making long, purposeful strides towards the goat-man. She pointed a finger in his face. "Have you no decency? Have you no honor? This kind of greed is what got this whole ball rolling in the first place. If you could get your brain out of your coin purse for one minute, maybe you'd see there are more important things than—" She stopped.

Gothart lifted his eyebrows. "Money? You must be joking."

Desert Rain tightened her lips. "Than thinking about yourself." She dropped her gaze, closing her hand into a fist. It was easy to say that she was responsible to fix the mess, but she was relying on others to do the work for her. She took a deep breath. She looked into Gothart's laughing eyes. "I'll take it."

"There we go! Now see, was that so hard?" He picked up and held out the sword to her again. Desert Rain snatched it, and found the sword to be much heavier than Gothart had made it look. Its unexpected weight threw her off balance, causing her to fall backwards onto her rear.

"How can anyone use this thing??" She sat up, setting the

sword in her lap. "It's so heavy."

"Oh, I'm sure you'd get used to it after a while." Gothart sat back in his chair, picking up his book again. "Tell you what. I'll keep it here in the bag, and any time you want it, you can reach in and pull it out. Easy transfer, no service charge. By the way, you might want to hold your breath."

Desert Rain cocked an eyebrow. "Huh?"

A splash of cold water hit her right in the face. After coughing and sputtering, she opened her eyes. She was no longer in the white room. She was lying on her back, staring up at the sky, and she was surrounded by the faces of Ahshi elves, and one scowling Quetzalin.

"What in the Eternal Deep happened to you?" Chiriku asked gruffly.

Desert Rain sat up and looked around in a daze. She was back in the palm grove, lying next to the lagoon. "I'm…not really sure," she replied.

"We found you passed out," Paki told her. "We carried you here. Are you not feeling well?"

"I'm fine." Desert Rain rubbed her head. Had she dreamt that whole thing? No, Gothart must have done something to her, must have used some kind of sleeping dust on her before booting her out of the pouch. She felt her pocket, and found it empty. Then she saw the black pouch land at her feet. She looked up at Chiriku, who had been responsible for tossing it at her.

"You should get rid of that thing already. Now wake up and come on." Chiriku grabbed Desert Rain by the arm and yanked her to her feet. "I found a friend of my old man's staying here. He says he was with Gramps when he and some others were being led to some sanctuary. It's a few towns over. Let's get going."

"Maybe you could give me a few more minutes," Desert Rain requested, trying to steady herself on her wobbling legs.

"You had a nap. Quit complaining and start walking." Chiriku turned her gaze to Paki. "Well? You're the guide. Start guiding."

Paki was polite and patient, but he didn't bother concealing his frown. He turned and led them past the lagoon, through the extensive rows of palms, and in ten minutes they were back in the serene forest, following a trodden path.

Chiriku went in the front of the line, since there was a clear path to follow. Desert Rain and Paki walked side by side in conversation, but they both kept their eyes on Chiriku, making sure she did not get too far ahead.

"What is this sanctuary that we're going to?" the Hijn asked.

"It is one of the garden temples dedicated to the wise Earth Dragon," Paki explained. "It is said that the elves and dwarves once worked together to build such structures, before the dwarves migrated to the mountains. Such an alliance has not been seen since those times."

"Is there a certain reason why Syphurians like Chiriku's grandfather would be taken there?"

Paki paused, his face as stoic as stone. "The temple is where we take travelers who have fallen ill."

CHAPTER FIVE
Chiriku's Past and a Ghostly Vision

When Paki, Desert Rain and Chiriku came to the next Ahshi town, Chiriku had finally become as exhausted as the other two from the hike, so this afforded them time to stay and rest a while longer. Paki had family in this town, his sister and brother-in-law who owned a small herd of young elk. They welcomed the three to a light lunch of wildfruit and tea, and then lent them three of their elks for the remainder of their trek.

With the elks, the trek was more enjoyable, and riding an elk was not all that different than riding a Laspher for Desert Rain. It was Chiriku who had difficulty with her elk, since she was used to controlling a mount with reins, and the elk were trained to take direction with light taps on their antlers. Chiriku tended to bang the antlers, causing the elk to turn too sharply. Most of the ride involved a myriad of squawking curses emitted by the frustrated Quetzalin.

It was early evening when they spotted a jade building through the trees. It had the strong, broad, enduring build like those of dwarven structures, with the fine designs and details of elven flavor. The temple was a step-pyramid, with a flat top that supported four glassy green trees, one at each corner of the roof. In the center was a great jade statue of a regal dragon, its lifelike image glimmering majestically. A breath-taking garden encompassed the temple, laced with flowery arches, stone fountains, and fruit trees of every kind. It was the closest thing to paradise that Desert Rain could imagine. Chiriku, as usual, made no outer show of being impressed—she just made a light huff that sounds like "harrumph."

The sanctuary was maintained by an Ahshi sisterhood of clerics, all dressed in flowing gowns and robes of light green. They did not possess any magical healing abilities like Clova, but they had profound knowledge of herbs and the natural medicines found in Ahshibana. Many of them had studied with Mage Skyhan, but they knew but a small fraction of the Healing Hijn's secrets.

The clerics welcomed the three warmly, while a pair of elves took their elks and led them off to a holding place. Paki had barely gotten through introductions before Chiriku cut him off, demanding to know if any of the clerics had seen a lone human male in his elder years, rather fat, rather loud, and probably reeking of cigar smoke. The elves were a bit perplexed by Chiriku's rapid talk, but one cleric attempted to gently take Chiriku by the hand—which Chiriku instantly snatched back—and led her down the entry hall into the temple. The others followed close behind.

They entered the great hall of the temple, a massive room often used for important prayer offerings to the memorial of Earthbelly, but now it was full of people, Syphurians of all walks of life, being tended to by the clerics. There were whole familes huddled together, and some who suffered alone. Most people, weary and shaken, sat or laid on mats and blankets. Some had legs or arms wrapped in bandages, having suffered wounds or broken bones during their flight from home. The clerics hurried about, supplying plenty of water, food and salves for their guests. There was a door on the opposite side of the hall where other elves were coming in and out. They carried clean rags, bandages, basins of water and full jars of salve in, and came out with bloodied rags and half-empty jars.

The elves offered Chiriku, Desert Rain and Paki mats to sit on, although space was sparse so they were placed in a tight corner. The clerics went off to look for any lone human that matched Chiriku's description, as clarified by Paki. The room was uncomfortably quiet, except for the soft whispers of tired children and one street minstrel who played a lute, despite a splint on his wrist.

"Thank Guerda-Shalyr that these people are able to receive such good care," Desert Rain said, mostly to Chiriku as reassurance about Hibbletom.

Chiriku shook her head. "Figures that the old man would come here. He probably got a cold or sprained a toe, and he'd act like he's got a foot in the grave. What a melodramatic baby." She leaned against the wall nonchalantly, clicking her beak out of habit.

Desert Rain watched the various guests, looking away as a few people gave her curious glances. She thought she even heard one child say something to his parents about "that lady in the corner must be real sick." She hid her face in her hair. After some time, a cleric came up to them, telling Chiriku to follow her. Desert Rain felt compelled to follow, and surprisingly, Chiriku didn't make any snide comment about it. She was looking unusually anxious. Desert Rain was praying that the cleric was not going to lead them through that ominous door in the back.

Her heart sank as they were led through that very door.

The corridor they entered was lined with doorways to small rooms on each side. There were draperies over the doorways, although it did little to muffle the sounds coming from the rooms. There were lung-wrenching coughs and painful groans, and it was enough to make Desert Rain cringe. Near the end of the corridor, the cleric drew back the drapery to a room on the left. Inside, there was a man lying in a hammock, lined with soft blankets. He was very pale, damp with sweat, and he wheezed as he breathed. In his hand, which hung over the side of the hammock, was a lit, but barely smoked, cigar.

Chiriku ran over and snatched the cigar out of Hibbletom's hand. The man jerked his head up, instinctively reaching out to get his cigar back. Upon seeing Chiriku, his expression softened, and he let out a heavy sigh. "Was wondering when you would get here," he rasped with a smile.

"Are you stupid, smoking when you're like this?" Chiriku was stern in her voice, but her half-smile drew the edge off her sharp tone.

"I wasn't smoking it. I was smelling the aroma. It comforts me." He tried to sit up, but he stopped and groaned. "Damn bones don't want to cooperate."

The cleric, satisfied that this was the correct person Chiriku wanted, dismissed herself to tend to other guests. Desert Rain decided to give the two time alone, so she let the drapery fall and sat down on the floor outside the room. Even without her sensitive hearing, she would have been able to hear the conversation going on inside, and despite knowing that it was rude to eavesdrop, she perked an ear towards the voices coming through the thin curtain.

"You look like crap," Chiriku said to her grandfather.

"You're one to talk. You look like something the griffin dragged in." Hibbletom coughed, and almost hacked up something, but fortunately kept it down. "Where've you been this whole time?"

"It's a long story."

"It's not like we got much else to do than talk, seeing as how I'm laid up in bed and all."

"Come on, it can't be that bad. You always make too much out of nothing." Chiriku felt Hibbletom's forehead, and found it hot. She found a water basin on the floor with a rag in it. She picked up the wet rag, wrung it, and laid the cool cloth on Hibbletom's forehead. "You might have a fever, but that would be the worst of it. It's nothing you haven't dealt with before."

Hibbletom sighed. "Don't feel like no fever I've ever had. One second I'm hot, then I'm cold…and my bones ache like there's no tomorrow." He managed a smile. "Although I'm feeling a bit better now that you're here."

Chiriku grinned. "You're so sappy."

"Glad to see this ordeal hasn't changed your attitude," Hibbletom said sardonically. "I would think that maybe you'd lose some of your sass after a demon attack. No such luck, I see."

Chiriku smirked, rocking the hammock gently. "You can't lose attitude. Might as well ask me to lose my beak."

"Which I wouldn't mind, you know. I could finally sell something without you squawking about how I'm overcharging my customers."

Chiriku was quiet, her smile drooping. "The shop…what if it's gone? What'll we do if we go back, and find that everything's been destroyed?"

Hibbletom folded his hands behind his head, with some

effort in moving his arms. "Well, we pick up whatever's left and start up again. Life's got to go on. That's what your dad always did when the going got tough."

"Yeah. Picked up whatever he had and got going." Her voice cut like a dagger.

Her grandfather let out a sigh, ending in a cough. "I could never rein that boy in like your mother could. The longest he ever stayed in the city without running off on some lame-brained adventure was when he was with her."

"And that was a *looong* time," Chiriku spat. "Do we have to talk about them? I'd rather chew off my foot."

Hibbletom knew Chiriku hated talking about her parents. He sometimes tried to sneak them into conversation, hoping someday she would finally expose her feelings about what happened. Chiriku, on the other hand, didn't believe there was a single thing to talk about regarding them. Her father, Hibbletom's son, was a self-made fortune-hunter, a man more suited to the wilderness than city life. Her mother, a Quertzalin as slender and graceful as an egret, had been a seamstress, well-liked by Syphurius' elite for her fine dresses and coats. She had fallen in love with the human adventurer who came to her shop regularly to have his traveling clothes mended, and he had found her exotic and beautiful. She had convinced him to stop the adventuring, to work in her shop with her. But it was not long before the call of exploration drew him away, leaving behind the Quetzalin and their newborn baby daughter. The mother, her reputation sullied by having birthed a half-breed, lost many customers and ended up closing the shop. Sure, the father sent them whatever money he earned on his exploits, but mostly the mother got by on any odd jobs she could find. In an attempt to save herself financially and socially, she married a Falcolin, but it was treated more like a business deal than a marriage. The Falcolin detested Chiriku, the little abomination, so the mother left her daughter in the care of her human grandfather. Chiriku would say, under her breath, how she hoped her mother had finally had a purebred child that wouldn't bring her shame.

Hibbletom didn't like his granddaughter staying cooped up in his shop all the time — mainly because he didn't like children underfoot — so he would take Chiriku to watch the gladiators at the local combat arena, which she took a surprising interest in. If there weren't any events going on in town, he took her on short camping trips to appease her rowdiness. He showed her how to make a fire, how to fish, any wilderness tricks that would be useful. This was all the fun Chiriku had in her life, since she didn't make friends easily. Hibbletom allowed Chiriku to have her odd interests, and even fulfilled her birthday request for a warhammer like the ones she saw the gladiators fight with — hers was forged to be lighter, of course. The other thing Chiriku looked forward to in life was receiving letters and little gifts from her father. He never wrote any indication of where he was, but he would write of his exciting exploits and how he would someday come back to see her. Then, when Chiriku was about eleven, the letters stopped. There was never an explanation. She never heard from her father again.

But that was that. The story was simple, it was sad, but who cared. Chiriku didn't.

"I always wished I could have done more for you," Hibbletom muttered.

Chiriku snorted a laugh. "Did you hit your head or something? Why are you so sentimental?"

The man looked forlornly at her. "I didn't know what

happened to you in the panic. For a while, I thought I'd never see you again. Can you blame an old man if he's happy at seeing his granddaughter safe and sound?"

"This is you when you're happy, huh?" Chiriku took the rag off his forehead so she could wet it again. "Besides, you knew you'd see me again. You can't get rid of me that easily."

Hibbletom did not reply right away. "You're resilient. You're stronger than I ever was." He stared off into space, his eyelids heavy with fatigue. "I'm very proud of you."

"Geez, listen to you. You're talking like—" She snapped her beak shut. She stared wide-eyed at him. Then she laughed. "What kind of herbs do they have you on? It's making you talk nonsense. You better take a nap. I'll be right outside. And you better not eye any of the elf ladies, because if I hear that you do, you're in serious trouble."

Hibbletom grinned.

Chiriku pulled aside the drapery and exited the room, to find Desert Rain sitting right outside the door.

"Will you die if you're farther than ten feet from me?" Chiriku sneered.

"I wanted to make sure everything was okay," the Hijn replied.

"Everything's fine." Chiriku took off down the corridor, calling for someone to bring a fresh basin of water for her old man.

Desert Rain smiled. It was nice to know there was someone who could get through that Quetzalin's tough exterior. She stood up to walk away, when she heard a heavy, torturous coughing. She pulled back the drapery and saw Hibbletom trying his best to muffle his uncontrollable cough with his sleeve.

"Should I get you a cleric?" Desert Rain asked.

"No…no, I'm fine," Hibbletom said after forcing the cough to subside. He looked up at her. "Say, you've been in my shop before, haven't you?"

Desert Rain nodded.

Hibbletom squinted at her, apparently no longer in possession of his spectacles. "Yeah, you're that woman who knows the Swordmaster. So, you were driven out of house and home too, eh?"

"Yes," Desert Rain replied softly.

"Come here a second." The man beckoned her over with a shaky hand.

Desert Rain came over to the side of his hammock. She noticed a blotch of blood on Hibbletom's sleeve. "What may I do for you?"

"Chiriku—you came here with her?"

"I've been with her the last few days trying to find you."

"Ah, I see." He shifted, clearing his throat. "Listen, I don't want you telling anyone what I'm about to say, especially not Chiriku, all right?"

Desert Rain nodded, although she wondered what he could possibly say to her that he didn't want his own granddaughter to know.

"Look, Chiriku doesn't have a whole lot of friends. She ain't too personable, if you know what I mean. But I'd like to know that she has someone looking out for her. Can you see that she doesn't get herself into any trouble?"

"Of course. But you don't have to worry about her. I don't think she'll be going much of anywhere until you get better."

Hibbletom shook his head. "Let's not fool ourselves. I've

known for some time that these old bones don't have enough energy left to make the trip back home. Barely had enough energy to make it here. I don't put much stock in false hopes." He coughed again. "I know Chi can take care of herself, but she's had a hard time. So maybe you could keep an eye on her every now and then. You know, make sure she doesn't pick any fights she can't handle."

"I'm afraid Chiriku doesn't like me all that much. Why ask me to do this?"

"You seem like a nice kid. Chiriku needs more nice people in her life. Don't want her turning into an old curmudgeon like me."

Desert Rain smiled, wondering if she should tell him she wasn't really a "kid." After all, she was older than he was.

"I'll do what I can," the Hijn reassured him.

Hibbletom gave a satisfied nod. He laid his head back, closing his eyes. "Thanks."

Desert Rain quietly left the room. She saw a cleric coming her way, with a bowl of clean water. The Hijn lowered her voice to address the elf. "May I ask what ails the man in this room?"

The cleric looked around quickly, then also lowered her voice to answer. "It is a disease that many of the people had when they came here. It comes from eating the meat of the wild boars that dwell in these woods. We were told that some of the travelers hunted down the boars for food while on the trail, and shared the meat with others."

"Is it very serious?"

"The younger ones recover from the disease in a short matter of time. The elder ones...we can never be certain. The human in this room has been one of the worst cases."

Desert Rain's ears drooped. She thanked the elf and walked away.

"Paki, thank you for your generosity and guidance, but I don't want to keep you away from your wife and home any longer than necessary. If you want to leave, you are free to do so."

The Ahshi did not look surprised at Desert Rain's words. "It is no trouble for me to assist you. You will need a guide to return to Kapokis, will you not?"

Desert Rain scooted closer to him so Chiriku would not hear, even though the Quetzalin was not paying attention to them anyway. "Yes, but not right now. Chiriku doesn't want to leave her grandfather, and I promised that I would keep an eye on her. What you could do for me is tell Clova where we are, so if she learns anything new from the Great Philosopher, she can send us word. Would you do that for me?"

Paki nodded once. "I shall leave in the morning, then. Sleep well, Hijn Desert Rain." He lied down on his mat, and shut his eyes. He was so suddenly still, it was possible he had fallen asleep instantly.

Desert Rain lied down on her mat as well, but she did not shut her eyes. She was trying to juggle all the tumbling thoughts in her mind. She pulled the black pouch out of her pocket, and slide her hand into the bag. At first, she felt nothing. Reaching in a bit deeper, her fingertips touched cool, smooth metal. She could feel the bumps of sapphires along the surface. She pulled her hand out and shoved the pouch back into her pocket.

She could sense someone watching her. She glanced over at Chiriku, who was studying her with suspicious eyes. The Quetzalin turned away.

Desert Rain wondered how she could gain the trust of someone like Chiriku when she didn't even trust herself.

Chiriku spent the following day with Hibbletom, leaving his room when he needed to rest or when she went to fetch them something to eat or drink. Hibbletom's appetite was waning, but Chiriku would assure him that he was looking better and to stop being so difficult.

Late in the day, a young messenger elf riding a deer arrived with a letter from Clova, written on the Philosopher's reed-pressed paper. The Ahshi did not use bird-carried messages like the other Noble Cities unless it was truly important. They did not like to overwork the animals that offered their services to them. He delivered the message to Desert Rain, who was walking around the gardens. The message was concise:

Dear Dezzy,
Paki says you would prefer to stay at the Earth
Temple for the time, and although I wish you were
here for us to talk, I understand. I am glad to hear
you found Chiriku's grandfather. The Great
Philosopher is currently resting from the
Flightspeak he sent out, and he tells me we won't
know if his communication was received until
someone responds. He hasn't sensed anyone trying
to send a response to him yet. I will let you know
when we get Flightspeak from the Elfë Tiagas.
Dez, I pray that you have truly forgiven me for
angering you the other night. I would never intend
to hurt your feelings. Now, more than ever, we need
to stick together. May Nature smile kindly on you.

With love, Clova

Desert Rain folded up the note and put it in her pocket. She thanked the messenger, and told him to tell Clova that everything was all right and she would wait for further word from her. The messenger nodded enthusiastically and rode off.

Desert Rain hoped Clova didn't think she was staying at the sanctuary to avoid her, since Clova could be sensitive to that sort of thing. She sat down by the edge of a rock-lined pool and ran her fingers over the water. Already she was feeling antsy, but what else was there to do for now? Her thoughts turned back to the black pouch. She pulled it out, and looked around to see if she was alone. There was a cleric tending to the flowers, but she was far off and not paying any mind to the Hijn. Cautiously, Desert Rain reached into the bag, and wrapped her long fingers around the cool, metallic hilt within. She withdrew the sword about half way, marveling at the silver and sapphire sparkling in the sunlight. It seemed surprisingly lighter.

"That's quite a weapon," came a voice.

Desert Rain dropped Silverheart back into the pouch, yanking the drawstring quickly. She snapped her head up to see an elderly man standing a few feet away from her. He was incredibly familiar, with his braided greenwood staff and his patient face. "You should be careful with that," he cautioned.

Desert Rain recognized him. Her hand unconsciously went to touch the blue bracelet on her arm. "You're…you're that shaman! The one who took Jubis."

The shaman nodded. He looked different from before, as when Desert Rain had first met him, he had appeared human. He now wore traditional Ahshi attire and he had pointed ears. He had become elven, but not quite Ahshi, for he had no Ahshibana, and his features were not so delicate. It was more like he was his own variety of elf.

Desert Rain stood up and bowed to him. "Please, tell me, what am I to do now? I feel like I shouldn't be waiting around here, but I don't know where to go or what—"

"Have patience," the elder said, coming over to the pool. "When it is time for you to act, you will know. For now, I have come to show you something."

"Show me…?" Dread bled across her mind. "It has to do with Katawa, doesn't it? What has he done? What did he do to the others?"

The shaman gestured for Desert Rain to calm herself. "There is no point for me to show you images that you can do nothing about. A comrade of yours needs to tell you something." He lifted his staff and touched the bottom of it onto the surface of the pool. The ripples vibrated across the water gently, then faster, then more violently. Desert Rain leaned over, and peered into the center of the pulsating waves. The waters became tainted dark, a midnight blue, and within this inky pool came faint, foggy whisps, like transparent ghost fish gliding through.

"What is this?" Desert Rain asked warily. She stared at the gurgling waters of night, and could see an outline of white haze that was hard to distinguish what it was. She stepped forth, kneeling down at the pool's edge. She got the feeling that she really didn't want to look, but she summoned the courage to look down into the water. What startled her was that she had no reflection; it was like staring down into a misty chasm.

She waited, not seeing or hearing anything coming from the dark water.

"What am I supposed to see?" she asked the elder.

"He cannot sense your presence," was the answer. "Call to him."

Desert Rain bit her lip, and took a deep, deep breath. *He who?* She warily reached a hand into the water, and her fingers passed through the outline of white haze. Retracting her hand, she gathered her thoughts and leaned over the pool. "I don't know if you—whoever you are—can hear me, but I hope you mean good by me and maybe have something good to say." She was feeling awkward with what she was saying, for she had no idea who it was she was supposed to be addressing—she still couldn't see anything in the pool. "The shaman says that you have something to tell me, and if you can speak, I'm willing to listen."

No reaction.

Desert Rain looked perplexedly up at the shaman. "What am I doing wrong?"

A hand shot up out of the pool and grabbed Desert Rain by the collar of her tunic. She gasped, but was too shocked to scream. Pulling himself out of the water, a bearded Ahshi knight general brought his pale, skeletal face close to hers. His face was not peaceful; it was tense with anguish. His hair was so matted with slimy seaweed that it was hard to tell if any of it was hair anymore. His eyes, most frightening of all, were blank-white, blind, staring at nothing. The hand that gripped Desert Rain was nothing more than skin stretched tight over bone, as cold and hard as ice. He gaped his mouth as if to speak, but bared two rows of bloodied teeth.

Desert Rain's eyes were about to pop out of her skull. The breath in her body was cut short, and her ears folded back flat agaist the sides of her head. She thought for sure, this time, she would faint. But she was held by those blind eyes, the face pleading for help. She managed to stutter the name of the elf she had known but a few weeks ago. "S-s-s-sir V-Valdrase!"

"He calls to them…" the ghost of Valdrase rasped, a trail of dark water flowing from his mouth.

"W-w-who?" was all Desert Rain could stammer.

"The demon…calls to those…he has claimed as his own…" Valdrase gasped, trying to breathe—if ghosts truly do breathe. *"My knights…he has them in his grasp…his Distorted…"*

"Your men…yes, I saw them! In the mayor's house…Katawa took them away?"

"They were drawn to him…to his words…He speaks poison…His Distorted…do as he commands…they have no choice…their pain…their minds are weak…"

The truth suddenly struck Desert Rain. She remembered what happened in the Grand Chambers, when Katawa had infected Rukna's mind with his touch. Those awful words he had spoken, the ones that made Desert Rain feel weak, the words that drove Rukna to attack his own sister.

"Valdrase, I understand. When your other knights return, I'll tell them—"

Valdrase gripped her tighter. *"In the night…the camp outside the city…his Distorted…destroyed them…in their sleep…"*

"Great Guerda-Shalyr…" Desert Rain trembled. "I…I'm so sorry. But what can I do? What do you want me to do?"

"They will come…for you…he calls…for you…" Pain contorted his expression, as he turned his head downwards. His fatal wound emerged, dark blood seeping from his gut. But it wasn't blood, for it hardened as it grew, slithering up his body towards his neck. It consumed him, eating away at his decaying flesh. It was clawing at

his face as he rasped his final words: "*You…must…balance…the dark…and the…light…*"

He released his grip, and plummeted back into the water. When the ripples settled, there was no elven Knight, not a trace of Valdrase anywhere. Desert Rain continued to stare at the empty pool, which cleared into its normal, clean water. It was some time before she was able to regain movement over her body.

"What was that all about??" she exclaimed. She turned to look up at the shaman, who was, naturally, gone. She looked about in all directions, to find the cleric still tending the flowers, and she was looking at the Hijn with a surprised expression.

"Did…you see anything strange?" Desert Rain asked her.

The elf turned and walked away towards the temple.

Just a crazy donkey-eared girl talking to herself, thought Desert Rain.

CHAPTER SIX
An Arrival and a Parting

Days passed, and Desert Rain couldn't get Valdrase's ghost out of her mind. She tried to keep herself busy by assisting the clerics whenever she could, either by helping to distribute medicines and food, tending in the garden, or telling stories to the children. She realized how much she had missed entertaining children, and it brought back her favorite memories of putting on plays or singing songs to the Ulomin children. This would lead to her remembering what had happened to those children and their families, to that poor mother afflicted with Distortion. She would spend the nights lying awake for hours, helplessly dwelling on those miserable thoughts.

Chiriku was dedicated to staying by her grandfather's side, insisting that he would be well soon and they could go home to open the shop again. By the end of the week, he was so frail that he could barely talk. Even the smell of his cigars made him retch. Chiriku ceased teasing him, for he no longer returned the sarcasm. She became quiet, not even making rude comments to Desert Rain when she sat beside her. There were times they sat on their mats in silence, but nothing needed to be said.

Then word came from the Tiagalands.

It was an overcast day, early afternoon, when Clova Flor

arrived at the sanctuary on elkback, accompanied by a cheerful but weary Mac Lizard. He had a few acorn-sized bruises on his forehead.

"Goodness, Mac, what happened to you?" Desert Rain asked.

Mac rubbed one of his sore spots. "Those bug people fight-tkk dirty," was all he said.

Immediately after jumping off her elk, Clova gave Desert Rain a tight hug, one that she didn't release how crushing it was until Desert Rain wheezed that she couldn't breathe. At first, it would seem that this hug was an indication of good news, for Clova was smiling her classic smile and her eyes were bright. But Desert Rain noticed that the smile was forced, and the brightness in her eyes was an artificial light.

Clova was off and rambling before Desert Rain could get a word out. "Oh Dezzy, it feels good to see you. I know it hasn't been long, but I was getting lonely without you. I was worrying about you the whole time. Yes, it's silly, but I was hoping that you weren't still angry with me. And Paki told me all about Chiriku's grandfather, and I worried about him too. Is he doing any better? I hope it's not too serious. If Mage Skyhan were here, then I'd have no reason to worry, but—"

"Clova, calm down." Desert Rain patted Clova's hand. "There's no reason to worry. I'm glad you're here. Why don't we go inside and you can rest for a while?"

"Perhaps for a minute or two." She pulled Desert Rain close. "We need to talk, in private."

The two Hijn sat under a young birch tree in the garden, surrounded by sun-yellow flowers swaying in the cool breeze.

Clova gently caressed the flowers, which became even more vibrant in color at her touch. Desert Rain waited patiently, giving Clova time to ready herself to speak.

"How's Chiriku doing?" Clova asked.

"She's holding up. You can never really tell how she's feeling, but I think she'll be fine."

"That's good. I'm sure she'll be fine too."

Silence.

Clova sighed with a smile. "It's really lovely here, isn't it? Sometimes I come here to spend whole days in this garden. It's so peaceful. I wish it were sunny out today."

Desert Rain nodded.

Silence.

"How's Anthron?" Desert Rain ventured to ask.

"Oh, he's fine. He was pretty worn out for a day or two, but he's back to his daily reading and nightly teachings." She paused. "He got a response to his Flightspeak yesterday."

"He did? That's great! I thought we might be waiting for weeks, or might not get a response at all."

From the look on Clova's face, it apparently wasn't all that great.

"Well? What did the Elfë Tiagas have to say?"

"It wasn't the Elfë Tiagas who responded." Clova twisted a lock of her long emerald hair in her hands. "It was Kidran."

Desert Rain was more than surprised by this. "Kidran? Where is he? Is he coming to help us? What did he say?"

"The Great Philosopher said that Kidran's reply Flightspeak was congenial, as to be expected. He's in the Tiagalands, in the elves' hidden city."

"If he's up north…did he even try to come to the Hijn

Council meeting?"

Clova sighed. "He claims that he couldn't. There has been a great fear that has swept over the Tiagalands. The Elfë Tiagas have forbidden anyone to leave the hidden cities, not even Kidran. He wouldn't explain any farther—or the Philosopher isn't mentally strong enough to fully understand it. Either way, he's been trapped up there for some time now."

"A great fear of what?"

Clova shrugged. She lowered her head and turned away from Desert Rain. "It was a risk for him to even answer Anthron's Flightspeak, since the snowland elves have cut all ties with the outside world, and won't talk to anyone. They don't even listen to Kidran when he tells them to reconsider their actions. He tried to send us a letter with one of his snowbirds, but it must have gotten lost, or captured…" She took in a deep breath, but her talk got more rapid and frenzied. "So the Elfë Tiagas won't even talk to us, let alone help us, and Kidran can't help, and who knows where in Luuva Gros Woasim is, and I have no idea what to do now…" She sunk her face into her hands, her body shuddering.

"Clova…" Desert Rain put her arms around her weeping friend. "Clova, it's all right. Don't cry, please. I know it looks bad, but we'll think of something else. Someone will help us. We have to think a little harder."

On the inside, though, Desert Rain was thinking something completely different. *Clova, you can't cry! You have to be the strong one here! I'm a mess and I can't think of a thing to do. You can't leave this up to me! For Guerda-Shalyr's sake, stop crying!!*

"I shouldn't have left him!" Clova turned back around and hugged Desert Rain as if she'd never let go. "I shouldn't have left Rukna with that monster! I should have gone back, I should have done something!"

"There was nothing you could have done. You had no energy left to do any magic, not that it could have done anything to fix what Katawa did to Rukna. If you had gone back, you would have been killed!"

"No, I could have snapped Rukna out of it. He wouldn't have killed me, no matter what kind of mind control he was under. He's my brother, and I should have fought to save him. I broke my promise to him, Dezzy!" She wept into Desert Rain's hair.

Desert Rain wasn't quite sure what to do, other than hold Clova. "You can't do this to yourself, Clova. I'm sure Rukna understands and forgives you. He would want you to be safe. We'll get him and the others back, and undo what Katawa has done."

"You don't understand." Clova sat back, wiping her tear-stained face. "When Rukna and I were children, we trusted each other, and that was it. When my mother and his father married, they were both ostracized from their families—you know how elves and dwarves feel about marrying others of different races. I was angry at my mother for making my relatives shun us, and Rukna was furious at his father for making him leave his home in the mountains to live here in the forest. But Rukna and I—we might as well have been brother and sister by blood, we were so close. We promised we would always be there for each other, and protect one another, no matter what. I broke my promise. I...I..." She couldn't finish, she was sobbing uncontrollably.

Desert Rain took off her bandana and handed it to Clova, who accepted it to wipe away her tears. "I know what pain you're going through. I had brothers once..." She trailed off, looking away. She composed herself and looked back at Clova. "We'll get

Rukna back. I promise."

Clova smiled weakly, returning the bandana. "You're a good friend, Dezzy. If you weren't here, I don't know what I'd do."

Desert Rain patted Clova's shoulder. "For now, maybe we should go inside and get some tea. We both need it."

Night crept in on silent, chilling winds. The two Hijn and the red-headed lizardman sat on their mats in the corner, eating a warm dinner of roasted nuts and cooked vegetables, freshly grown in the sanctuary's garden. There wasn't much talk except for Mac going on about his fairy-hunting exploits, which he made sound much more exciting than they actually were. Clova had been offered a private room in the temple, courtesy of the clerics, but she had politely turned it down. She preferred that they kept the room ready for a guest who might need it, and who knew who might come through the temple doors next, seeking aid.

Clova must have had unusual foresight, for the sanctuary did indeed receive more guests that night, ones in desperate need.

A group of humans came shuffling into the main hall, escorted by a pair of elves. Judging by their clothing, the humans were most likely squatters from one of the reclusive villages outside Juka Basin. In front was a disheveled man, most likely a farmer judging by his physique and clothing, carrying a small girl wrapped in a dirty blanket. He was followed by an equally disheveled woman and two young boys. Behind them was another man who lugged sacks of personal belongings. He was well-hidden in his wide-brimmed traveling hat, cascading mantle and muddy-brown apparel. His arms and hands were wrapped in worn leather strips, showing the dirt-caked fingers. He didn't seem burdened by the sacks he carried, yet his posture reflected a tired, dejected individual.

"Please, we need medicine," wheezed the farmer with the girl in his arms. "We have been driven from our village, and my daughter is sick. We did not know where else to go. Please, we do not have much money, but my daughter must have medicine."

The clerics quickly guided them towards a room in the back. Desert Rain watched the family walk past. *Driven from their village? By who? Was no place safe anymore?*

As the humans were being led through the door, Chiriku was coming out of it. She bumped into the baggage man, and she squawked a quick curse at him. The man barely seemed to notice her as he disappeared through the doorway. The Quetzalin dragged her feet as she walked, and she plopped down on her mat as if she had lost all feeling in her body. It wasn't exhaustion that caused this behavior. It was clear from the intensity in her eyes and the rigid frown in her beak what the matter was.

Mac was the unfortunate one to be sitting next to Chiriku, and he was not picking up on the air of extreme hostility the Quetzalin was generating. "So there's-ssck the eye-pecker. Saved you a plate-ttk." He extended to her a bowl of vegetables that, evidently, had been plucked of some of its contents. Chiriku dealt the bottom of the bowl an upward slap that flipped it out of Mac's hand and sent the vegetables into his lap. He was fazed for a second, and then he scooped up the food and deposited into his own empty bowl, which constituted as his third helping.

"You should eat," Desert Rain advised Chiriku. "You haven't been eating much the last few days."

"Like you care," was the snippy reply.

"I do care. You're running yourself ragged, and you're

going to get sick if you don't eat something."

"Who are you, my mother? Knock it off."

"You may think no one cares about you, but you're wrong."

The Quetzalin wrapped her arms around her knees. "Shut up."

That remark shouldn't have made Desert Rain angry, yet she found herself slamming her bowl of food down on the floor. "If you think no one cares about you, it's because you drive everybody away!"

She had not meant to say "drive;" she had meant to say "push." She did not know how severely that one mistaken word would hit Chiriku. The bird girl was paralyzed, staring at Desert Rain with wide eyes full of shock and hate. Her beak trembled, and her breath grew heavy, as if she was about to screech. She stood up and stormed away, straight out of the temple and out into the night.

"Goodness-ssck, Gila Gul, what did you go and do that for? Not that she doesn't-ttk deserve a scolding, but for swamp sod's sake-kk…" He popped one more walnut into his mouth and then went after Chiriku.

Desert Rain lowered her gaze, rubbing her aching forehead. Clova placed a hand on Desert Rain's shoulder. "It's been a long week. I think everyone's tired. Give her a little while."

Tired…it's more than being tired, Desert Rain thought.

A few minutes later, Mac came back in, holding a hand over one eye. He sat down on his mat. When he removed his hand, the skin around his eye was fresh red, and his half-closed eyelids twitched.

"Best we leave her alone for now," he confirmed. "And don't-ttk bring up any quotes about chickens in front of her. *Ever.*"

It was later in the night, when all in the sanctuary were asleep, that Chiriku snuck back inside the temple. Desert Rain, who had never been that sound a sleeper, twitched her ears as she heard the Quetzalin quietly walk by, and sit down on her mat. Desert Rain didn't open her eyes, deciding that they both needed a good night's sleep before talking again.

Chiriku nudged Desert Rain, and when the Hijn didn't react immediately, she gave her a light punch in the arm. Desert Rain shot up, flinching away from Chiriku. "A little shake would have been fine," the Hijn said.

"Look, Ears, it's not like we like each other or anything." Chiriku scratched the back of her neck. "But I was thinking that if I've managed to piss you of all people off, than I must be really…you know. And this isn't really an apology or anything, but I'm too tired to start fights with people I barely even know. So, can we act like what happened earlier didn't happen?"

Desert Rain smiled at her. "I'm sorry too. I know it's a difficult time for you right now. I shouldn't have talked to you the way I did."

"It's nothing new to me. It's not like people haven't called me a crow before." Chiriku lied down and turned her back to Desert Rain. She looked over her shoulder. "Tell Mac I'm sorry for punching him in the eye. It'll look stupid if I say it."

Desert Rain lied back down, insulating herself under her blanket. She was beginning to think that Chiriku might be the most confusing person she'd ever known — but, then again, she herself was not so different.

The next morning, Desert Rain had an overwhelming curiosity to learn more about the humans who had arrived the previous night. She felt odd in asking the clerics if they knew anything about them, since she didn't want to seem nosy. She figured that she herself should go check in on them, in a friendly neighbor sort of way, to see if there was anything she could do for them. Perhaps it was because she had once been a normal human long ago that she was drawn to this family, or maybe she wanted to feel like she could actually do something to help someone—anyone.

She hunted out the room the family was staying in, cautiously sneaking a peek around each drapery that she passed. She eventually came upon the room she was looking for. She quietly watched the family huddled around the hammock the sick girl was lying in. The girl could not have been older than six or seven, and she was cute even with her dirty hair and face. Her parents, eyes closed, sat wearily on the floor beside the hammock, while the two boys were still sleeping after their long trek. The other man—a farmhand, Desert Rain surmised—had seemingly not slept at all. He was standing against the wall with the bags of belongings at his feet, mending a torn tunic. He was still hidden inside his cloak and hat, the brim coming down to his brow, so all that could be seen was his scruffy lower half of his face. On one side of his face was an indistinguishable blotch mark, but much of it was covered by his prickly facial hair.

The man snapped his eyes up towards the drapery that Desert Rain was peering from behind. He said nothing, but his gaze was fixed. Desert Rain figured he must have felt her watching, and it would be rude to not relieve his apprehension. She drew aside the drapery and stepped into the room. "Excuse me, I don't mean to snoop, but I was wondering if there was anything I could do—"

Her eyes met the man's, and she froze. They were both petrified for some time, staring into one another. Desert Rain's heart nearly leapt into her throat. His eyes were spellbinding, ensnaring—and gray-blue. They had a surprising piercing, familiar effect, even within the shadow of the brim of his hat. Desert Rain could not move, could not even twitch an ear. When she finally could move, it was to dash out of the room and vanish down the corridor.

I'm losing it, she thought. *I'm actually losing it. Funny, I shouldn't know that I'm losing my mind. But clearly, I am. Pull yourself together, Desert Rain. He's a farmhand, a common, everyday man. No one you know. No one, living...or dead...*

She stopped in her tracks. She gave her brain the chance to sort itself out. It was like Clova had said. Clearly, she was tired, and it was causing her to not think straight. She couldn't let her haunting memories turn her into a paranoid wreck. If she was ever going to help anyone, she had to get over herself. She clenched and unclenched her hands for a minute, calming herself, and then she turned around and headed back to the family's room. She was about to draw aside the drapery, but the farmhand thrust it aside for her before she could lay a hand on it.

Once again, Desert Rain was unable to move when her eyes met his, but this time she recovered from the petrification swiftly and rationally. "Forgive me," she apologized, dropping her gaze to the floor. "I didn't mean to be rude, walking out like that. I was startled."

"Who is that, Gabriel?" The mother came into view behind the farmhand. She was a plain woman, half of her auburn hair pinned on top of her head, the other half loose around her face. She had a frazzled, neurotic air about her, and she seemed to be washing her hands with some invisible substance.

"Oh," the mother said when she saw Desert Rain. "What do you want from us?"

The desert Hijn was taken aback by the mother's instant distrust. "Is there anything I could do to help you?"

The father — a brawny man with calloused hands — came over to stand beside his wife, and he made an obvious jerk backwards when he saw Desert Rain. "Who are you?" he inquired suspiciously.

"My name is Desert Rain. I'm a guest here as well."

"You not like any elf I've ever seen."

Desert Rain chuckled, tugging on one of her ears. "No, I'm not an elf. I'm human…I mean, I was, once."

The two boys, now wide awake, poked their heads out from behind their parents. The boys looked so alike, they might have been twins — their hair color was the primary difference, once a mousy brown and the other blonde. "Are you a witch that put a spell on yourself to make you look like that?" the blonde one asked with immense fascination.

"Not quite — although I don't know any witches who'd want to look like this." Desert Rain smiled at the boys, seeing that they had an interest for the bizarre.

The father narrowed his eyes. "You ain't one of them magic dragon people, are you?"

Desert Rain's ears folded back. She wasn't sure whether or not to answer truthfully. The tone of the father's voice was brusque, and his gaze was stone cold. Squatters probably didn't care much for magic-users, Desert Rain thought.

"I am Hijn," Desert Rain reluctantly answered.

The father crossed his arms over his chest, a smirk of scorn on his face. "So, now you want to help, *after* our village was burned to the ground. Can you rebuild our house with a flick of your hand?"

Desert Rain didn't like where this was going. "If you want me to go away—"

"Go away? Ha, like you great and wise Hijn are ever around to help the likes of us. Sure, you're always there when those in the fancy Noble Cities need you, but what about us in the woodland villages? Where's the Rain Hijn when our crops are dying from drought? Or that glorious Swordmaster when our village was ransacked by the Zi'Gax? Can you tell me that?"

The Zi'Gax. Desert Rain knew of them. They were a breed of goblins, rather monkey-like, but as quick and deadly as vipers. They made their living by hiring themselves out to do the dirty work for less scrupulous individuals—it went without saying that the Zi'Gax weren't smart enough to survive by thinking for themselves. Sometimes it was bounty hunting, sometimes disposing of "thorns" in the side of their employers. Most of the time, the Zi'Gax were hired by the Wretched to plan sneak attacks on the Knighthood. There were certain members of the Noble Races who would stoop low enough to hire these goblins for private purposes.

Desert Rain's face faded to a pale cream-yellow. "The Zi'Gax destroyed your village? Why?"

"How should we know? All I know is, it would have been nice if one of you all-knowing Hijn had been there to drive 'em off. So, unless you know if that Healer is around here, we don't need your 'help.'" The father grabbed the drapery and yanked it to mask the doorway.

Desert Rain stood there, bewildered. She knew not

everyone like the Hijn, but it hadn't ever entered her mind that the Hijn were selective to whom they chose to offer guidance and protection. No, the Hijn couldn't be like that—not all of them. Certainly not Clova, or Mage Skyhan, or…*Swordmaster Skyhan.* As she turned to leave, she saw a gray-blue eye peeking out at the edge of the curtain. She grinned sheepishly at the farmhand—Gabriel, was it?—and then walked away dejectedly.

One bad experience was piling on top of another. She couldn't stand trying to sort it all out in her head—she wanted to forget about it for a while. There was a simple method she always used to get her mind off things, and that was music. She didn't know how much it would please her now, since her artistic spark was gone, but it should at least calm her nerves. Upon entering the main hall, she found the minstrel with the sprained wrist. He had given up on trying to play his lute, his splint inhibiting him too much. She respectfully inquired if she could borrow his lute for a while, since he was not using it. The minstrel observed her long, slender fingers, and hesitantly handed his instrument over—after she promised to handle it with extreme care.

She carried the lute as if it were a newborn baby. She took it over to her mat, sat down, and began to pluck a few notes, reacquainting herself with the strings. Once she was warmed up, she began playing a sweet, sad tune, one that she had learned as a child. It wasn't long before she had drawn a small crowd—much to the chagrin of the minstrel, who hadn't ever drawn such a crowd when he played, but he couldn't deny that she was good. Desert Rain's fingertips glided over the strings like the graceful lapping of waves on a beach, creating currents of soul-moving sounds across the whole room. Soon she was softly singing along with her music, and, although she wasn't sure why, this captivated her audience all the more. She became so enthralled in her music, she did not even notice that the brunette and blonde twin boys had joined the crowd.

When Desert Rain finished, she received a round of timid applause. The two boys stepped up past the crowd, right up to Desert Rain.

"Our sister loves music," the brunette boy told her. "But she has to stay in bed. Would you come to our room and play for her?"

Desert Rain paused before answering. "I don't think your parents would like me getting in the way."

"You won't get in the way. Please, weird lady? Maybe it will make our sister feel better."

Desert Rain couldn't refute a request like that. This was, perhaps, a way in which she could help this family. She got up and followed the boys back to their room. Granted, the father was not pleased to see Desert Rain again, but the mother seemed to open up, especially when the boys told her that it was the Hijn who had been making that lovely music they heard down the corridor. The woman went over to her daughter, nudging her gently. "Alana? Would you like to listen to some music?"

The little girl opened her eyes, having not been asleep but resting. "Yes, Momma. I heard music playing outside. It was nice."

Desert Rain sat down on the floor next to the hammock, and started to play an old Ulomin folk song on the lute. Alana leaned her head over the side of her hammock to see who the mystery musician was. She was not surprised by Desert Rain's appearance. She smiled, paying all attention to the odd woman with the lute. Desert Rain even spotted the father tapping his foot, unbeknownst to him. Gabriel leaned against the wall across the room, his head lowered in what looked like contemplation. The desert Hijn found herself staring at him, and once she realized this, she quickly looked away. Alana suddenly coughed, hard.

The mother turned to the farmhand. "Gabriel, could you find one of the elves, see if they could bring Alana some more of that tea that soothed her cough?"

Gabriel nodded, and quietly left the room.

Desert Rain's fingers slightly slowed down, the music slightly softened. She continued playing, though, as she asked the mother, "I don't mean to pry, but who is that man?"

"Gabriel? He's a drifter we took in. He helped us escape the Zi'Gax and find our way here."

"He must know his way around the forests pretty well, then."

"He's the best," Alana said. "He's really smart, and really strong. He can lift a whole cow!"

"He pushed a cart with a cow in it," her blonde brother corrected her. "A small cow."

"Did he say where he comes from?" Desert Rain was hoping she was not being too inquisitive.

"We all got something to hide," the father replied. "You got any other songs?"

Desert Rain lowered her eyes and began to play another song, one of her own composition. While it sounded wonderful to the others, the music was stale to her — it may have been that she was thinking about the one audience member that wasn't there.

When Desert Rain was done with playing, she bowed a good day to the family and departed into the corridor. She remembered Hibbletom, and walked down the hall to his room.

She pulled back the curtain, and saw Chiriku sitting against the wall next to Hibbletom's hammock. The Quetzalin stared into nothingness, sitting as still as an ice statue. She didn't even acknowledge Desert Rain as she entered the room. The Hijn stared at her curiously, and then turned her gaze to the sleeping old man.

It was then she realized he wasn't sleeping. She came over to his hammock, observing his ash-white face, his still body. His chest did not rise and fall with the rhythm of breathing. She placed a gentle finger to his neck, searching for a pulse. His skin was clammy, and cold. She could feel no blood moving through his veins.

She drew back her hand with an impulsive flinch. She bit her lip, her shoulders slumped under the weight of sudden sorrow. She took Hibbletom's lifeless hand, held in in hers as she said a silent prayer. She placed his hand gently down at his side, and slowly pulled his blanket up to cover his face. She turned and knelt down in front of Chiriku. The bird girl was oblivious to all around her.

"Chiriku…" Desert Rain placed a hand on her shoulder.

Chiriku turned away from Desert Rain, resting her head and shoulder against the wall. "Go away," she rasped.

Desert Rain lingered there a moment, but then slowly stood up and left the room. She leaned against the wall outside the doorway, and because she knew Chiriku would never expose her grief, she silently lamented for her.

Her lamentation stirred up old feelings, and an even older sadness than Desert Rain thought she had put behind her. She, too, knew what it was to lose a loved one, a guardian, someone who had been as much a part of her as she had been to that someone…

***

Ninety years ago.

"Grandma Luna! It's me! Are you home?"

Desiree bounded down the steps into the underground temple, grateful to get out of the hot sun. She had been riding almost nonstop the last few days, having rented a horse in Syphurius, where her family was spending the month. She had left the horse in Ulomin, fearing that the stifling open desert would be too much for the steed, even in the dusk hours when the desert was cooler. Now her feet were sweaty and blistered, and she removed her traveling boots with great relief. Upon glancing about the room, however, she found it lacking a hostess. It was not like Grandma Luna to not be home, and it made Desiree worry. An elderly woman like Luna should not be out in the desert alone, away from the temple's water and shade.

Coming back up the steps, Desiree scanned the sand dunes, coated in a warm tangerine hue by the setting sun. She called for Luna, watching carefully for any footprints her mentor may have left behind. It did not take too long for the girl to find the old woman seated on top of one of the dunes, eyes fixed on the sky above.

"There you are, Grandma. What are you doing out here?" Desiree ascended the dune, the sand still a little too warm for her bare feet. She sat down next to Luna, wondering when her teacher was going to acknowledge her presence.

Luna let out a deep sigh. She watched the stars seeping out through the dying rays of the sun, the vibrant scarlets and oranges of evening fading into the purple of night. Desiree thought Luna looked very tired, even somewhat ill. Luna's hair, usually so fine and soft, was dull and frizzed. Her face was gaunt, yet her eyes were as bright and lively as ever, shining their beautiful sea green.

"What's wrong?" Desiree ventured to ask after some time of silence. "Do you want me to go away?"

"No, Desiree. Please, stay." She folded her hands in her lap, a tiny smile gracing the corner of her lips. "It's lovely, isn't it? This has always been my favorite time of day. Where day and night cross, they make such wonderful colors." There was a note of sadness in her voice, although she looked upon the heavens with wonder.

"Yes, it is lovely." Desiree rubbed her arms, the night chill creeping in. "I'm sorry I've come so late, but I didn't really have enough money to stay at an inn in Ulomin, and besides, I wanted to see you right away—"

"It's all right. I'm glad you came tonight. Tomorrow would have been too late."

Desiree furrowed her eyebrows. "What do you mean?"

Luna let out another sigh—or maybe it was labored breathing. "I am afraid, my dear Desiree, that we must part tonight."

The girl did not understand—or perhaps she did, all too well, and did not want to face it. She leaned in close to Luna, placing her hand on her arm. "No…no, don't say that. Are you sick? I can run back to Ulomin, I can get a doctor—"

"Oh, Desiree, you know better than that. There's no need to fuss over an old woman like me…" She trailed off, turning to look at Desiree. She smiled kindly. "Although…I shouldn't leave you thinking you've been fussing over an old *woman* now, should I?"

The way Luna emphasized the word "woman" made Desiree both curious and nervous. In a way, Desiree had always known she wasn't being tutored by an ordinary woman. She had tossed around the thought that Luna was a witch—a good one, of course—or maybe a shaman who had been blessed with great insight by the power of the temple she lived in. She had once even pondered if Luna was truly as human as she appeared, but it did not matter much to Desiree, not then. Now, though, it looked as if she was going to find out, and she was not sure if she wanted to know.

"Grandma Luna..." Desiree felt a pressure in her head, and tears forming in her eyes. "All I look forward to is seeing you. I don't want things to change..."

"But they must, my dear. I have been around for longer than you can imagine, and believe me when I say nothing remains the same for long. It is the nature of the world. It is the very spirit of life itself. Nothing is ever finished; it continues to change. Even when we descend into the Eternal Deep, we do not remain there. We come back again, different than the times before. Thus we learn, through many different eyes, the many lessons the world has to offer us." She gestured for Desiree to sit in front of her, facing her. Desiree did so, and found herself locked in Luna's eyes. The connection was so strong, the girl felt Luna's very heartbeat, beating in synch with her own.

"I don't want us to part. I want to help you..." Desiree bit her lip to hold back a sob.

"And so you shall, if you truly wish to. What I am about to ask you is important, Desiree. You must answer honestly, and without fear. If you feel any doubt, any fear in your heart, then you must not consent. However, if this is something you know you can face, then I give you my blessing, and we shall not have to part. I will always be with you, guiding you, and I will bestow on you my greatest gift."

Desiree was overcome by grief, wonder, anxiety, and some sensations she couldn't quite label. As she stared into Luna's eyes, she could feel a change. There was a new sense of courage she hadn't ever known, a courage that wanted her to face whatever it was Luna was going to ask of her. Luna could see this in Desiree's eyes, and knew that she could reveal the truth now. Then another change occurred, this time with Luna. Desiree did not notice it right away, for Luna's eyes remained the same enchanting green, but everything else of her was slowly shifting, slowly morphing, slowly blending into the design of another form. She was growing, her neck extending, her body expanding, yet her eyes remained level with Desiree's. Luna's hair was enveloping her whole body, changing from soft wispy hair into moonlight-blue scales, edged in gold. Her skin, which was visible from her chin, along her long serpentine neck to her underside, was warm golden ochre in color. Wings flared from her shoulder blades, stretching after many centuries of hiding beneath a human guise. The delicate membranes were gossamer, almost sparkling in the fading light of day. Before Desiree now laid a dragoness, about a hundred feet long from the tip of her equine nose to the end of her tail.

"Now you see me as I truly am," came the soft, tender voice Desiree knew so well, and yet it spoke inside her mind.

Desiree was not afraid. In fact, she was now less afraid than she had been a minute ago. There was no denying that this was a shock, and yet, Desiree knew in her heart that she had known all along. She reached out a gentle hand, placing it on Luna's muzzle. "You're so beautiful," she said.

Luna smiled—as best as a dragon can smile. She lifted her head with some difficulty, but managed to touch her nose to

Desiree's forehead. "I give you this gift, with full trust, with full love. May it guide you, and help you in guiding others. May the path of knowledge lead you to wisdom, and thus shall you find truth. May you listen to the voices of life around you, so you will know you are never alone on your journey."

Desiree could feel a tingle in her forehead. At first it was sharp, but it quickly turned soothing. Desiree closed her eyes, peace and joy filling her.

"Thus I, Bellaluna of the Blueshine, make you, the human Desiree, my heir. I grant you all I have obtained over time, all that has given me wisdom, all that has given me life. I bestow on you the words of Dragontongue, the secrets no other shall know." She did not speak these secret words aloud, but somehow Desiree instantly knew them, knew how to speak the dragon phrases, knew the secret of Blueshine in her heart.

Luna withdrew her nose, lifting her head high, casting her gaze to the sky. *Ia Ternaut* was bright in the heavens now, its silver light shining down. "You must understand the gift I have given you. I have little energy and time left, but I will show you the Blueshine."

Her wings outstretched, her neck fully extended towards the sky, Luna spoke the words of Dragontongue in melodic, moanful tones, and released a howl unlike any Desiree had ever heard. A gentle blue aura enveloped them, enveloped all that Desiree could see, as if everything had been caught up in an ocean of moonbeams. She could see wisps of light and shadow dance before her, the ghosts of good and the apparitions of evil. In the ever-growing magic of Blueshine, the evil presences melted away, the terrors of night overcome by the hopes of dreamers. There were swords, spears, tea leaves, books, birds, ships, wolves, stars, clouds, a menagerie of shapes that whirled through the blue aura around them, but all were good, driving away darkness. It felt both cool and warm, frightening and comforting. She could understand the Blueshine: it dissolved all things evil, left the good untouched.

The blue aura suddenly dropped away, and Desiree sat there as if nothing had happened. Luna went limp, falling to the earth, sending up a cloud of sandy dust. Desiree immediately got to her feet, coughing as she scrambled through the lingering dust. She knelt next to Luna, placing a hand on her neck. Luna opened an eye, and looked at Desiree. She smiled weakly.

"Do not be afraid, Desiree. Remember to listen to your mind, and to your heart." The light of her green eyes faded. She closed her eyes for the last time.

Desiree was paralyzed, but then came the torrent of tears. She put her arms around Luna's neck, weeping bitterly against the soft scales. Then she was holding nothing, for Luna was no longer a physical body, but was now pure essence, a swirl of fading light and smoke. It floated around Desiree, mixing into her own essence, seeping into her body. It was not invading, not to Desiree. Her sadness ceased, and she was relaxed, at ease. She sat there for some time, watching *Ia Ternaut*, the Traveler's Lantern, as clouds passed across its glowing face. She arose from the sand, walking back to the ruins of the temple. Once inside, she had a drink of water from the well, and then sat down in one of Luna's chairs. Draped on the chair, there was a blanket, and Desiree covered herself with it.

Tomorrow she would go back to Ulomin, retrieve her horse and head back to her family's camp. Tomorrow she would leave, thinking she would never return to this place again. Tomorrow, she would realize she was different, and she would have to invent a story to explain the new moonstone on her forehead.

But that night, she would sleep, dreaming of the Blueshine.

CHAPTER SEVEN
The Hunt

Mac wasn't used to staying in any one place for long—such was the life of a wandering merchant. He had learned one thing in the last few days, and that was Juka Basin was a poor selling spot. The Ahshi had little need for much of anything, and they were not interested in luxuries. Mac did not have anything much to sell to them anyway, except for the few minor trinkets in his pockets, and the elves considered them impractical and frivolous. All of Mac's good wares he had left with Kurl, back on the outskirts of Syphurius. He didn't worry about his strongback, for they had always had an understanding of what to do if they got split up. They would make their way back to the Bayou and meet up there, even if one of them should take a particularly long time. He imagined that Kurl was probably there already, if not close. The strongback had a good sense of direction, if he didn't have sense with anything else.

It had been four days since Chiriku's grandfather had passed away. Chiriku was spending her time alone by the plot in the garden where old Hibbletom was buried. Everyone was keeping their distance from her—even Mac knew better than to approach her during this time. Gila Gul and Miss Clova had spent the last few days in deep, serious deliberation, trying to figure out what the next course of action should be. Mac had eavesdropped from time to time, and the two Hijn did not seem to worry about his presence. Desert Rain had said how they needed to find a Knight who stood a chance against that demon fellow, and Miss Clova kept bringing up someone named Kidran and how they should try to convince some elves up north to release him. There were also mentionings of someone named Woasim, different leaders of the Knighthood, and wizards or witches that could be located. It really wasn't much of Mac's business, not having much knowledge in the ways of Hijn or Knights or wizards, but he was starting to wish that they would decide what to do and get going with it. If he had to go much longer without meat, he was going to start chewing on his tail.

He also noticed that Gila Gul had taken an interest in that particular human family, and a special interest in that guy in the big silly hat. Mac was observant by nature—he had to be for his line of work. He saw how anytime that fellow passed by, Desert Rain was watching him, or how she was making daily visits to that family when she needed a break from thinking about the future. It didn't bother Mac in any way, for he was glad that she had something to do in this boring place. Miss Clova spent her off-time puttering in the garden, causing flowers to grow or collecting seeds for her magic pouch. It was Mac who was running out of things to do, and he was not going to go fairy-hunting again. His head couldn't take it.

It was late evening, nearly night, when Mac got the excitement he had been craving.

It was after dinner, the usual fair of vegetables, nuts and fruit, and Mac thought he would sit under a tree outside to enjoy the cool breeze. He leaned back against an apple tree and closed his eyes, crossing one leg over the other. He hummed a little tune to himself, day-dreaming about the things he normally dreamed about: the mansion he would one day have, the finer threads, his own lounge—something more upscale than the Mudpuddle Oasis. His day-dreaming was interrupted by something flittering by his ear. He swatted at it, thinking it to be a bug, but then he was swatted on the nose. Shooting open his eyes, he instead saw a very large bug—a bug person, floating on rapidly-beating wings of translucent blue-white. It was about four inches tall, female in shape, but it had enormous black eyes and two feathery antennae coming out of its forehead. It was dressed in a flimsy dress made of spider silk, and it was staring at Mac impatiently.

Mac rubbed his nose. "What do you bug people have against-tkk my face?" he asked casually, as if this were no surprise at all.

"I am *not* a bug," the moth-fairy squeaked. "I'm a Twiight, you twit."

Mac sat up, yawning. "So, one of you li'l buggers-ssck is finally surrendering, eh? Knew that one day ol' Mac was gonna get-tkk you?"

The moth-fairy laughed, spinning around in the air and darting around Mac's head. "Get *us*? You can't even get a clue. But I know something you don't know."

Mac cocked an eyebrow. "Unless-ssck it's something profitable, I'd rather get back-kk to my nap."

"I guessed you would say that. But you gave us Twiights such a good laugh, trying to catch us in your silly cage and all. We like it when someone can make us laugh—you mortals never appreciate the value of laughter. It's what makes us Twiights live so long, you know."

"I'll keep that-tkk in mind. Now unless-ssck you're gonna let me catch you, you can just-tkk fly on outta here."

"My point is," the moth-fairy huffed, "that I thought I should warn you about what's coming, since you made us laugh. You like to trade, right? Consider this a fair trade."

Mac scratched his nose, sighing. "What're you talking about-tkk? Warn me about what?"

"About the Zi'Gax. They're coming this way. They'll be here tonight."

Mac shot up in alarm. "ZI'GAX-ssck! Good toads, not Zi'Gax-ssck! Anything but that-tkk!" He paused, and leaned back against the tree again. "What are Zi'Gax-ssck?"

The Twiight flitted about cheerily. "We saw them in the forest. They don't look too happy."

Mac stood up, stretching. "Well, that's nice-ssck and all, but I don't-tkk have a clue as to what you're talking about-tkk."

"Your friends might," the moth-fairy said with a grin. "You might want to tell them." Then the Twiight fluttered upwards into the tree and vanished into the leaves.

Mac scratched his head. "Bug people…go figure." He walked back into the temple, finding Desert Rain and Clova on their mats. Desert Rain was playing a light tune on the lute, as after-dinner entertainment for the children. Mac sat down next to her and poked her in the arm.

Desert Rain continued playing as she acknowledged Mac. "Is something wrong, Mac?"

"Not really wrong, I don't think-kk. Wondering if you knew what a Zi'Gax-ssck is."

Desert Rain stopped playing. Her eyes widened. "Why do you ask?"

"Funniest thing happened. You know those li'l bug people I was-ssck trying to catch? One of them flew by my head while I was outside, and she was-ssck saying something about a Zi'Gax-ssck something or other coming here tonight-tkk."

Desert Rain dropped the lute. It landed with a loud thunk on the floor, causing everyone nearby to turn their heads. Clova's jaw dropped, and her hands began to tremble. Most of the children who heard what Mac had said looked confused, but two of them, Alana's twin brothers, went pale. As children will, they saw no reason to keep this information private.

"THE ZI'GAX!" They were off like wild horses, running as fast as their little legs could carry them, shouting the warning to everyone within audible reach. "THE ZI'GAX ARE COMING HERE TONIGHT!"

A buzz of panic spread like wildfire on dry wood. Some brushed the warning off as a prank of two reckless boys. Others huddled closer to one another in petrified clumps. A paranoid few immediately began gathering up their things in order to get out of there. The elves tried to calm everyone, but the murmurs crescendoed into urgent and fearful chatter that echoed throughout the room. Clova tried to shout words of reassurance above the roar, but no one could hear her, or they weren't paying her attention.

"Thanks, Mac," Desert Rain said under her breath.

As the packed-up group was about to scramble out the front door, they were blocked by Chiriku standing in the way. When they moved to push past her, the bird girl produced her warhammer from a sheath on her back, and held it defensively. Everyone halted.

"Move it, kid!" a Falcolin ordered. "We gotta get out of

here!"

Chiriku was set like stone, resting her warhammer on her shoulder. "So is this how Syphurians are? You always run away when someone threatens you? I thought Syphurius was a city of proud, brave nobles. Even *I* expected Falcolin to have more backbone than this."

The people glanced at one another, mystified.

"I'm sick of running away. I'm sick of Syphurians being scared. This time, I'm staying and fighting." Chiriku grasped her warhammer in both hands. "If you people would stop acting like frightened mice and start acting like Syphurians, we can show these Zi'Gax who's boss."

"But we're not fighters," a Syphurian woman said.

"No," Desert Rain interjected, coming to stand next to Chiriku. "But you forget that you have two Hijn here. We aren't going to let anything happen to you. We'll find a way to hold them off."

"Oh no, you're not cutting me out," Chiriku declared. "I'm a fighter, and I intend to fight."

Desert Rain wasn't sure how to feel about Chiriku's sudden determination to battle. Chiriku was still in mourning, and this didn't seem to be the right way to cope with her loss. On the other hand, it did not look like anyone else was willing to help. Even the few Falcolin in the room, who don't like to be accused of cowardice, weren't stepping up.

Clova came to stand in front of the crowd. "Listen to me, everyone. I know you've all been through a lot. I know it must seem like the world's turned upside down. But this is a sanctuary, a place of peace and security. There is no safer place for you to be. The elves will take care of you, and I'll take care of the Zi'Gax.

Everyone, stay inside. If anything should go wrong, the elves will take you to safety. The worst thing you can do right now is panic." She donned a smile, to the best of her ability. "So why don't you all go back and get comfy cozy, all right?"

"Unless you would *like* to go out into the cold, dark forest this time of night, so the Zi'Gax can find and catch you before you even know they're coming," Desert Rain added.

The Syphurians still looked doubtful, but they turned around and went back to their designated mats.

Clova sighed in relief. "Dezzy, maybe you could play some music to calm everyone down. I'm going to go outside and grow a wall up around the temple. If I make the vegetation thick enough, the Zi'Gax will hopefully give up trying to hack through it before they get in here."

"But Clova, for you to grow a wall big enough and thick enough to cover this whole temple…that would take all the magic energy you have," Desert Rain remarked. "Not to mention we don't know how many Zi'Gax there are. A good number of them could slice through in a short time."

Chiriku snorted. "Yeah, really, a stupid wall? That's the best you can come up with? Those Zi'Gax won't give up unless we bash some heads."

"I'm not going to start a battle here," Clova retorted, placing her hands on her hips. "I'm not going to let *you* start one."

"That's because you're a scaredy-elf!" Chiriku squawked.

"Both of you, stop it!" Desert Rain stepped between the Forest Hijn and the Quetzalin. "We're not going to solve anything by arguing."

"Gila Gul's right-tkk," Mac said, strolling over to them nonchalantly. "I don't know much about these Zi'Gax-ssck fellows, but maybe there's a way to deter them before they get-tkk here."

Desert Rain perked her ears towards Mac. "Do you have a plan?"

"Well, I don't mean to boast-tkk," he said, tucking his thumbs into his belt, "but we folk-kk down by the Bayou have our li'l tricks-ssck of the trade. We get plenty of nasty critters-ssck that we have to bamboozle, and I might have something that'll throw those Zi'Gax-ssck off track-kk. Now, do any of you know if there is some gigam spice and pop-buds-ssck around here, so I can make some blast-tkk powder..."

The forest was soaked in shadows, the trees shrouded in obsidian black. The leaves shivered in the night wind, howling the coming of intruders. There was no clear path, even for the nocturnal sight of the Zi'Gax, who silently stalked past the trees. Everything was outlined in a reddish light to their eyes, sometimes the red bleeding blue or violet, depending on if there was an intense source of heat or cold close by. So far, everything was still, and they could smell no strong scent of living flesh.

There were about two dozen Zi'Gax, half skulking along the ground, the other half traveling by hopping from tree to tree — their powerful legs being their primary appendages. They were mummified from ankle to neck in six-inch wide bandages, their typical clothing choice, for skin-tight clothing kept them streamlined and agile. One Zi'Gax, a grimy mud-yellow in skin color, wrapped in bandages of dark gray, hovered near the leader of their pack. He kept his sensitive ears warm with his stocking cap, striped gray and brown, settled low over his brow, and trailed behind him, almost scraping the ground. His bare feet and hands, like the other Zi'Gax, were used to extreme weather, whether hot or cold. His palms and soles were leather-tough, with sharp fungus-encrusted nails that could rip through the thickest flesh. His face, half-masked by a bandage that covered his left eye and forehead, displayed a smushed nose, blistered dry lips with protruding teeth, and beady eyes of black irises and red pupils, sunk into sockets rimmed with deep wrinkles.

"Is that stupid device even working?" the stocking-capped Zi'Gax hissed to his leader. "We've been in this forest for days, and that blasted piece of junk hasn't shown us anything." His tone shifted into his usual whine, as he was prone to complaining and blathering. "I'm hungry, and my toes are freezing, and this is the most boring hunt ever."

The leader, a much taller Zi'Gax wrapped in the defining blood-red bandages of his position, snarled at his comrade. His skin shade was that of an older goblin, a gray-green, and he possessed two sickles hanging from his chain-belt. These were given to Zi'Gax who had proven themselves, compared to the stocking-capped Zi'Gax, an underling who wielded two iron daggers. The leader held a strange, compass-like device, enscribed with bizarre markings all around the inside rim. There was a small metal ball inside the compass that hovered in the center, and it was designed to levitate towards the presences of magic. Not the flimsy, flashy magic of common spellcasters, but the deeper, more potent Ancient Magic that a rare few possessed. However, the ball had slightly shifted one way or the other the last few days, not verifying anything concrete.

"Watch your tongue, Spiggat, before I tear it out," the leader spat to the other Zi'Gax. "They said we must use this device to find our prey. Do not question to orders of our employers."

Spiggat ground his crooked teeth. "I don't doubt their power, Cryle. But that thing has led us to villages that have had no sign of what we are looking for. I don't mind the looting, of course—" He licked his lips at the memory of enjoyment he had when pillaging a human village—"but I don't like these woods. And what if we're spotted by those elves?"

Up to now, the Zi'Gax had tried to avoid any elven villages, since the elves were master archers and as good of shots in the dark as in daylight. The magical device had also not indicated that there was anything to be found in the Ahshi towns they passed, and they didn't want to risk any elves escaping to warn the neighboring towns. But they couldn't leave Juka Basin unchecked. It would be the kind of safe haven their prey would hide in, Cryle thought, and as soon as they found it, they would strike swiftly before the elves realized it.

"Don't worry about the elves," Cryle assured his comrade. "If any are foolish enough to cross our path, we will dispose of them as we would anyone else." He tapped his compass, wondering if, indeed, the device had ceased working.

Suddenly, the metal ball drifted to the right, and slowly made its way to the edge of the compass, rolling upwards slowly. Cryle halted his pack, waiting for the ball to stop rolling. The other Zi'Gax sniffed the air, searching for any strange smells. Cryle scanned the trees, his eyes looking for any outlines of violet, an indication of body heat in the immediate area. They all quietly crept to hide behind trees, or stayed low to the ground, blending into the shadows of night. Their eyes glowed dimly, like those of wild animals. Cryle closed his eyes to focus his sense of smell, and he detected the potent smell of lilac.

He inched forward slowly, crawling with his belly dragging

along the ground. The others followed, and the ones in the tree tops jumped down, guarding the rear. They came closer and closer to the sweet smell, finding a wall of lilac bushes about twenty feet in front of them. Cryle wrinkled his nose, and lowered his brow. Funny, his sense of smell should have picked up something that stunk this badly from a mile off. It was as if these lilac bushes had suddenly appeared out of nowhere…

A sudden blast of bright light erupted on the ground in front of them. The brightness blinded the Zi'Gax, causing them to scatter in all directions, screeching like frightened monkeys. Cryle jumped to his feet, shielding his eyes and baring his teeth. Another blast of light landed right at his feet, causing him to spring backwards and land on his ratty tail. He heard rustling all around him, as if the forest was moving of its own accord. Once his eyes adjusted, he saw that vines were rising from the earth, curling around his legs and body. Enraged, he grabbed one of his sickles and sliced away the vines, freeing himself and jumping up into a tree before the vines could regrow. Glancing around, he spotted another Zi'Gax, ensnared in vines, pinned to the forest floor.

"You fool!" Cryle leapt down from the tree, dashing over to cut his subordinate loose from his bindings. "Find whatever is doing this! NOW!"

The freed Zi'Gax slithered away, staying close to the shadows. Cryle sniffed the air, trying to smell past the stench of lilacs. Whoever was responsible for this ambush must have placed those lilacs there, knowing their fragrance was strong enough to mask their own scent. He checked his compass again. Now the ball was rolling all around the rim, as if magic was coming from everywhere. There must be magic traps set up all over the place, but they were plants, for Hob's sake. How could plants possibly —

He heard a loud crack, not too far from where he was. He stayed low, scurrying silently towards the noise. His eyes caught the outline of something glowing violet, lying on the ground. It was a body—a Zi'Gax's body, its head smashed in. The body still twitched, and the hand loosely clutched a dagger. Cryle inspected the lethal blow to the head. From the depth of the hit, it had been caused by a warhammer. He was more than confused, since dwarves were the ones who used warhammers, as far as he knew. What would a dwarf be doing here? Sniffing the air again, he did not pick up the scent of a dwarf, but that of a bird—no, it was either Falcolin or Quetzalin. He curled his lips back over his gums, and continued with a rapid pace through the woods.

"We got-tkk them on the run!" Mac whispered, hiding in a tree next to Desert Rain. "Did you see their faces-ssck when that blast powder hit-tkk?"

Desert Rain put a finger to her lips to shush Mac. "Shhhh. You stay here, Mac. It's my turn now."

Desert Rain jumped down from the tree, her prehensile feet landing on the the forest floor soundlessly. Mac had done his part perfectly. His blast powder had caused all the Zi'Gax to be separated from one another. Desert Rain's role was, to put it plainly, live bait—she was to draw each Zi'Gax into the plant traps Clova had devised. Her part was risky, but she was the fastest person in Luuva Gros, and it was very unlikely that any Zi'Gax was going to catch her. She prayed that if any of them was to throw a weapon at her, she would be fast enough to evade it. Chiriku had self-assigned herself to sneak attacks, hiding behind trees in wait for a Zi'Gax to come by and fall to her warhammer. There was the possibility of Chiriku taking a mistaken swing at

Desert Rain, but Desert Rain should be fast enough for Chiriku's swing to miss her and hit whoever was chasing her instead.

Desert Rain moved swiftly around the trees, the night vision in her right eye guiding her through the blackness. Her ears were ever attentive, listening for any movement in the brush. She breathed through her mouth as to be more silent, but her breath was quick and short in her nervousness. She had no idea where Clova was at this moment. The Forest Hijn had created several pre-set traps, ones that triggered as soon as someone stepped upon them, but Desert Rain knew where they were and could easily jump over them. If these did not work, it was Desert Rain's duty to lure the Zi'Gax into Clova's "big" trap that was located near a small clearing.

Judging from the number of Zi'Gax they had seen, this was to be no easy task.

Something sharp zinged past Desert Rain's ear, cutting off a few strands of her hair. It landed solidly in a tree trunk, and she could see that it was a dagger. She heard fast-approaching footsteps behind her, and without looking back, she took off with lightning speed. She darted towards the nearest trap she knew of, deftly leaping over it, not stopping until she heard a noise like several whip lashes and a quick yelp. Turning to look, she saw a Zi'Gax tangled up in a mass of vines, snarling as he wiggled helplessly.

Desert Rain stopped to regain her composure, telling herself that she had to do that about twenty more times.

After creeping around for two minutes, she stumbled upon three Zi'Gax grumbling in discussion. They were too involved barking at and punching each other to notice her at first. Desert Rain wasn't sure if any one of Clova's pre-set traps would catch all three of these goblins at a time, but she knew the big one would. Trouble was, she wasn't close to the big trap from here, and she might run into more Zi'Gax on her way to it. Maybe that was a good thing, as long as none of them caught her. She picked up a stick with her foot, took it in her hand and flung it at the three Zi'Gax. The stick bopped one in the head, and instantly the three whirled around to face Desert Rain. She waved mockingly at them, and was off like a pursued rabbit.

The forest blurred past her as she ran, and she heard the Zi'Gax cursing her as they gave chase. In her rush, she nearly tripped another of Clova's magic traps, but remembered to jump over it in time. She heard another yelp behind her, but the running footsteps still followed. She saw the trees being to part, indicating that the clearing was coming up. She sped up—and then two new Zi'Gax jumped out from the shadows to block her path, daggers at the ready.

Desert Rain veered sharply to the right to dodge the goblins before her. She was now being followed by four Zi'Gax—at least that she knew of—and she was going the wrong way. The footsteps and snarling was getting closer, and she felt a sharp pain in her arm as a flying dagger skimmed her. Clutching her wound, she kept running, her brain scrambling for a plan. She heard a loud smash, and the startled shrieks of the Zi'Gax behind her. Darting a quick glance back, she saw Chiriku, a bloody-headed Zi'Gax at her feet, and the three others baring their teeth at her like dogs ready to pounce.

Desert Rain stopped dead. There was no way Chiriku could handle three Zi'Gax at once. Where was Clova when you needed her?

Chiriku made a broad swing at the goblins, forcing them to

back away. This didn't deter them. One pounced at her, and she blocked with the handle of her warhammer. She kicked the beast in the groin, which sent him flat down, moaning. The other two rushed her at the same time, and she managed to crack the jaw of one with the head of her weapon, but the other tackled her, trying to yank the warhammer from her hands. He snapped his teeth at her, but she held him back by jamming the handle of her weapon under his chin. Then there was a crack, and the goblin went limp. Throwing the Zi'Gax off her, Chiriku looked up to see Desert Rain, holding a rock in her hand.

"Nice one, Donkey Ears," Chiriku commended her. "Didn't think you had it in you."

A long, curved dagger dug into Chiriku's ankle. She screamed, dropping her warhammer. The Zi'Gax, the one she had kicked, yanked his dagger from Chiriku and readied it to slash again. Desert Rain grabbed the Zi'Gax, throwing him away from Chiriku, but he grabbed Desert Rain's arm, pulling her to the ground. He got up and kneeled over her, bringing his dagger over his head for a swift fatal strike.

A thick branch whacked the Zi'Gax in the face. He tumbled backwards, holding his bloody nose, growling a whole slew of curses. Desert Rain sat up quickly, scrambling backwards. She saw the figure who was wielding the branch, who now faced the Zi'Gax. He was cloaked with a hat shrouding his face, his leather-bound hands handling his make-shift battlestaff expertly.

"Gabriel??" Desert Rain couldn't believe her eyes. What was he doing here?

The Zi'Gax hissed, standing up and charging with his dagger high overhead. But before he could bring it down, Gabriel swung his battlestaff at the goblin's legs, tripping him flat onto his face. The Zi'Gax didn't even have a chance to get up, for Gabriel brought the butt of his battlestaff down sharply onto the nape of the beast's neck, snapping it like a twig. The goblin didn't even twitch; he was instantly dead.

Chiriku rolled onto her side, grasping her bleeding ankle. "Divine Beasts damn it!"

"Chiriku!" Desert Rain went over to her, inspecting the wound. It wasn't too deep, but it was serious enough. She took off her bandana and wrapped it around the ankle tightly. "We need to get you someplace safe."

"Don't coddle me," Chiriku spat, leaning against a tree to stand up on her one good leg. "I'm not gonna let a little cut stop me."

"Then stay here," Desert Rain ordered. She turned to Gabriel. "Keep an eye on her. I'll come back after I make sure some more Zi'Gax are out of the way."

"You can't go alone."

Desert Rain blinked, surprised. She hadn't heard Gabriel speak before. His voice was soft, demure, the tone of a shy poet. Yet there was a hidden assertiveness in his tone, and his eyes locked steadily onto hers. "You can't go by yourself," Gabriel repeated.

"We can't wait here for the other Zi'Gax to find us," Desert Rain argued.

"I'll go, then."

Desert Rain delved into those gray-blue eyes, looking for that glint of pride and valor that she once saw in another man. There was a flame of bravery, certainly, but it was small, surrounded by the smoke of self-doubt. It was the inner light of a young man who had a heart of goodness and generosity, but no faith in himself. It made her heart sink, for some reason. This was not the soul-fire of a Swordmaster. It was a normal pair of blue eyes.

There was a rustling a few yards away. The three of them froze. Gabriel gripped his staff, holding up a hand for Desert Rain to keep still. He crept slowly, methodically, ducking low behind trees as he went. He suddenly darted out of sight. Desert Rain wanted to follow, to help Gabriel if he was ambushed, but she couldn't leave Chiriku alone.

"What, are you going to let that guy have all the fun?" Chiriku tried to steady herself on her good leg. She carefully bent down to pick up her warhammer. "How about a little help here?"

Desert Rain came over and let Chiriku put an arm around her, leaning on her as a crutch. Chiriku limped along, wincing as she went, and Desert Rain remained alert, scanning the woods for signs of danger. Everything around them was uncomfortably quiet. Sweat dripped down Desert Rain's face, and her ears shivered. Chiriku whispered for her to cool it, since Dez's shaking ears were ruffling up against her feathers.

They limped on and on through the dark wood. Then Desert Rain spotted something ahead, in the middle of a tight ring of trees. It was a silhouette of a man with a long battlestaff in his hands. She and Chiriku ducked down behind a bush. They peered out, watching Gabriel, who stood rooted there, in a defensive position. His feet were spread wide, his battlestaff held across his chest. The two women were not sure what he was doing. He looked stuck.

Then they noticed that he was surrounded by pairs of red-glowing eyes.

A blur of black whooshed out of the trees, a flash of light off of metal headed straight for Gabriel. The boy dodged the attack, bringing his battlestaff upwards and knocking the dagger from the Zi'Gax's bony hand. More blurs lashed out, hungering to smother Gabriel in darkness, but the man jumped aside, twirling his battlestaff around to block the multiple assaults. The battle was difficult to follow, the combatants darting this way and that in a jumbled foray, but Gabriel was fending off four Zi'Gax at one time.

"He's going to be killed!" Desert Rain gasped.

"What an idiot," Chiriku stated. She tried to stand up, but her ankle was throbbing. "Damn it. If you could get a couple of those suckers to come this way, I could whack 'em."

Desert Rain knew what she had to do. She had to get those Zi'Gax away from Gabriel, had to lure them into the big trap, not too far away. She left the bush and started towards the fight, and that's when she noticed something. Gabriel was no longer handling his weapon like a battlestaff. He held it at one end, perrying and swinging it like a club. No…like a…

"He knows how to use a sword," she realized. Her hand reached for the black pouch in her pocket, thrusting her hand into it. She found the hilt inside, wrapping her fingers around it, getting as firm a grip on it as she could. She withdrew the magnificent sword, and it shined even in the overpowering darkness. She dashed towards the battle, holding the sword before her. Its radiance gleamed brightly, catching the eyes of the four Zi'Gax. They gaped their horrid mouths wide, squinting their beady eyes against the silver light. They shrunk back, raising their arms against the terrifying sword.

Chiriku's beak dropped open. "You had that sword this whole time, and didn't think to use it??"

"Gabriel!" Desert Rain lifted the sword as best she could, as it was a bit heavy for her. "I have a sword you can use! Here! Take it!"

The expression on Gabriel's face was not one she expected. His eyes were wide in fright. He gripped his battlestaff tightly, and stared at Silverheart like a deer facing a wolf. He backed away, his knees shaking. He dumbfoundly shook his head.

Desert Rain couldn't understand. Why didn't Gabriel want the sword? Maybe he didn't know how to swordfight; maybe she was mistaken about him. She didn't have any time to contemplate. The Zi'Gax were staring at her with skeptical eyes. She could think of one thing to do: bluff.

"Stay back!" she commanded, coiling her fingers around the hilt so to hold the sword before her, blade extended towards the goblins. "This is Silverheart, the Wretched-slayer! One slice of this sword will kill every last one of you!"

Three of the Zi'Gax cowered at her declaration. "That *is* the evil sword!" one of them cried. "The one of the horrible Swordmaster!"

The one not-so-scared Zi'Gax bared his teeth. "Maybe, but that ain't no Swordmaster. I bet she don't even know how to use it." He twirled his daggers in his hands, and then gripped them for attack.

Desert Rain's ears drooped. *Forget this!*

She ran like she had never run before. She knew those Zi'Gax would be chasing her now, would kill her so they could get their hands on Silverheart. The weight of Silverheart was slowing her down, and she almost considered dropping it. But no, she couldn't. She couldn't lose it, not for anything. The big trap wasn't too far. If she could make it...

She saw it. Straight ahead was a break in the trees, and

what lied beyond was screened by a veil of blue mourning glory vines rising from the ground. Desert Rain was running so hard, her legs were burning in pain. She could feel the Zi'Gax right on her heels, laughing maniacally in anticipation of capturing their quarry. They could tell she was tired, and it would be more fun to catch her by hand then throw daggers at her. She made one final sprint, and made a mighty jump through the curtain of mourning glories, vanishing from the Zi'Gaxs' sight. The Zi'Gax, blinded by their lust of the hunt, leapt through the vines after her like lemmings.

They stopped. Not of their own free will, but because they ran headlong into a wall. They were plastered against something spongy, something fuzzy, something sticky. When they tried to pull away, they found their entire fronts stuck to the adhesive-coated prickles of the wall. If they could have turned their heads to see what they were stuck in, they would have seen the face of a gigantic scarlet flower, with petals large enough to cradle full-grown men. The fleshy petals were lined with spines — no, teeth, and they were splayed like the jaws of a bear trap. The Zi'Gax barely had a chance to scream for help before the petals of the carnivorous plant snapped shut around them. It swallowed them all down into a massive bulbous digestive sack, which in terms of size, could have held a large bull. Through the membranous skin of the plant, Desert Rain could count about five other goblins as well — which Clova was most likely responsible for — encased in the jelly acidic juices of the plant. The goblins inside couldn't move, as the sticky gel held them fast.

Desert Rain plopped down onto the ground, landing on her back. She breathed heavily, her legs shaking from the exertion. Silverheart laid at her side. After a few minutes, she sat up slowly, panting. She held her head in her hands, a massive headache pounding in her skull. She was still for some time, until she heard someone approaching. Snapping her head up in alarm, she saw Gabriel, carrying Chiriku in his arms.

"Dummy wouldn't let me walk," Chiriku scowled.

"Are you all right?" Gabriel asked.

Desert Rain nodded tiredly. "I'm fine. The Zi'Gax fell for the trap. We should be okay for a while."

"Looks like we rounded up a good bunch of those suckers." Chiriku looked at the giant carnivorous plant, counting the bodies she saw inside it. "Let's see…nine there. And I bashed at least six others, and Dummy Boy here got one. I spotted two or three others caught in the vine traps. Yep, I say we got the upper hand."

Desert Rain nodded. "It was a good thing Mac had the seed of this giant plant in his pocket so Clova could grow it. If these things really grow all around the Bayou like he said, I don't think I want to visit that place." She stretched her legs, rubbing her burning calf muscles.

"So, are we going back for another round?" Chiriku asked eagerly.

"I'm going to find Clova. Hopefully, once the remaining few Zi'Gax can't find the rest of their group, maybe they'll run off to wherever they came from—"

"*I wouldn't count on it.*"

Five figures rained down from the trees overhead, landing right next to them. Two of the figures grabbed Gabriel, causing him to drop Chiriku to the ground. Before she could reach her warhammer, one of the Zi'Gax, taller than the others and wrapped in red, kicked Chiriku in the jaw, snapping her head back and knocking her out. The remaining two accosted Desert Rain, threatening her with their iron daggers.

The tall Zi'Gax surveyed his captives, curling his upper lip at them. "This is pitiful. To think we were almost tricked by a pair of wenches and a boy with a stick. Spiggat—" He addressed one of the goblins by Desert Rain, an underling wearing a stocking hat— "Cut open that giant dandelion over there."

Desert Rain squeezed her eyes shut, not believing how their plan had suddenly gone so horribly wrong. The Zi'Gax called Spiggat went over to the meat-eating plant, and after a few good stabs of his daggers, cut through the thick membrane and sawed open the side of the digestive sack. The trapped Zi'Gax spilled out in a pool of acidic goo. By now, some of their bandages had been eaten away to reveal large holes, and their skin was raw and burned. This made them all the more enraged at their enemies, and many moved in to do away with these impudent insects.

Cryle growled a warning to them, and the Zi'Gax held back, grudgingly. "Not yet, comrades. You'll get your revenge soon enough. But we have to keep our minds on our business." He turned to Gabriel, and pointed at him. "We need to catch our bounty, and you're going to tell us where it is."

Out of nowhere flew two green spiders, near the size of human heads, and they smacked into and coiled around the faces of two Zi'Gax, cutting off their air and sending them wriggling to the earth, suffocating. Desert Rain blinked in surprise, and could see that they were not quite spiders—they were spider plants. With her sensitive ears, she thought she heard the whisper of a spell, and another spider plant came soaring by, ensnaring the Zi'Gax guarding her.

"Run, Dezzy!"

The lead Zi'Gax snaked towards the direction of the call, spotting a female figure hiding behind a tree. He withdrew a sickle from his belt, and charged.

Clova reached into her seed pouch and murmured a quick spell, tossing a bulb that instantly morphed into a spider plant. The Zi'Gax's sliced through the enchanted weed in midair. Before Clova could begin another spell, the red-bandaged goblin jumped her, impaling the pouch, scattering all her seeds. In the blink of an eye, he was holding her from behind, his spindly but steel-hard arm around her rib cage, his sickle against her throat.

"Now I've got you," the Zi'Gax hissed into her ear. "You're coming with me, Hijn, and if you try anything funny, I'll slit your throat."

CHAPTER EIGHT
Wielding the Sword

"Clova!" Desert Rain lurched forwards to her friend, but two Zi'Gax thrust their daggers at her face, keeping her down on the ground. She glowered at them, but they cackled at her.

Clova was rigid with fear. The sickle jabbed at her skin, and the slightest movement would cut her. She was also drained, sweating profusely — her excessive magic use to set up all the traps had taken its toll on her. The head Zi'Gax bared his teeth in a wicked smile, and turned his gaze to the sword lying at Desert Rain's side. He looked back at his own sickle, and wrinkled his nose. "I want that sword. Bring it to me."

"No!" Desert Rain went to grab Silverheart, but Spiggat pounced, spitting a rattling hiss at her.

"I'll do it, Captain Cryle," Spiggat announced fervently. He grasped the sword in his grimey fingers, and made a surprised shriek as the sword flashed a white light, shocking him and rendering his fingers numb. He staggered back, tucking his hands under his armpits and chittering curses. The other Zi'Gax had become distracted by the flash of light, and Desert Rain took a chance. She grabbed Silverheart, receiving no shock at all, and once again coiled her fingers around it awkwardly. She got to her feet, and the other Zi'Gax near her skittered away from the deadly blade. She held the sword before her, and it took her a second to realize that Silverheart was lighter. Much lighter, as if it had adjusted its weight to suit her. The hilt subtly shifted in her palms, adjusting so her lengthy fingers could get a better grip on it. Even the blade looked different, shorter than the longsword she thought it to be, and elliptical in shape rather than linear. She faced the head Zi'Gax, sword pointed at his wrinkled, pug face.

"Let her go, now!" Desert Rain bellowed.

"Dezzy, no!" Clova tried to raise her hands, but the sickle pressed harder against her.

Cryle narrowed his beady eyes at the donkey-eared woman. He sneered in contempt. "I'm supposed to be afraid of a scullery maid, am I? Not even a good-looking one, at that. You're out of your league, wench."

Desert Rain held Silverheart in both hands, feeling a seering energy flow through her arms. "You're going to look far worse than I do, when I'm done with you."

Cryle paused at this remark, and then let out a weasely laugh. The other Zi'Gax joined in, creating a cacophony of wild hooting. Desert Rain didn't take her eyes off of her enemy. Every inch of dread inside her was gone. There was a burning drive to get that ugly imp away from Clova, to teach all these little monsters a lesson. She planted her feet firmly on the ground. She clenched her teeth, and flattened her ears back against her head like a maddened mare.

"You're a feisty one," Cryle said after his laughter subsided. "But I don't have time to play around. Why don't you be smart— give me that sword, and maybe I'll be nice enough to let you and those two others over there go. After we beat a little sense into you, of course."

Desert Rain gripped the sword tighter. "Let Clova go. She's never done anything to you."

Cryle smirked, amused by the would-be heroine. "We got nothing against the Hijn witch. We're doing what we're paid to do. There's a good reward to bring back this one."

"Who sent you, and what do they want with her?"

"That would be their business, now, wouldn't it?" Cryle snapped his teeth at her. "I'm not being paid to answer questions."

Desert Rain began to advance on him. "You're going to answer mine."

"Don't," Gabriel warned her, as he struggled against the Zi'Gaxs' grip.

"You better listen to the boy," Cryle advised. "If you want to leave this forest alive, you better forget about this Hijn and we'll be on our way. I admit, I expected the Hijn who belongs to the Distortionist to put up a better fight."

Desert Rain's ears perked up like a startled rabbit's. "The Distortionist…"

Spiggat, taking any opportunity he could to talk, cut in. "The Distortionist is the enemy of our masters. They thought they were rid of him, but he's returned, and the word is that a female Hijn was the one who brought him back. Our employers gave us this handy little device to hunt her down and everything—"

"Shut your trap, Spiggat!" Cryle growled. "You're not supposed to educate the prisoners."

Desert Rain's face went stoic, cold. "The Distortionist you speak of is Katawa of the Darkscale."

Cryle gnashed his teeth, his eyes wide and wild. "How do you know the Twisted One?"

"Because Clova's not the Hijn you're looking for." Desert

Rain raised her head high, defiantly. "I am."

There was an uncomfortable pause.

"Sh…she's a Hijn too??" Spiggat glanced back and forth between Clova and Desert Rain. "But…but they didn't say there would be two of them!"

Cryle tightened his lips. He, too, was perplexed. He looked at Clova. "This one does magic." He looked back at Desert Rain. "I didn't seen *you* do any magic."

The desert Hijn's voice grew as dark as dragon's blood. "Let go of her, and I'll show you what I can do."

The Zi'Gax began to snicker, but there was a nervous twinge in their chuckling. Cryle was not amused anymore. He was getting impatient, and did not like being talk to in such a way, especially by some female. "If you *are* a Hijn, we'll take you both and let our employers sort out the two of you." He gestured with his head for his brigade to take the insolent girl.

Three of the Zi'Gax moved towards Desert Rain. One removed his length of chain belt, holding it ready to tie her up. The panic returned to Desert Rain. Silverheart became heavy again. She shook violently, her body frozen in place as the Zi'Gax advanced on her. She closed her eyes, biting her lip until it bled. She could feel the cold iron of the chain touch her skin—

She heard the sound of flesh impaled.

She opened her eyes. Silverheart was still in her hands, but it was no longer directly in front of her. Somehow, it had shifted, and now the blade was half-way through the Zi'Gax with the chain. She couldn't even recall having moved an inch, and yet she was staring at the Zi'Gax, shock on his smushed face, black-red blood seeping out of his gut. He dropped the chain, and fell to his knees. Yanking the sword from the goblin's body, Desert Rain watched him fall over, lifeless.

Dead silence.

Desert Rain did not believe what she had done. She had…*killed* someone. No, wait, she didn't. She couldn't have. She didn't do anything, she wasn't even sure how it could have happened. It was the sword, it had to be. But how could Silverheart stab somebody, by itself? Maybe she truly had done it, unconsciously. Maybe in her fear, her body reacted, despite having received no orders from her brain.

Her mind reached back in time to the memory of some frightening words, spoken by a certain indigo-skinned demon, his yellow slitted eyes staring wickedly down at her. *Do you know what happens to people without souls, little girl? They become feral. And that's exactly what will happen to you. You will fall apart, piece by piece, until there's nothing left.*

Was it true? Was she becoming feral?

A roar of rage escaped Cryle's lips. He threw Clova aside, into one of the other Zi'Gax, who seized her tightly. He removed his other sickle, clashing his weapons together in a rusty, horrible clang. "You want to spill some blood," he rasped through crooked, clenched teeth. "I'll have to take you as a corpse, then."

He made a running start, and then launched himself at Desert Rain, his sickles hungering to rip her open.

Desert Rain went numb from head to toe. *Great Guerda-Shalyr, I'm going to die!!!*

An air-shattering clash resounded through the still forest. The two combatants were locked in time, like a work of art, their blades grinding against one another. Once again, Desert Rain couldn't explain how, but Silverheart had risen to block the attack, its pure, silver steel a streak of light against the dirty, dark metal of the sickles. Its weight was barely anything now, but that may have been because she felt nothing at all. There wasn't a single ounce of physical nerve in her whole body. It was like being in a dream, or in the Eternal Deep, so she supposed. She could feel something — well, "feel" wasn't really the right word, for she couldn't describe it in terms of hot or cold, pain or pleasure — in the moonstone on her forehead. It pulsated like a warrior heart ready for battle, shimmering in a milky moonbeam glow. The sapphires on the hilt of Silverheart responded to this heartbeat, glistening in blue fire. Her right eye glowed its intimidating emerald green, with a gaze so penetrating, it was as deadly as the sword she held.

Cryle was being devoured by an unknown horror as that green eye bore into him. He had never felt this kind of dread from anyone, not man or beast, nor even the ones who had hired him to capture this Hijn female — and they had been the most terrible beings he had ever encountered. He did not like being afraid, and it made him loathe this girl all the more. He didn't care if his employers had demanded that he brought back the Hijn alive. He was going to kill this one.

His sickles slid across the sword with a metallic hiss. He swept them to the right, bringing them around to slice her in the side, but his strike was met again by the sword. He thought he spotted confusion in the girl's face, but it must have been a trick to lure him into a false sense of security. The sheer speed of her block showed that she was well-trained with a sword, and he did not become the alpha Zi'Gax by being fooled.

Desert Rain, on the other hand, had no idea what in Luuva was going on. She was seeing what was happening, but had no control over any of it. Every time the Zi'Gax lashed out with his sickles, her heart stopped for half a beat, every bite of blade on blade rang sharply in her ears. If she could feel anything in her body, her stomach would be churning from the fear of what gashes she was going to receive. Before any gash could be inflicted, however, Silverheart opposed the sickles, driving them back with excellent proficiency. The swordfight grew increasingly rapid, and the percussion of clashes and the whistles of razor-sharp blades cutting through air wove a gruesome battle hymn. The spectators—Zi'Gax, Hijn and human alike—watched in breathless awe of the raging opponents, barely able to keep up with the movement. Desert Rain would have vomited if she had been given a moment to do so, but the sword wasn't allowing her to stop. It would have been frightening enough if there was nerve in her body while this sword dueled for her, but being completely numb gave her no amount of command whatsoever. For all she knew, she might have been sliced already and not even known it.

The head Zi'Gax snarled like a wild dog, his fighting growing more violent the longer they continued. "Not bad, for an ugly toad," he spat.

Not bad, if I had any say over what I'm doing! thought Desert Rain. *I'm possessed!*

Cryle swung one sickle down on top of the sword, his other sickle came up from under, and he caught Silverheart in a claw grip. With a quick twist, he flipped the sword right out of Desert Rain's hands, sending it off to the side, twirling like a windmill. It bounced once on its hilt, and then landed flat a few yards away. He could see the faltering panic in his opponent's eyes. She was defenseless.

As soon as the sword left her hands, Desert Rain could feel again, and what she felt rack her whole being was the chill of approaching death. She shivered like a sheep ready for slaughter, her eyes hazing over as the Zi'Gax brought his sickles up over his shoulder, to swing them down in an arch to slice open her chest.

Instinct kicked in. She fell back, away from the Zi'Gax's swing, but the tips of the sickles snagged her tunic and ripped it. She landed smack on her back, but then she reached her prehensile feet towards him, grasping his ankles and yanking with all her might. She sent him down onto his back, causing him to drop his sickles. She got up swiftly and scrambled after Silverheart, but the goblin gathered his weapons and was up on his feet, hot on her tail. He brought his sickles up to the right to slice at her again. Desert Rain lunged at Silverheart, scooping up the sword with one hand, using all her strength to lift it as she twisted around to face her adversary. Before the nerve left her body again, she swung that sword with all her might—

Silverheart met the two sickles, and sliced through the inferior weapons like warm butter.

To say Cryle was stunned would be an understatement. He gawked at his broken sickles, the sliced-off ends glowing hot orange. He looked up at Desert Rain, who was also gawking at the damage she had done. She was transfixed, as if waking from a dream. With the fight coming to a complete halt and the physical nerve returned to her, her body caught up to the extreme effort she had given. Everything ached and burned inside her, and she made the mistake of showing this by letting her body slump.

Cryle was aching as well, but he took this opportunity. The end of his split sickles still burning, he thrust the hot metal of one into the flesh between Desert Rain's shoulder and neck. With a painful scream, she staggered back, fell, and grasped firmly at her excruciating burn. This was it. She squeezed her eyes shut, knowing that the Zi'Gax was over her, and was going to make her suffer before he killed her.

This would have been Desert Rain's fate, but as she had been told before, there were forces that would keep her safe. One of these was the Forest Hijn.

Clova was still exhausted from her magic use, but her heart pounded as if she was running for her life. It was her friend's life that was at stake, however, and she was twisting up inside as she watched helplessly from the sidelines. She had no idea Desert Rain could wield a sword like that—quiet, shy Desert Rain was fighting as well as any Knight! So well, in fact, Clova felt the seed of optimism grow within her, becoming ever more confident that Desert Rain would win. When she saw Silverheart decapitate the sickles, a burst of elation filled her, and she would have jumped for joy if she wasn't being held. Then she watched as her friend was stabbed in the shoulder, and fell to the ground in pain. Tears filled her eyes as she witnessed the alpha Zi'Gax laugh in wicked delight, and used his broken blades to slice at Desert Rain's tunic, cutting her arms and backside as the desert Hijn curled up into herself. There wasn't intent to kill, yet. The Zi'Gax enjoyed wounding his adversary, scarring her with long red streaks along her skin as she flinched with each strike.

Clova couldn't take it anymore. This was too cruel for her. Maybe other Hijn had seen this kind of brutality before, the ones who battled the Wretched, but she couldn't bear it. Deep down within, she summoned up all the energy she had left, balling it up into a mass of aura-fire. It seered raw and hot in her chest, and she was about to explode from the intense magic she was mounting. She knew the words of Dragontongue to speak, ones she rarely if ever spoke, but she was shaking with such fury that she might not be able to pronounce the spell correctly. The Zi'Gax holding her must have felt something was wrong, for his grip slackened, and he inched away from her, keeping her at arm's length. The words Clova spoke started out in a death whisper, for she was trying so hard to keep herself steady and mentally focused. As the words leaked out, her emotions took over. Her voice rose, her speech quickened, until she was hollering the spell at the top of her voice, and the final word, as well as all her remaining magic, was released in a scream of pure anguish.

The scream resonated like a banshee wail, the pitch warping into something otherworldly the longer Clova held it. All the Zi'Gax clasped their hands to their ears, crying in panic as they hunched over in agony. Desert Rain's ears took it even worse, but it distracted her from the pain of her wounds. Clova's wail was echoed by the trees that howled and writhed in reaction to Clova's magic. The whole forest was thrashing about them, the icy wind stinging every body it blew against, rattling the leaves like hollow bones. The ground began to quiver. It deepened into a shake that caused everyone to wobble on their feet, and it worsened until a thunderous cracking erupted around them.

The earth beneath them was splitting apart.

Desert Rain managed to prop herself up on her arms, her senses returning as fissures rippled across the ground around her. She wasn't sure how Clova was doing this. Rukna was the Hijn who commanded magic over stone and earth; Clova was mistress of flora and vegetation. She shouldn't have the power to crack the earth like this. Then Desert Rain saw how it was being done—roots were crawling up from the fissures, pushing the earth apart.

The Zi'Gax were too bewildered to react at first, but then when one of them lost his footing and fell into one of the fissures, the others were triggered to move. Some attempted to run, but the ground shifted too violently beneath them and they plummeted down into the depths of the earth. Others had their legs snatched by the invading roots, and were pulled down into an underground lair. Cryle snapped his head around, unable to budge from his spot. The earth split between his legs, and he moved aside before the crack opened wide enough to swallow him. Unfortunately for him, a root shot out of the earth and coiled around his arm, yanking him down so suddenly that he dropped his sickles down the fissure. Try as he might to pull the root off, he could not get free.

Nor did he get a chance to, for five seconds later, he had a sword lodged in his chest.

His black eyes froze open in his death. The last thing he ever saw was the woman standing over him, her green eye burning away his blackened soul.

Desert Rain pulled the sword from the goblin, her breathing so heavy that her body lurched with each gasp. She steadied herself against Silverheart, driving the blade into the ground, grasping tightly as the earth continued to shake. Then, as abruptly as it had all started, the earthquake stopped, and the screams of the trees faded into silence.

She could not move at first. Every movement was like knives piercing her muscles. She forced her head to rise, and she surveyed the clearing. There wasn't a living Zi'Gax to be found. The earth was riddled with extensive cracks, and the roots had receded back underground. Gabriel had stood his ground, somehow—he held Chiriku in his arms, and the two of them were stranded on a chuck of ground surrounded by crevices on all sides. Clova was standing, paralyzed, her eyes blank and glossy. The muscles in her body relaxed slowly, and she breathed a moan of relief.

Desert Rain slid Silverheart back into the black pouch and tucked it into her pocket. She limped over the broken ground, and she tripped as she walked.

Clova, coming back to reality, blinked her eyes. She saw Desert Rain struggling to reach her. She moved, wobbling, but began making her way to her friend.

"Dezzy..." she whispered, her voice sore and dry from the scream. "Dezzy, don't move. Stay there..."

A grimy hand slinked out of one of the fissures, clawing at the ground with chipped fingernails. Straining, Spiggat pulled himself up, freeing himself half-way from the cavernous gap below him. He panted as he rested his elbows on the ground, squinting through his dirt-caked eyelids as he lifted his head. He caught movement — the green witch was walking about twenty yards away from him. Spiggat bared his teeth, as he reached down towards his belt for one of his daggers.

Desert Rain knelt on the ground, her eyes closed as she rocked herself back and forth. She tried to calm her body, to relax every muscle so the pain would lessen. By closing her eyes, she amplified her other senses, including her hearing. She picked up a faint sound, a snarl. Raising her head and opening her eyes, she saw a Zi'Gax groping his way out of the earth, a dagger raised over his head, his gaze focused on Clova.

There was no thinking. There was no pang of panic. There was reaction, although everything seemed to be in slow motion. Desert Rain thrust a hand out before her, a word forming on her lips, a word she was not aware that she was speaking. The Zi'Gax let the dagger fly, the jagged rusted metal spiraling through the air, aimed right for the Forest Hijn.

Desert Rain uttered the final breath of Dragontongue as Clova turned, seeing the dagger coming, right at her heart. She had no time to dodge. The dagger's blade hit her chest—

It shattered into a thousand pieces.

Clova did not move. Perhaps she thought she was dead on her feet. She felt the spot on her chest where the dagger had hit, but there was not the slightest puncture mark. She looked down, finding not a dagger, but thousands of tiny shards. They sparkled like diamonds, but were an ice-blue color. Yet it wasn't ice or gem. It was more like glass, and when Clova bent down to pick up a shard, it disintegrated in her fingers. She looked over at the Zi'Gax, whose eyes were wide in fear and confusion. He pulled himself fully out of the fissure and ran off, disappearing into the forest.

Clova turned to Desert Rain, who still had her hand held out in front of her. After a beat, the desert hermit dropped her hand to her side. Both the Hijn were motionless for a full minute, and then a smile graced Clova's face. It broadened into a joyous laughter, as she ran over to Desert Rain, helping her to her feet and hugging her close.

"Dezzy, you did it! You did it, Dez, I always knew… you…could…" Clova's voice trailed off as her whole body went limp, and Desert Rain caught her before she fell over.

"Clova!" Desert Rain knelt again, cradling the unconscious Clova in her arms. The green hue of Clova's skin was almost solid white, her body shaking from the result of her final spell. Gabriel, carrying Chiriku—who was regaining consciousness—gradually made his way over to Desert Rain. Desert Rain didn't say anything. She held the Forest Hijn, praying to Guerda-Shalyr that she would be all right.

She checked her fingers, and saw the tips of them were encrusted in a glassy ice blue. She sighed, having expected this. It was like the last time…

"There you all are," came the lighthearted voice of Mac, who appeared at the edge of the clearing. He had leaves stuck in his hair, and he plucked them out. "Leaving me up in that-ttk dang tree, with all those nasties-ssck running around. And I think-kk a storm's coming, that-ttk wind was blowing mighty hard —" He immediately stopped talking when he got a look of the area in front of him. The ground was broken into chunks as if a herd of strongbacks had rampaged through there. His buddies were huddled together. Miss Clova was out cold, Gila Gul looked like she had wrestled with a croc, and there was a dead, bloody Zi'Gax lying on the field.

Mac raised his eyebrows, innocently asking, "What'd I miss-ssck?"

CHAPTER NINE
Designed Destiny

The cleric stepped quietly into the room, carrying a bowl of fresh rose water and a clean cloth. She glided over to the hammock, dampening the cloth as she approached. She removed the dried cloth on Clova's forehead and replaced it with the new cold one. The Forest Hijn was burning up, her breathing uneasy as she lied in the hammock. The clerics had tried to make her as comfortable as possible, giving her the finest of their blankets and cushions to line her hanging bed. The medicines they gave her were easing the fever a little, but Clova's ailment was mostly attributed to extreme fatigue. Rest was the best remedy for now.

Desert Rain was sitting on a mat beside the hammock. She had been well-tended to, the wounds on her arms and torso soothed in salves and wrapped in strips of cloth. She, too, was exhausted, but she had no desire to lie in her hammock in the adjoining room. She preferred to sit next to Clova, humming to calm her nerves. The elves brought her food and drink and offered her fresh salve and bandages every time they came by. The clerics may not have known what exactly had happened with the Zi'Gax, but Clova had told them in her moments of consciousness that Desert Rain had saved her life, and the clerics could not find enough ways to thank the desert hermit. They even gave her a beautiful pale-green tunic with a pressed-flower trim to replace Desert Rain's shredded one. Desert Rain had never been given so much attention, and she wasn't exactly comfortable with it, but she was glad that the ordeal in the woods was over.

Chiriku, who had been unconscious during the swordfight, couldn't believe what she heard about Desert Rain slaying an alpha Zi'Gax. Gabriel confirmed the story for her, but the Quetzalin shook her head. As if Donkey Ears could take on anyone, let alone a goblin bounty hunter. Once she saw Desert Rain's wounds, she changed her tune. She had to admit, Donkey Ears had guts, no doubt about that. If Chiriku had been awake at the time, she could have joined in on the fun and cracked open some skulls—maybe saved Desert Rain from a few of those gashes.

Mac, meanwhile, had already committed the story (at least mixing what he had heard from Clova and his own imaginative flair) to memory and was regaling the other guests of the sanctuary with the tale of Hijn heroism. He didn't like to boast, but he had lended a hand in defeating the Zi'Gax—it had mostly been his plan, after all. He also didn't mean to be a bother to Desert Rain, but he asked her if she wouldn't mind saving her bandages when she replaced them with fresh ones—he bet he could get a coin or two selling "Bandages of Bravery" to a couple of the awestruck Syphurians.

Desert Rain crinkled her nose, thinking how gross that was.

She sat, deep in thought. The image of the dagger flying at Clova haunted her mind, including a vision of what could have happened if Desert Rain had not reacted in time. She was going to have to decide about what to do from here on out. The fight with the Zi'Gax had made one thing very clear—she couldn't let something like that happen to Clova again. Clova may have more power than she did, but this had been a battle none of them should have had to get involved in. What the Zi'Gax had said proved that Desert Rain was the target— they had been sent to get the Hijn who had befriended Katawa. She had a good idea who had been the Zi'Gaxs' employers, and her suspicions were confirmed when Gabriel came to her with an odd-looking compass in his hands.

"This was on the Zi'Gax leader," he explained. "I thought this might help us find out who sent them."

Desert Rain studied the large compass, not being able to tell what symbols were engraved in the face of it. The little metal ball had been smashed into the surface of the compass. She remembered what that Zi'Gax in the stocking cap had said: *"They gave us a device to find her and everything..."* This must have been used to detect Hijn, or maybe their magic. She turned the compass over to look on the back, and there was a carved image of three waves of water over a ball of flame. The mark was frightening familiar, for she had seen it before, as a tattoo on a Wretched's chest.

"The Darkscale," she said to herself.

"What? Those Wretched sent those creeps?" Chiriku said when Desert Rain revealed the information to her and Mac outside of Clova's room.

"No surprise-ssck to me, Eye-pecker," said Mac, smiling as his term of endearment made Chiriku glare. "They all are Nasties-ssck, whether they're demons-ssck or goblins. I'm sure they all are in cahoots-ssck with one another."

"Don't you understand?" Desert Rain held the compass out to them in a tight grip. "The Darkscale sent the Zi'Gax to capture *me*! I put all of you in danger!"

"Now that doesn't-tkk make sense, Gila. Why would those

Nasties-ssck want anything to do with you?"

"Because they think I'm working for Katawa. If they got me, they'd get one step closer to him." She stuffed the compass into her pocket and wiped a hand over her face. Her head was throbbing.

Chiriku shrugged. "So why didn't those Darkscale dummies come to get you themselves? Why send those stupid bounty hunters?"

Desert Rain paused. That was a good question. Surely, the Darkscale could have handled hunting her down. They would have beaten her, too, being much more proficient in magic than she was. Maybe they were afraid of encountering Katawa while looking for her. Or maybe…it wasn't just Katawa they were worried about.

"It was a test," she surmised. "They wanted to find out how dangerous I am, if I might be a threat. And that one Zi'Gax got away! He's going to go to the Darkscale and tell them what I did — Great Guerda-Shalyr!" She plopped down on the floor, holding her head in her hands.

Mac knelt on the floor next to her. "Relax-ssck, Gila. We're all safe now. Frankly, if I heard about someone who could take-kk down a whole pack of goblins-ssck, and make a dagger break-kk into li'l pieces with a word, I would stay as far away from her as I could!"

"Yeah, maybe you'll make those Darkscale jerks break out in a sweat," Chiriku said with a smirk.

Desert Rain sighed. "I doubt it." She rubbed her sore arm, tightening her lips as she thought. "Now you see, I can't be around anyone. I bring trouble wherever I go. The Darkscale will send someone else after me now, someone worse than the Zi'Gax. And

Katawa…I know I haven't seen the last of him." She stood up, looking at the two of her friends in all seriousness. "That's why I'm leaving. Right away. By myself."

Mac and Chiriku looked at one another. The lizard sighed, shaking his head. "We've already been over this-ssck, Dez. You runnin' off alone doesn't-tkk do anybody good. And what about Miss-ssck Clova—"

"Clova is exactly why I have to go on by myself!" Desert Rain began pacing furiously. "Look what I did to her! Yes, I know that I would be dead right now if it wasn't for her. But what if this happened again, and it's another dagger, or arrow, or sword, and I'm not able to stop it from killing her? No, I won't let it happen. This was never her fight. It's always been mine, and mine alone."

"If you wanna go and ditch us that badly, then go ahead," Chiriku replied sharply.

"I'm not ditching you. But I…" Desert Rain let out a deep sigh, collecting herself. "You two shouldn't have been forced into this either. For that, I'm forever sorry. I couldn't have come this far without you guys—" She hesitated, knowing how true that was. She struggled to continue. "What I can do to repay you, as a friend, as more than a friend, is to free you from this burden, to let you go back to your own lives."

"Go back? Back to what?" Chiriku crossed her arms. "What's back in Syphurius for me?" Without waiting for a reply, she turned away, running off down the corridor.

Mac scratched the back of his neck, giving Desert Rain a sad smile. "If that's-ssck really what you want Dez, then you do what you think is best-tkk. But don't push us away 'cause-ssck you think we can't go down the road you have to walk-kk. If it's one thing you learn growin' up in the Bayou, you should never need to walk-kk alone. And, frog gone it-tkk, I've walked this far with you. What's a few more miles-ssck?"

Desert Rain still could not understand why Mac wanted to stay by her side. No one ever wanted to stand by her, not in her entire life. Yet here was this kind lizard, someone who must have been taunted more than once by the Noble Races for being a Lejenous, but he was more understanding and patient than any Noble she had ever known. She put her arms around him and held him close, feeling tears of thankfulness run down her cheeks. "I don't want to send you away, but I don't know what I'm supposed to do, Mac."

"Dezzy…" A weary voice came from the room behind them. "Dezzy…are you there…?"

Desert Rain released Mac, giving him a smile of gratitude, and turned to enter the room. She lifted the curtain and walked through, seeing Clova sitting up in her hammock. She still didn't look too well. Her greenish hue had returned somewhat, but there were dark rings around her eyes.

"How are you feeling?" Desert Rain asked.

Clova sighed with a smile. "Better. A good sleep was all I needed. And you? How are your wounds healing?"

"Fine. I didn't get cut too deeply." Desert Rain came to stand next to Clova and felt her forehead. "You're still pretty warm. You should keep resting. I'll go get you some tea."

Clova's smile weakened. "No, I need to talk to you about something. That sword you fought with — that was Swordmaster Skyhan's, wasn't it? That was Silverheart?"

Desert Rain dropped her gaze. "Yes."

"Then it really is true, what you said. Swordmaster Skyhan is…?"

Desert Rain closed her eyes and nodded. She felt Clova take her hand. When she looked at the Forest Hijn, there was a sad sparkle in Clova's eye.

"And he gave you his sword," Clova said wistfully.

The hermit's ears went rigid, and the mismatched eyes shot wide open. "Wait, Clova, that's not quite—"

"I always knew," she whispered, donning that same dreamy grin she had when she had seen Desert Rain and Swordmaster Skyhan in Syphurius. "I knew he was in love with you. You always had a thing for him, I could tell. You two would have been so perfect together. And if he knew what a swordswoman you are, how excellently you wield Silverheart..."

"Please, Clova—"

"I'm glad that it was you who was with him in his last moments. He must have known that deep down inside, you had the same fire in your soul as he did. He knew that you could take up his sword for him. Oh, Dezzy..." She gripped Desert Rain's hand tighter, her eyes brimming with tears. "He would be so proud of you, as I am."

Desert Rain was quiet and squeezed Clova's hand gently. It had been hard enough for Clova to accept Skyhan's death. There wasn't any point in telling her how awful his demise really had been. How in Luuva could she possibly explain what happened when she had held Silverheart, that she hadn't really been the one fighting at all? Perhaps it was better to leave Clova with her notions. They were certainly sweeter than the bitter truth.

The dreamy look left Clova. "He was such a patient, honorable man. He held up his virtues undyingly, which is more than I could say for the rest of us Hijn. I wish he had been at the council meetings more, to remind us how we should have conducted things."

Desert Rain raised her eyebrows at Clova's words. "Things couldn't have been that bad —"

"Dezzy, you saw how we were," Clova said, her voice getting intense. "We were squabbling like children! I don't exclude myself — I shouldn't let Fierno get to me. It amazes me that Merros can keep his cool, but he never liked having to head the meetings, I don't think. And V'Tanna can be so…apathetic. Woasim doesn't even send word of his whereabouts most of the time. And Fierno, oh, don't get me started with him!"

"I know what you mean," Desert Rain admitted.

"And that's exactly why that Wretched got the upper hand. None of us are connected with one another like we used to be. With so few Hijn left in Luuva Gros, the bond has become so very weak."

"I guess it didn't help that I never went to the meetings." Desert Rain hung her head.

"It's understandable. The Hijn don't gather at all anymore for fun. It's when a crisis comes up. We don't have the grand celebrations we used to have. We don't dance the Summons of the Elementals, we don't enjoy being with one another. That meeting in Vaes Galahar was maybe the first time in a long time most of the Hijn were in the same room together."

Desert Rain found it all hard to believe, but Clova was serious. Then again, she understood what Clova meant by a "weak bond" between the Hijn. Desert Rain never really formed any connection with the Hijn, but now, her bond with Clova was the strongest it had ever been.

"We'll have to reinforce that bond between all of us again," Desert Rain decided. "Once we rescue the others, we'll work together to stop Katawa."

"I know," Clova sighed. "But we still haven't decided where to start. How can we fight a demon that we can't even touch?"

"Perhaps I can offer some insight into that, Hijn Clova Flor," a familiar voice stated.

The two women turned their heads to see the Great Philosopher standing in the doorway, a bundle of thick books under one arm.

"*Lorihalynir Athro-kos,*" Clova gasped. "What an unexpected pleasure it is to see you—*outside* of Kapokis."

"It's an equal pleasure to see you as well, although it saddens me to see you in such a condition. And you, Hijn Desert Rain—" Anthron gave her a bow. "I have heard the tale of your heroism from one of your enthusiastic companions—the red-headed merchant."

Desert Rain blushed a little, not so much from modesty, but from embarrassment that Mac would make such a big deal over the story. His version must have been obviously exaggerated, probably with false details, since he hadn't witnessed the fight firsthand.

"You'll have to excuse Mac. He's a bit of a bard," Desert Rain said. "It's so kind of you to come visit Clova. I'm surprised you heard about our confrontation with the Zi'Gax so quickly. Or was this another one of those 'disturbing a thread in the web of magic' sort of things again?"

"When the forest itself quakes and howls, it is hard not to notice," Anthron replied. "But I was actually already on my way here when that occurred. While I do bestow condolences to Hijn Clova, that was not my primary intention in coming here."

"Oh." Desert Rain looked back at Clova, who rested her head back on her pillow and half-closed her eyes in weariness. "Sir Anthron, I understand if you have important matters to discuss with Clova, but she is exhausted right now. Perhaps it could wait until morning—"

"You misunderstand me," Anthron answered, lowering his voice in confidentiality. "It is *you* with whom I must converse. If you would come with me, please. It won't take too much of your time."

Anthron led Desert Rain into the last room at the end of the corridor that was empty except for another, smaller door. It was covered by a jade curtain that blended almost seamlessly with the walls. Beyond this curtain was a staircase that descended into a passageway lighted by bioluminescent crystals, shimmering a hazy rose color. The walk down the passage grew chillier as they walked along. The room that Anthron brought her to was not a grand one. A large circular rug, woven and dyed with many hues, covered almost the whole floor, and in the center was a rounded slab of stone, polished and flat on the top. On this stone table were three more glowing crystals, this time shining the color cerulean. Upon her nocturnal eye adjusting, Desert Rain saw that this room was home to plants all around the edge of the rug. These were not like the flowers in the garden, however; these had no colorful blooms, and were all thorny and dark-leafed. It was like a greenhouse for a nightmare jungle.

"What is this place?" she asked. "How can these plants survive in the dark and cold?"

"Plants are not so unlike people, Hijn Desert Rain. While many in this world thrive on the warmth of light, some are born to the quiet and solitude of darkness. These plants have the crystals to supply them with the energy they need." He went over to the crystals and touched each one of them, causing them to brighten considerably. The plants seemed less intimidating then. In the bluish light, they looked like art made of cobalt glass.

Anthron sat down at the table, and Desert Rain sat down opposite him. The elf placed his books on the table, taking one and leafing through the pages casually.

Desert Rain cleared her throat. "Sir Anthron, if I may be honest, I don't see what you need to tell me that you wouldn't want to tell Clova—"

"Do you believe that there is a design to the events that befall us, Hijn Desert Rain?" Anthron asked.

Desert Rain thought that was a bizarre question for him to ask out of the blue. "I—" was all she got out before Anthron cut in again.

"Most of my life, I did not believe so. As much as I studied the concept of Fate, I couldn't find any conclusive proof that such a theory directed our lives. It wasn't that Elf or Man was in constant control of his life, but that did not verify that what befell him was predestined." He paused, looking up at her. "You, however, may change my opinion about that."

Desert Rain lifted an eyebrow. "I'm afraid you'll need to explain," she replied.

"Do you know what it is that the Elfë Tiagas fear?" he asked.

The Hijn took a moment to change tracks in her mind. "No, I don't. And what does that have to do with—"

"Nothing," Anthron cut her off again. "The Elfë Tiagas have feared nothing in all their extensive, unchanging lives."

"But Clova told me that you told her that Kidran told you…" Desert Rain backtracked, realizing how confusing that was. "Kidran said that the elves were keeping him confined up north because they were afraid of something."

"That is true." Anthron gazed upwards into space, sighing. "Many do not understand this, not having the longevity of our kind, but the Ahshi, the Elfë Tiagas, the nomadic elves, and the elves who live in the Noble Cities all once lived together in harmony. We lived in one beautiful city, a combination of our passions and knowledge. I remember that time, living in the same house as my northern cousins. I was a mere child then, but I remember my childhood as clearly as this moment. The last time we elves felt the unrelenting claws of fear, the deep shadow that instigated us to become irrational and even cruel, was because an age-old secret that I am about to reveal to you."

Desert Rain's jaw hung slightly. That was an awful big fact for her to accept, for the Philosopher to reveal a secret of such monumental importance to her. "Why tell this to me, if it's such a deep secret? I would never reveal it, of course, but I'm the wrong person for this sort of thing."

"I take a great risk in revealing this to you, I admit, one that defies a pact older than you can imagine. But I have weighed the options, and I believe this to be a logical action to take," Anthron assured her. "I cannot tell you the deeper meaning of it, but it has to do with the Taming of the Wild Magic, and while you may think that it's silly to take stock in a legend, there is much truth to it—"

Desert Rain shook her head like a fly-bothered mule. "Woah, woah, woah. You're getting way too far ahead of me already, Anthron. What is this Taming of Wild Magic? Do you mean the Great Manifestation?"

Anthron got a perplexed look on his face. "You must know the legend of the Sage Dragons taming the wild magic of Luuva Gros. It is the story all the Hijn celebrate during the Red Eclipse."

Desert Rain suddenly felt small. "Well, I don't really ever…talk to the other Hijn. I don't think I've ever gone to the Red Eclipse Celebration. They're every ten years, so I kept forgetting." Of course, Desert Rain didn't really forget—she found no reason to ever go.

"Surely your Sage Dragon mentioned something of it. It is part of the Dragons' history."

Desert Rain knitted her eyebrows. That was odd, Bellaluna had not brought this up at all, not that Desert Rain could remember. If this was part of the Sage Dragons' history, why not teach her about it? Luna had taught her things about life before the Great Manifestation, and afterwards, but the Taming of Wild Magic was not something Desert Rain had ever written down, and she would have written about it if Luna had told her of it. Maybe Luna did not find anything of value in that legend—or maybe it was something she did not want Desert Rain to know.

"No, she didn't," was all Desert Rain could say in answer.

"I see." Anthron was not disappointed; he looked suddenly eager. "To think you, of all the Hijn, don't know the legend."

"And I get the impression that you're going to tell me."

"For now, I'll make it as brief as I can. But you will know it all someday, I am sure." He took a deep breath. "When the Sage Dragons came to Luuva Gros, the land was fertile with a chaotic magic unlike their own. It was so fragile, that upon the Sage Dragons' foreign presence in the land, it teetered on lashing out and uprooting everything. But the Sage Dragons, beings of pure magic, believed they could tame this chaotic energy and blend it into their own, so they could remain in Luuva Gros and maintain the balance. It took many years, but they were able to find a way to tame the magic and be linked to the land through it. Thus, could they mold the land and influence the forms of the inhabitants of it, to become the Luuva Gros it is now. It is believed that this period of magic-taming is what caused the Great Manifestation."

"Okay, I think I understand that." Desert Rain paused to soak that in. "And this is something all the Hijn—except me— know?"

"Not exactly. While they know that the Sage Dragons brought the wild magic under control, they do not know the means in which they did so. The dragons created a powerful item for that purpose. The old elven texts have refered to it as the Equanume Balance, the first and last Machine of Ancient Magic. It worked on the principle that all magic types were in one of two groups: love and fear, or light and dark. Somehow, the Equanume Balance was broken, and one half was given to the elves, since the dragons believed they would be the one race that would not try to use it to further their own purposes. It is an object that has remained untouched, uncorrupted, since the time it was bequeathed to the elves, and remained in the safekeeping of the Elfë Tiagas when we Ahshi and the nomadic elves left. I conclude that the reason for the Elfë Tiagas' frightened behavior is because this item has once again *tipped*."

"Tipped?" Desert Rain asked blankly.

"Tipped," Anthron repeated. "The magic of the Elfë Tiagas revolves around the aura from the piece of the Equanume Balance. When it tips, it is certain that their possession of their magic is threatened."

He turned the book he had in front of him to show Desert

Rain a picture. It was a crude drawing, of something that looked mechanical, alien, yet a hint of the organic.

"The Lightscale," Anthron whispered, as if it were a curse.

"The what?" Desert Rain observed the picture more closely. It did look like a measuring scale — except it was much taller than a normal scale, the chains of it looked little more than thread, and the plates had a strange shape, more like globes than plates. It was drawn as if the artist didn't quite know how to interpret all the parts, except for one piece: a symbol on top, an orb — perhaps a jewel?--around which two sculpted dragons intertwined.

"It is the Lightscale, the embodiment of all the good magic strewn throughout Luuva Gros, once pure chaos, tamed to be used by the Sages and mortals alike."

Desert Rain studied the picture a little longer. "So the elves know of this device, and they are sworn to secrecy. That means the only Hijn who would know of it would be…"

"Those of elven heritage," Anthron confirmed.

"Clova and Kidran." Desert Rain rubbed her chin, pondering. "Wait, if there's a Lightscale, and that's half of the…the Balance, and you said it was to maintain light and dark, then there must also a—" The next word stuck harshly in her throat. "—darkscale." Her fingers coiled into fists. "The Darkscale clan have something to do with this, don't they?"

"Sadly, they are the ones who got their hands on the other half of the Equanume. No one is quite sure how — most say the demons stole it from the dragons. There is also the possibility that an adversary of the Sages, one who opposed what they stood for, gave it to them."

"The…Lifescourge?" Desert Rain remembered what Merros had told her back in the Grand Chambers of Vaes Galahar, and his words still sent shivers throughout her body.

Anthron shrugged. "It is possible. I have heard of an ancient entity called the Lifescourge. I find the rumors insubstantial. There are no records of such an evil creature existing except through hearsay."

"I need a moment, please." Desert Rain stood up and began to slowly pace back and forth. What kind of twisted fairy tale was this? Some ancient item of magic, created by dragons—this was about as fantastic as any story she had ever written. She could even tell where this was going—something as powerful as this Lightscale could stop the Wretched, but the Darkscale device could destroy the Noble Races as well. But was this Lightscale something that could help her stop Katawa? And if it really was so great, why hadn't the elves ever used it to fight the Wretched? Or why hadn't the Darkscale demons ever used their scale against the Knighthood? Was the Lifescourge really tied into this, as the other Hijn had feared? Despite her rising mountain of questions, right now she wanted to know what this Lightscale had to do with her.

"I know that for you, this is all baffling," Anthron apologized. "But the reason I tell you all this is because if the Lightscale has indeed tipped like I theorize, then it either means that a presence of darkness is weakening it, or a presence of light is strengthening it. There has never been anyone to activate the power of the Lightscale in centuries, so the northern elves presume that a great darkness is coming there way to destroy them. But there may be one who can show them that this tipping is due to a presence of goodness, and can get the Elfë Tiagas to release Hijn Kidran."

Desert Rain's ears perked up in relief. "Really? Who is this person? Where can I find him?"

"Her," Anthron corrected the girl. "And she's standing across the table from me."

Desert Rain's first reaction was to laugh, but the laughter wilted into a strand of incoherent phrases. "But I…no, that's not…I think you're…that's the most…what in Luuva…" She sat down, composing herself. "Sir Anthron, I think you make too much of me. I'm a desert dweller. I don't have magic. I don't have any special skills. I am absolutely, positively, the last being in Luuva Gros who could possibly activate any kind of machine of Ancient Magic."

"Not according to your merchant friend," Anthron said. "I believe he said you shattered a dagger with one word?"

"Yeah, but that was…that was a fluke. I didn't even know what I was saying."

"True magic is never a fluke," Anthron replied firmly.

"For the love of Guerda-Shalyr — why not Clova? She's much more powerful than I am, and she was born elven. The Elfë Tiagas would respond to her more willingly than to me —"

Anthron sighed in exasperation. "What you must understand is that there are many kinds of magics in the world: elemental magic, like those of Hijn Clova; magic of the mind and body, like that of the Healing Hijn; and then there is a rarer kind — since there were few dragons born of this nature — a magic older than earth, the seas, the skies, time itself…a light surrounding this world that can never be quelled. The Moon Dragoness was one such Sage."

"You know…who she was? Who I am?"

"That is a moonstone on your forehead, is it not?" Anthron brushed that one troublesome strand of hair from his face. "Legend has it that it was a celestial dragon who built the half of the Equanume Balance that is the Lightscale. Therefore, it is *you* who can activate it."

Desert Rain could feel a drop of sweat trail down the side of her face. "But this is all a theory, right? I mean, there's no proof that a Hijn like me could do anything with this Lightscale. We're *assuming* it's possible, right?"

"Yes, it is a theory. But you wanted to know of a possible means to defeat the Wretched who distorts all he touches, true? Since you dismiss your own magic as a 'fluke,' the Lightscale would be the best weapon to fight your adversary, without bringing harm to the other Hijn."

"But if the Lightscale is with the Elfë Tiagas, that's all the way up in the Tiagalands, hundreds if not thousands of miles from here! And I'd have to go through the Inbetween, and I'm dead meat if I go there. And even if I could get through there to the Tiagalands, I'd freeze to death before coming even close to finding the elves' hidden cities!"

Anthron took back his book, shutting it with a quick flip of his hand. "So you find this information worthless?"

Desert Rain bit her lip, having not expected that retort. "No, of course not. It's something to go on, more than I could have come up with. But it's…it's a little unbelievable, you know? I mean, this sounds like a mission for heroes, for knights, for great wizards, not for…" She gestured with both hands to herself. "Well, look at me!"

Anthron did as she requested, observing her for a long moment. "And what do they have that you lack?"

"Everything!" Desert Rain stopped, and calmed herself, surprised that she had raised her voice. "I'm sorry, I didn't mean to yell. But would you tell me what it is that you see about me that I don't—" Her eyes suddenly narrowed on Anthron. "Or do you even really see anything? What is this really about, Anthron? Why are you breaking such a sacred pact to tell me something that is merely a 'theory'? Why tell me all this when you can't even guarantee that I can do anything with this Lightscale? Or is this pact not important to you anymore—is this a secret that lost its value when the Ahshi left the old elven society?"

A glint of nervousness crept into Anthron's eyes.

Desert Rain, eager for the truth, prodded further. "You don't like your northern cousins, so you've been waiting for an opportunity to truly bend some control over them. What better way than through an age-old secret, one that means everything to them, but means nothing to you anymore? *You* don't have the Lightscale, but why should they? What makes them worthy and not you? But you couldn't go blabbing about it to anyone—not to humans or dwarves or whoever else might want the Lightscale for themselves. But here *I* am, a Hijn of a celestial dragoness, and you think you have a justified reason to tell *me*, to have *me* force them to hand it over. Oh, you broke a centuries-old pact, you spilled a secret more precious than life itself, but you did it in the name of goodness and justice. All so your cousins will no longer hold the power, and you can feel satisfied knowing that they're squirming in their—"

Anthron slammed his hands on top of his books. The crystals at the table flared a bright red, throwing a monster light on his face. "THAT IS NOT THE REASON!"

A silence hung in the air after the echo of his shout died away. Anthron looked more shocked at his outburst than Desert Rain. His hands were shaking, his loose lock of hair dangling over his left eye. With an unsteady hand, he tucked the strand of hair behind his pointed ear. The light of the crystals changed to match the clear blue of his eyes, which were cast down at his books, seeking comfort in their familiar covers and bindings. He placed his hands on them, slowly steadying himself.

"You seek truth," he finally said, in a voice less steady than it had been. "I cannot deprive you of that. You are worried about my intentions."

"Yes, I am," Desert Rain admitted. "It's not that I don't think you honorable, Sir Anthron, but people don't go telling such valuable secrets just to be helpful."

"No, I suppose they don't." He sighed, clenching and unclenching his fingers. "Desert Rain, there are many reasons I could give you for my actions here. Perhaps I overwhelm you with my explanations, and that angers you. If I must simplify this to its most bare, basic reason, it would be that…I fear."

The intensity in Desert Rain melted into curious sympathy. "You fear what?"

Anthron's lips trembled. He closed his eyes. "I fear what is coming. Elves fear change. Change is going to happen—great, dark changes. All my knowledge, all my logic, all my intellect can't halt or redirect it." He opened his eyes to look at her. "It is out of my control. It is Destiny at work, and all I can see, so clearly, is that you are in its design. Where more powerful Hijn failed, you endured. Where Death chased you, you escaped. Where others are alone, you are protected by forces beyond my comprehension."

Desert Rain's hand floated up towards the shaman's bracelet on her arm. It all did seem illogically in her favor.

"Forgive me if my reasons may be selfish," Anthron continued, "but this is all I can do to direct the future, to instill hope for my people. For elves of all factions. All I can do is guide one who may be able to stop the darkness who could bring about another change throughout Luuva Gros, one that could bring its end."

That hit Desert Rain between the eyes like a rock. She blinked to clear her head. "Its end? This is between Katawa and his clan. How would this affect all of Luuva Gros—"

"He destroys the Darkscale Court, he becomes possessor of the Darkscale. With it, he can reshape all of Luuva Gros to his wicked design…and everyone in it."

CHAPTER TEN
The Plan

It was not that this whole situation had been even remotely good before, but now Desert Rain saw how bad it really was. Katawa, who was already impervious, getting his hands on an object like the Darkscale—he could extend his distortion as far as he desired. In the back of her mind, she hoped that his drive to get revenge on his clan was his sole intention, that maybe the Darkscale device meant little to him. But who was she kidding? Of course he'd use it, if he had it.

She had been handed the impossible duty of being the one to stop him, because this elven philosopher, sitting so nonchalantly in front of her, had categorized her as a unique Hijn. This certainly explained why he had treated her so oddly when they first met. As if being a Hijn wasn't rare enough, now she had to be told that she was even rarer than that—an heir of a celestial dragon. What was that supposed to mean, anyway? That she was supposed to be able to do something incredible, colossal, world-changingly extraordinary with her gift—why not drop a ton of bricks on her shoulders and ask her to swim across the ocean to the Otherlands? Why hadn't Bellaluna, for all the knowledge and words of wisdom she had given her, told her about any of this?

She knew it was useless to think it, but the words flickered across her mind anyway: Swordmaster Skyhan must have been a Hijn of celestial magic too. He was master of Purelight, the most powerful magic anyone in Luuva Gros possessed. If there really was a twist of Fate at work here, then *he* should have been the one to activate the Lightscale. Or maybe Fate liked to have a good, hard laugh. Fate would say something like, *eh, the Swordmaster's too obvious. Hey, let's tell that donkey-eared freak that* she's *got to fight that Wretched that she was foolish enough to care for! It'll be a hoot!*

Anthron waited in silence, apparently having nothing more to say.

"Thank you for telling me all this, Sir Anthron. I know it must not have been an easy decision for you, to break your pact. But you must have a lot of faith in me, and I'm very grateful for that. But I'm going to need time alone to think all this through."

Anthron nodded. "Very well. Although I should perhaps warn you, it may be tricky for you to think alone, when your friends are so adamant to know what you're doing at all times."

"Oh, no, Mac and Chiriku would give me privacy if I said I needed it—"

She paused, noticing that Anthron's words had a meaning behind them. He smiled wryly at her. Desert Rain lifted a questioning finger to point towards the entrance of the room. Anthron nodded once. Desert Rain wiped a hand over her face. "Mac? Are you out there?"

She heard a faint Bayou curse word come from outside the door.

Desert Rain lifted her head up. "Mac, you have to stop this habit of eavesdropping on everyone's conversations! This was supposed to be private!"

Mac appeared in the frame of the door, throwing an

accusing finger to point behind him. "Hey, it all wasn't-tkk my idea! Chi saw you following that philos'pher fellow and talked me into going after you!"

Chiriku came up behind him, swatting the back of his head. "You two-faced belly-crawler! It was your idea! You were so curious to know what was going on—"

They bickered for a good six seconds before Desert Rain cut them off. "All right, all right. I don't care whose idea it was. How much did you both hear?"

Mac and Chiriku shifted their eyes to gaze around the room in an act of ignorance.

"You heard everything." Desert Rain cast Anthron an apologetic look. She turned back to Mac and Chiriku. "Neither of you can ever, *ever* tell anyone else what you heard, understand? Anthron would get into real trouble if the Ahshi knew what he's done."

"Calm yourself, Hijn Desert Rain." Anthron gathered his books and stood up. "It is good that they know. After all, it would be rather confusing to them to join you on your journey, not knowing where they were going or what they were searching for."

Desert Rain snapped her head back to the elf. "What? Oh, no, no, no. They can't come with me. This is all so…I've already put them through too much."

"Yeah, that's great. Talk about us as if we're not here." Chiriku crossed her arms in her usual defiant way. "Look, I'm going to go with you, whether you like it or not."

"Chiriku, this is serious—"

"I *know* it's serious! Don't you dare treat me like a kid! It's not always about you, you know. I got a score to settle with that demon. If that son of a maggot hadn't driven us out of Syphurius, my grandfather wouldn't have gotten sick and he'd still be alive." She reached a hand back to place it on the handle of her warhammer, gripping it as the feathers on her head and neck fluffed up. "I've lost everything I had because of that Wretched. You want me to go home? What home? There's nothing for me back in Syphurius, nothing for a half-breed with no family. All I want now is to bury my hammer in that demon's face for what he's done to me. Are you going to stand there and have the gall to tell me that I can't come along? Who in the Eternal Deep do you think you are?"

Desert Rain went rigid at this verbal assault. Chiriku may have normally been short-tempered and stubborn, but there was a look of vehemence in her eye that dared Desert Rain to tell her not to come. The more Desert Rain thought about it, it might be unwise to turn her away. Desert Rain couldn't be sure she could fight the way she did against the Zi'Gax again, but Chiriku knew how to fight, and fight well. It would be good to have Chiriku along, both as a fighter and someone who was street-wise, something Desert Rain was not. Whatever obstacle should arise, whether it would be man or beast, Chiriku would be able to face it head on without hesitation. Plus, Desert Rain had promised Hibbletom that she would keep an eye on Chiriku. Who else did the Quetzalin have to look out for her now?

The Hijn turned to look at Mac. Did he feel the same way? He did not look fazed by anything he had heard. He gave her a wink, one that spoke for itself: *I told you that you had something special about you, didn't I, Gila?*

It was evident to Desert Rain that she couldn't turn either of them away. She had been afraid that she wouldn't be able to protect them from danger if they came with her, but it had been *they* who had protected *her*—from goblins and Wretched, but also from her own self-doubt. If she went alone, she would never get far, and where would Mac and Chiriku go in a land where Katawa and his manipulated minions, his Distorted, could show up at any turn? As long as they were all together, they would all protect each other.

"You're right, Chiriku," Desert Rain replied. "Who am I to tell you, either of you, what path you ought to take? If this is what you really want to do, Hij-Urawran know I can't stop you." She gave the Quetzalin a half-grin. "A whole pack of Zi'Gax couldn't stop you."

At that moment, Desert Rain could have sworn that the corner of Chiriku's beak lifted a little, into a barely noticeable smile—not a sardonic one, but of the genuine kind. Maybe it was the dim light playing tricks.

Mac was smiling too. "Glad to see you've come around, Gila Gul. Like we Bayou folk-kk say, 'It's easier to wade through the swamp with—'"

Chiriku slapped a hand over Mac's mouth. "Say one more stupid Bayou proverb and I'll live up to that name you gave me and peck your eyes out."

Desert Rain, learning that Chiriku was more squawk than peck, surpressed a chuckle.

Mac nodded, saying a muffled "okay" so that Chiriku would release him. He rubbed his hands together in enthusiasm. "So, all we gotta do is go up north, find this magical whats-its-ssck and use it on that-tkk big ol' Nasty. Sounds-ssck easy enough. What do we do first, Dez?"

Sounds easy enough? What would Mac consider hard? "It's not that simple, Mac. The first problem is even getting to the

Tiagalands. It's not exactly right next door from here."

"Then we just-tkk sit down and think-kk about it some," the lizard responded. "I don't suppose-ssck we could make it a li'l brighter in here?"

The room instantly brightened as Anthron touched each of the crystals on the table, the dim blue glow becoming a warm yellow radiance. He sat down at the table, not saying anything as the others came to sit around the table with him.

"Let's take that big buzzard of Clova's to fly up there, problem solved," Chiriku said more as an instruction than a suggestion.

Desert Rain shook her head. "Gust isn't ours to take. I'm not going to take away Clova's Roc from her, and unless you know how to command a Roc, it wouldn't do much good anyway."

"Not-tkk to mention I hear that no birds'll go near that cursed Inbetween place-ssck," Mac pointed out. "I heard that birds fly over that-tkk place when they're ready to go to the Pond of the Beyond."

"That's superstition," Chiriku retorted.

"No, he's right. Woasim the Wind Hijn told me about it a long time ago," Desert Rain said, shifting restlessly. "He says that there's a kind of awful smog that hangs high over the whole stretch of the place. It's the waste of all the dark magic the Darkscale create, combined with the fumes generated by the Bloodburn smelting furnaces and machines. It creates acidic rain, and smoke so thick, no sunlight can fall on the Inbetween. Woasim called it something funny…the 'Malaise Cloud,' or something like that. Anyway, he says the few flying animals who dare to go near it are Kidran's snowbirds, because they're endowed with protective frost magic. Even they sometimes don't make it through." She thought about the snowbird Kidran had supposedly sent out to bring the council a message, and had been lost. She couldn't imagine what might have happened to that bird in a smog-cloud of raining acid. "I'm not even sure how he and Kidran can travel through that smog—they must ride winds that take them high enough above it or have warding-off spells to protect themselves."

Chiriku shrugged. "So, Clova must know some spells. Since you apparently don't have a clue about how to do any magic tricks when you want to, it would help to have a magic-user along who knows what she's doing."

Desert Rain felt prickles on her neck. She bit her lip and shook her head. "She's too sick, and we don't know how long it will take for her to fully recover. Every day we wait, Katawa could be closer to finding the Darkscale clan, and when he does, he won't hesitate to force the Hijn council to fight against his family."

"And I don't-tkk suppose Clova would feel too good being up in the icelands, where nothing grows," Mac thought aloud.

Desert Rain hadn't even thought of that. Even if Clova was in perfect health right now, she'd have absolutely no power up in the Tiagalands. Everything would be too cold for her to use her plant magic—seeds wouldn't germinate in ice. She'd be even more helpless than Desert Rain—at least Desert Rain had Silverheart, if anything. Knowing Clova, she would insist on braving the arctic lands with them anyway, magic or no, and Desert Rain would not put her at risk like that.

Chiriku could tell what Desert Rain was thinking by the expression on her face. "Then what, you want to walk all the way there or something?"

"Maybe we could get the elf folk-kk here to lend us a few of those deer they ride," Mac suggested.

Desert Rain shook her head. "Riding or walking through the Inbetween is even worse than trying to fly over it. Unless we have highly trained bodyguards who have braved the Inbetween before to come with us, we'd never get through there without getting lost or killed." *Great Guerda-Shalyr, the Tiagalands alone will be bad enough for getting lost or killed!*

"Well, is there even a third option?" Chiriku asked haughtily. "Do you know some magical way around the Inbetween, because, I hate to break it to you, we'll have to go through it to get to the Tiagalands."

"If we had a—" Before Desert Rain could finish her sentence, Anthron placed a scroll in front of her. Unrolling it, she found that it was a detailed map of Juka Basin and its surrounding regions, with the Land Ablaze to the south, the coast to the east, and the Inbetween to the north.

"Thank you," she said warily to the elf who apparently could read her mind. She spread the map out in front of her, looking at the area of the map labeled the Inbetween, but this area was, of course, blank of any routes or landmarks. The Inbetween stretched all the way from the east coast to the west, from northern borders of the Forest Overlooking the Sea to the opposite end of the Azokind Mountains. By the Divine Beasts, Kidran and Woasim must be the bravest people in the world to be able to cross that expanse of unknown wilderness, as they sometimes had to do. Anyone else determined enough to pass through there always brought experienced guards or Knights with them, as many as they could afford. Even then, they would find the thinnest stretches of the Inbetween to pass through to make it in and out of the territory quickly, but even then it could take days to make it across. It was unfortunate geography that kept northern Noble Cities so cut off from the southern ones.

"See?" Chiriku said, as she and Mac looked over Desert Rain's shoulder. "No way around it. We have to go through the Inbetween somewhere."

"Or we could take a boat-tkk to go around it-tkk," Mac cut in.

Desert Rain and Chiriku raised their eyebrows at him. Desert Rain checked the map again. Sailing by boat on the eastern ocean would be faster than going by elk or on foot, and they would avoid the Inbetween that way. "But Mac, the closest port is all the way south by City Cindrea, and that's a few weeks' trek in the wrong direction."

"That would take us even longer, muck-eater," Chiriku said in the way a little sister may mock an older brother.

Mac put his hands behind his head and smiled, although he had nothing to lean back on. "Not if you got a boat-tkk in the Bayou."

Desert Rain went slack-jawed. "There's a port in the Bayou? I've never heard of a port in that territory."

"Well, maybe if the Noble Race types-ssck ever came to give us Bayou folk-kk a visit, then maybe you all would know about our port-tkk," Mac replied, a bit pointedly. "But then I suppose Nobles-ssck wouldn't want to set foot-tkk in one of our boats-ssck, would they?"

Desert Rain looked down at the map. "According to this, the Bayou is practically a straight shot east of here, right on the coast! It would take a few days to get there!" She poured over the map for a few seconds. "There we could take a boat, up to the Coast Keepers' Islands, where we could resupply before crossing over to the mainland, to the Ring of Springs, and from there to the Tiagalands."

"Great," Chiriku sighed. "So we have to go tramping through a swamp to find a rickety junk boat. Fantastic."

"And that's only our first problem." Desert Rain slouched, scratching her forehead. "We still don't know how we'll find the Elfë Tiagas once we get up north."

Mac and Chiriku thought about this, but they both came up empty of any suggestions.

Desert Rain drummed her fingers on the table, and Kidran popped into her mind. He may have been an Elfë Tiagas born, but he was not like the other elves. He would have been more suited to be an Ahshi with his open-armed, personable attitude, but he was heir to the Frost Dragon, and thus the local Hijn of the winterland dwellers. She knew that if Kidran had any control of his situation right now, he would help her. Maybe he still could help…

She turned to the philosopher. "Anthron, do you think you could send another Flightspeak to Kidran? If he knew we were coming, maybe he could find a way to sneak away from the Elfë Tiagas and meet up with us somewhere. Then he could help convince them to help us, if we explain to them what you told us."

Anthron tucked back the loose strand of hair that had freed itself once again. "I can send another Flightspeak, but it was by chance that Kidran received the first one. I cannot guarantee that he would be the one to receive it again. If the Elfë Tiagas were the ones to sense the Flightspeak first, they might triple their wards to prevent you from finding them. I don't think they would take to my theory so readily."

"Good toads-ssck, those snow elves sound real cold," Mac said. "Guess that's-ssck why they like living in the ice-ssck."

"With their cities shrouded by warding magic, we could be hunting through the Tiagalands for months…" An idea poked inside Desert Rain's mind. Her hand shot into her pocket and pulled out the Darkscale compass. She inspected the dents and scratches in it, shaking it to hear a few loose parts clink around inside.

"Didn't you say that thing could detect magic?" Chiriku asked.

"That's what that Zi'Gax said," Desert Rain answered. "It might hone in on Ancient Magic, or this compass might detect Hijn…which means we could use this to find Kidran! This could lead us right to him, if it wasn't busted."

Anthron plucked it from her hands without even asking. He looked it over, tapping it in certain places, and then selected one of his books and started flipping through it. He eyed a page and took a small clay pallet knife from a fern-leaf-woven bag tied at his waist. He started prying the glassy top of the compass off. "It's a fairly standard compass mechanism. I'm sure with a little studying and patience, I can figure out how it works and fix it. There's probably a specialize crystal involved, if its purpose is to detect magic."

"Well, that fixes that, hoping that the stupid compass doesn't keep pointing to you," Chiriku pointed out to Desert Rain.

Desert Rain scratched her head. "Well, maybe as long as *I* don't use any magic, it won't point to me. With the elves' guarding spells being so strong, and much of the magic is provided by Kidran, it should get the compass's attention." Desert Rain paused, mentally running through all they had so far discussed.

"Sounds-ssck like we're good to go, then," Mac said, satisfied. "I guess-ssck the next thing to do is start-tkk heading to my home sweet home. I know the perfect folk-kk to pick up some supplies from."

"And get a boat with a crew?" Chiriku asked skeptically.

"Relax-ssck, Chi. I got it all in hand."

"I don't suppose we can buy coats and hiking gear in the Bayou?" Desert Rain asked. She was already shivering with the thought of that cold, snow-laden place she would be facing, a place that was the exact opposite of her desert home.

Mac patted her shoulder. "You're talking to the best-tkk merchant in the Bayou. If I can't get it-tkk, nobody can."

Chiriku stood up. "When do we hit the road?"

"I advise you to be patient, Quetzalin," Anthron said, not looking up from his work. "I would assume that you would prefer to gather supplies and food, and have an elven guide and elk take to you the edge of Juka Basin, rather than set off on foot unprepared."

"I guess," Chiriku replied smugly.

Mac tilted his head at Desert Rain. "Dez, you *are* going to tell Miss-ssck Clova where we're gonna be going, right-tkk?"

Desert Rain's ears twitched. She lowered her head. "I...I don't know if I can, Mac."

"But she'll be all worried about-tkk you."

"I can't say goodbye to her. She'll argue and..." Desert Rain shook her head. "I can't do it."

"Well, aren't you nice," Chiriku said dryly. "You're going to leave behind a sick friend without saying goodbye."

Desert Rain didn't reply, but she knew that she was going to have to face many hard situations soon, and this was one she couldn't avoid.

***

The desert hermit stood by Clova's hammock for a good minute, watching her sleep peacefully. She almost didn't want to wake her up. This was going to be so hard, to tell her goodbye — possibly the last goodbye for a long, long time. What would she do if Clova protested? Given that Desert Rain didn't want to go on this quest, Clova might convince her not to go. But she had to.

"Clova?" Desert Rain gently nudged her shoulder. "Clova? I'm sorry to wake you, but I need to tell you something."

Clova gradually awoke, fluttering her eyelashes and groaning softly. "Dezzy?" She suddenly shot wide awake, apprehension seizing her. "What is it? What's wrong?"

"Nothing, nothing's wrong. Everything's okay." She placed a hand on Clova's arm. "Clova, I've been talking with Anthron, and the others and I have discussed a plan for what we should do next."

Clova tried her best to sit up. "That's wonderful, Dezzy. I wish you had woken me up sooner, so I could have joined in. But I know you wanted me to rest, you're such a sweetheart. So, what are we going to do?"

Desert Rain gulped silently. "Clova, I want you to get well so badly, you must realize that. And, and I can't...you can't..." She couldn't hide the muddled mix of emotions on her face. Clova picked up on it instantly.

"Dezzy, you're not going to leave without me, are you?" Clova reached up to take Desert Rain's hand. "Give me a few days. I'll get better, I promise. I'm a little tired, that's all. Then we can go together."

"You don't understand." Desert Rain squeezed Clova's hand. "Where we're going — where I'm going — it would be dangerous for you. You wouldn't be able to use your magic, and you might become deeply ill. I can't do that to you. I won't let what happened with the Zi'Gax happen again, with you unable to protect yourself."

Disappointment crossed Clova's face. "What are you talking about? Where are you going?"

Desert Rain released Clova's hand, turning away so she wouldn't see the Forest Hijn's sad eyes. "Anthron told me an important secret of the elves, one that you know, I think. He has a theory, and I know it seems dumb to invest so much in just a theory, but it's all I have to go on right now. At any rate, I have to go to the Tiagalands to find the Elfë Tiagas and get Kidran's help."

"The Tiagalands? But why would Anthron advise you to go—" Clova stopped, and leaned back in her hammock. She was quiet for a while before speaking again. "The secret...he told you *the* secret?"

Desert Rain nodded.

Clova stared at Desert Rain for a long time, and the desert Hijn wasn't sure if Clova was looking at her or staring into space. Then the Forest Hijn closed her eyes, sighing. "Dezzy, does Anthron think you can awaken the Lightscale?"

Desert Rain, once again, nodded. "Yes."

Clova was quiet again, but then she made a tiny smile. She opened her eyes. "Anthron does not make theories blindly. I think what he sees in you is truly there. I've seen it too, in your eyes, in what you did to save my life. You are right, I would be powerless in the snowlands." She shifted onto her side, casting her eyes down to the floor. "You're not going alone, are you?"

"No. Mac and Chiriku are insistent on coming along. Chiriku has convinced herself that she has a personal vendetta against Katawa, and Mac...I don't know, he likes adventure, I guess."

"Good." Clova looked up at her. "I believe you will find them. I will trust in the spirits of the Hij-Urawran to guide you. Kidran will figure out a way to find you, I bet."

Desert Rain couldn't help but smile at Clova's optimism. "How is it you can be so hopeful?"

Clova laughed lightly. "Dezzy, shouldn't you of all Hijn put faith in hope? They say — I really don't know who 'they' are, but I've heard it — that moonbeams are the wings of hope, flying over all at night, reminding us that even in darkness there is light, and that despair will be dispelled by morning. That's awfully pretty, isn't it?"

Desert Rain nodded, but sadness filled her. How ironic that saying was, that in truth it was the heir of the Moon Dragoness who had started this whole mess to begin with.

Clova sat up again, reaching out and taking Desert Rain's arm. She pulled Desert Rain to her in a tight, smothering hug. "Travel safely with my blessing. May Nature guide you and show you kindness. Know that I will keep you in my prayers and heart." She lingered on the hug a moment longer before releasing her friend. She reached towards her neck for her seed pouch, but then remembered she had lost it in the confrontation with the Zi'Gax. She removed a ring from her finger — a simple ring of silver and jade, a circle of teardrop-shaped leaves — and took Desert Rain's hand. She slipped the ring onto Desert Rain's slender finger. "This is so you'll remember to come back after you find what you're looking for. Then we can save Rukna and the others together, right?" She smiled warmly.

Desert Rain looked at the ring, and nodded. This time, she couldn't reply, for if she opened her mouth, she knew she would cry. She paused, wishing there was something else she could say or do, but then she turned, and left the room. She heard Clova whisper a soft "goodbye" behind her. Desert Rain mouthed the word, but couldn't bring herself to say it aloud.

She was half-way down the corridor when she heard a child's voice. "Miss Lute Lady?"

Desert Rain turned to see the little human girl, Alana, coming out of her room. She quickly gained composure, wiping away a tear from her eye. "Hello there, Alana. How are you feeling today?"

"Much better, thank you." Alana went up to her, shining a youthful grin. "Gabriel told me how you fought the goblins. You must be very brave."

Desert Rain smiled but shook her head modestly. "Gabriel fought very bravely himself. You're very lucky to have him with you. Is he in your room right now?"

Alana nodded happily.

The Hijn thought a moment, and then bent down to be more eye-level with Alana. "Could you tell Gabriel goodbye for me?"

"Okay." It took Alana a second to realize the meaning of that. "Are you leaving?"

"My friends and I have to leave in the morning, and I don't know if I'll get a chance to say goodbye to Gabriel, or thank him again for all he did to help us."

"Why don't you tell him yourself?" Alana took Desert Rain by the hand, but Desert Rain slipped quickly out of her grasp.

"It's…" Desert Rain stood at full height, wringing her fingers. "If you could tell him for me, I'd appreciate it. Thank you." Desert Rain turned and glided down the hallway, keeping her gaze down at the floor. Why she couldn't tell Gabriel herself, she couldn't say. Maybe one goodbye was all she could handle right then.

She went to her mat in the main hall, to find Mac already snoring away on his, and Chiriku sitting on hers. The Quetzalin looked up at her but said nothing. She looked weary and seemed to be in deep thought. Desert Rain lied down on her mat slowly, for her back wounds still ached even with the salve the elves had put on them. She shut her eyes, but her mind continued to work for a while. Tomorrow was going to be the beginning of a whole new chapter in her life, one that was going to lead her down a trail she had never trodden. Questions persistently echoed in her thoughts. Was this going to work? Could she really do this? Was there really a twist of Fate directing these events? But there were also the voices of affirmation mingled in with her questions. Time was of the essence. Katawa was getting nearer to his goal with every passing day. She had been the one to return his memories, who gave him the power to spread his poison. The Knighthood must be out there right now, trying to stop him, but it was her responsibility. She would keep her vow. She would find this Lightscale, and find out how to use it to undo the Distortion.

Interlude: The Birth

Ninety years ago.

Desiree stood with her toes planted in the warm sands, facing the ruins of the temple she had visited so often in the past. Even now, she felt the comfort that Grandma Luna gave her, even though the temple was now empty, and had been for some time. Desiree had not been here since the night Luna had passed away, after giving her the gift of Blueshine. Now Desiree had wished she hadn't come on that evening, had not been here when Luna had died. For then, she would not have gained Blueshine, which she discovered was not a blessing, but the greatest curse of her life.

There were images still fresh and vibrant in her mind. They did not quite link up somehow, the events between the images blurred in her desperation to forget. But she still saw the faces — all the faces. The ones she loved: her mother, her father, her sisters and her brothers. These faces were twisted in fear, because *they* had come. The event replayed again and again in her head, in a neverending cycle that filled her with ever-increasing pain. It was so clear, that she may as well have been living it all over again…

***

She awoke on the ground, her body aching, her fingers burning as if stricken with an intense frost bite. She was lying on her stomach, and she slowly raised herself up on her shivering arms. Everything she saw upon waking— the wagons, the sleeping tents, the clearing around it all—was awash in glassy, bluish crystal, like a tidal wave had tumbled through and paralyzed all it touched. Even the fire that had been crackling in the fire pit had become a jagged statue of shimmering glass. She looked at her sore fingers, which she swore looked a bit elongated, and even a bit yellowish. The tips of her fingers were caked in the crystal that swathed the artists' camp, and it hurt to flex them. She rubbed her fingers together, the crystal dissolving off in a fine powder. Looking around the crystal-stained clearing, she did not see anyone at first, not her family, not the other artists that traveled in the company, not even the rogues that had attacked their camp.

Then she spotted them. The thieves were still here, but they were no longer a threat. They, too, had become encased in the wash of crystal, frozen in their last moment of shock and fright as the magic had swept over them. Desiree had not been able to tell who or what they were when they had first assaulted the camp, but now she could see their horrid, inhuman faces petrified in the blue glass. They were goblins—two had gotten away before the Blueshine had caught them, but the unfortunate ones would never harass another traveling cavalcade again.

Desiree was bold enough to touch one of the goblins, to see if it was still alive underneath the crystal, but it crumbled into a pile of tiny shards as soon as she laid her hand on it. The goblins had not been encased in the Blueshine; the magic had completely altered their bodies into the strange, gem-like glass.

This was not supposed to have happened. That was not what the Blueshine should have done. It was supposed to have driven away the evil, protected the camp in the moonlight aura of goodness. But it had devoured everything with its crystalline touch, and she had been left alone. Where was her family? Where were the other artists? Had they all, too, been entrapped by the Blueshine?

She heard something shatter. She turned to see the door of one of the wagons had been kicked open from the inside, but the crystal-coated door had crumbled into pieces, like the goblin had.

"Desiree, what have you done??"

The voice was her mother's. The middle-aged artisan, still as exotic and beautiful as she had always been, crept out from the wagons, along with Desiree's haggard father and little sisters, and the others hiding in the giant canvas-covered carts. The artists gawked at the scene before them, at the landscape eaten away by glassy blue crystal. Some let out short shrieks and they stepped on patches of crystal and it gave way beneath their feet, dissolving into sparkling sand. They all turned to stare at Desiree, a new sense of fear in their eyes.

Desiree was speechless and scared. She had never been the most popular performer in the company, and had spent a good deal of time trying to stay out of sight when not on stage. But now they all stared at her, so transfixed, so scrutinizing. All Desiree could do was look down at her feet, which she had noticed had started to change during the past few months—they were starting to look more like hands. She had hoped it was her imagination, but others had noticed it too.

Then she realized who was missing. The ones who had refused to hide from the goblins, the young men who had stood their ground and tried to fight them off. Those boys included her older brothers. Where were they all? Where had happened to Andeas, Lionel and Tandre?

They found the boys quickly. At the very edge where the crystalline wash ended were six figures, three of which were her siblings. The force of the Blueshine must have pushed them away, instead of washing over them. *They weren't frozen because they are good people*, Desiree thought, *and the Blueshine won't hurt good people.* But she saw how wrong she was. Her brothers had not been left unharmed. They lied in the frost-tipped grass, shaking, gasping for air. Their skin had turned ice-white, and their veins were visible through their skin, outlined in crystal-blue. It was as if all the color had been drained from their body — even their hair and eyelids were caked rigid with powdered crystal. Most of their clothing was broken off, having succumbed to the same brittleness as everything else touched by Blueshine.

Desiree rushed to her fallen brothers, falling to her knees beside them. She ventured cautiously to touch Tandre, the youngest of the three, and to her relief, he did not shatter like the goblin had. Yet it was painful to touch him — it wasn't like a burn or frostbite, but it sent a surge of sharpness through her arm that made her withdraw her hand with a yelp.

Desiree couldn't describe the horror that swallowed her as she looked at that terrible sight. How could this have happened? Her Blueshine wasn't supposed to do this to good people! Unless, she wasn't worthy of the power; she wasn't good enough to use it.

There hadn't been any sympathy for Desiree as someone yanked her away from her brothers, and others came over to the young men and wrapped them in blankets. They lifted and loaded the boys into the wagons, placing them onto their shabby cots. Desiree heard the raspy, furious voice of one of the elders, a stout old woman who jabbed her wooden cane at her.

"What have I been telling you all along? This child is

cursed! I knew it as soon as she came home with that mark on her forehead! Bought the stone from a jeweler and stuck it on with face gum, she says. I've never seen her take that stone off. It's the mark of Demons, I tell you!"

Desiree backed away from the prodding cane. "No! That's not true!"

"That's not all that's wrong with you. Look at your skin! I swear, you're turning more sallow by the day."

Other voices blended into the cacophony of anger. "And her hands! She's got the cursed ice on her hands!"

"She's been with demons!"

"They've turned her into one of them!"

"She's become a Wretched!"

The girl held her hands up, as if to ward off the verbal attacks. "No, I'm not! You know that's not possible. Please, listen to me, this was an accident…It wasn't supposed to happen like this…" Desiree ran over to her father and mother, who were standing by the wagon that their sons were lying in. "Mother, Father, you believe me, don't you? That I didn't mean to do this? I meant to help. I would never do this on purpose. Please, say something…"

Her parents didn't look at her. They both looked so shaken and upset, even the colorful beauty of their costumes and makeup would not be able to mask their emotions. They did not seem angry or afraid, but heartbroken. Desiree tried to take hold of her mother's hand, but the woman jerked away from her touch. That shudder made Desiree feel as cold as the crystal on her fingertips.

Her mother and father both slowly turned and walked into the wagon. They sat down on one of the tattered cots where their half-frozen sons lied. They didn't look back at Desiree — they never looked at her again.

Desiree whimpered, "I'm sorry…"

A small rock hit her in the shoulder. She whipped around to face the rest of the artists and artisans, who had now gathered into a tight mob.

"We don't want demon witches here!" yelled one of the artists.

Desiree made one last attempt to defend herself. "I didn't mean to…I was trying to stop the thieves. I was trying to protect us!"

"Look at what you did! The goblins would have taken our money and some of our possessions. *You*'ve gone and destroyed everything!"

"You've hurt your brothers with your dark magic, witch!"

Desiree was blinded by her tears. She wrapped her arms around herself as each accusation pierced her like prodding spears.

"She's gone and killed her own brothers!"

"We can't have a wicked changling live with us!"

"Get rid of her!"

"We don't shelter witches!"

"She's a Wretched!"

"Demon!

"Witch!"

"WRETCHED! WRETCHED! WRETCHED!"

Desiree had run away from the accusing voices and the pelting stones, fleeing with an inhuman speed that no other in Luuva Gros could match. She did not plan where to go at first, and for some time hid in the dark corners of towns she passed, without a home and without money. Even the beggars faired better than she did, for her gradual physical changes made her too afraid to speak to anyone. Eventually she had found her way back here, to this temple in the desert. She had sought refuge here before, and now it was her one haven. She couldn't live anywhere, not in the cities, not where people would fear her or mock her. After what she had done, what pain she had caused, she could not risk living among people. She could not hurt anyone like that again.

Bellaluna had made a mistake. Desiree shouldn't have been her heir. Something with the Blueshine had gone horribly wrong, and it wasn't the magic's fault. It was Desiree. She wasn't fit to use the magic. She was not strong enough, was not good enough. There must have been a great wickedness inside her to make the Blueshine act like that. She feared this power. She couldn't control it. Without Luna, she would never learn how to control it. As she stood there, staring at the remains of the temple, feeling the warm sand between her toes, she made a firm resolve:

She would never summon Blueshine ever again.

A cool drop fell on top of her head. Desiree thought she imagined it, but then she felt another drop land on her ear. Looking down at the sand, she watched as tiny dark spots began to freckle the landscape. Lifting her eyes to the sky, she saw gray clouds gather overhead, but not the dark ominous ones of a storm. The rain trickled down softly, the gentle weep of a light shower, cool and refreshing in this desolate land. Desiree could not understand it. Luna had told her rain almost never came here in the desert, maybe once or twice a year. Of all days for it to rain, when Desiree had returned after all this time.

Peace descended upon her as each raindrop bathed her hot, golden ochre skin. She would be all right out here. This was a sign. Luna had taught her how to survive in the desert, how to find food and water, how to avoid dangerous animals, how to bring them to her trust. Desiree had thought Luna taught her these things for the sake of knowledge, but maybe there was more to it than that. Maybe Luna knew that Desiree would return to this place, and the desert was to be her new home.

As Desiree watched the rainfall, she decided to relinquish everything about her old self, to begin anew out here in the Golden Dragon Desert. She would shred away every last detail, as much as she could bring herself to do. Some things about her she may never discard, but the being of Desiree would be sanded away.

Desiree…the name had never been right for her. Her mother had always said it was perfect, that it meant "Desire," or "Love." Look what love had done. The people she loved, she had hurt. Even as a little child, she had always felt the name was somewhat off. It was close to who she might be, but not quite.

She would become what was around her. She would become part of this place Luna had once held domain over, the place bequeathed to her.

Desiree…

She would endure the heat of the sands. She would rebuild this temple to be her home. She would become a mystery, something that could appear and vanish in the blink of an eye, like rain in the desert.

She inhaled deeply, and stretched her arms out to welcome in the new self, the birth of the spirit she had created within.

I am Desert Rain.

CHAPTER ELEVEN
Meeting in the Woods

Desert Rain…

She could feel his presence pressing down on her.

Desert Rain…I'm here…

She couldn't open her eyes. She couldn't move at all. She felt a chill invade her body as his breath stung her neck. His teeth raked over her throat, his lips brush against her ear. A trembling filled her chest as the frightening and intoxicating presence overwhelmed her. Suddenly she felt his hands plunge into her belly, and the electrifying pain of the Distortion twisted her inside out.

You are mine!

Desert Rain awoke with a start. She was drenched in sweat, and the trembling in her chest was still there. The presence was gone. She sat up on her blanket, one of the several provisions the Ahshi had given her for her journey through the forest. She looked around, finding no one other than her two companions. Chiriku was asleep, her warhammer in hand. Mac was still awake, although it must have been late, judging from the placement of *Ia Ternaut* in the sky, which could be seen through the gaps in the canopy. He sat by the campfire, roasting pieces of an apple on a stick, popping the pieces into his mouth happily.

She instinctively checked herself, feeling her stomach for any sign of deformed skin or muscle. There were none. She checked her pockets, making sure she still had her possessions. In one pocket was Gothart's black pouch—he had been quiet as of late, but he could entertain himself, she was sure. In the other pocket was the Darkscale compass, which Anthron had figured out how to fix after a few hours of inspecting it. The inner workings were much like a normal compass, as he had predicted, and there had been a small crystal prism inside that had been knocked out of place, but not broken. After shifting and securing things back into their alleged places, and tapping out the dents, the compass had the appearance of being functional. The little metallic ball hovered in the center of the compass, which Anthron could deduced that this was how the device would be in a neutral state. There was no real way to test if the compass was working, although the ball did occasionally hover towards Desert Rain. She hoped that up north, the compass would be more responsive to the presence of the Elfë Taigas' magic.

She winced slightly as she moved, her wounds still burning a little, but they were healing well thanks to the Ahshi medicine she had been given. The medicine had healed Chiriku's ankle wound as well, and she could once again walk without limping. It had also helped that she had kept off her feet the last few days, since they had been riding on elkback with the Ahshi up until yesterday.

It had been three days since she, Mac and Chiriku left the sanctuary. Their elven guides had been with them up to the afternoon of day two, for they had led them to the edge of Juka Basin, where they had parted. The elves had made it clear that they would bring them as far as the outskirts of the Basin, for beyond was the swamplands, a land of which the elves were not too fond. Mac would have to be the guide from here on out, to which Chiriku bluntly verbalized that they were all going to get extremely lost and probably eaten by something.

Desert Rain was already missing the comfort of their elven bodyguards and elks. She trusted Mac to lead them, but it had been nice to know that the elves had their archery for protection. There had been an occasion where their elven guides had to fend off some large animal—a wild cat, it had looked like—with a few arrow-shots. Mac had a few handfuls of spare blast powder with him to scare off animals, but not much, so they were trying to stay as quiet and unnoticeable as possible.

"Are you all right-tkk?" Mac asked when he saw Desert Rain jerk out of her sleep.

Desert Rain rubbed her eyes. "Yeah, I'm fine. A bad dream, that's all." She sat cross-legged, and let out a yawn. "What're you still doing up?"

"I was feeling a bit-tkk peckish," he replied as he popped another slice of apple into his mouth. "And I figured someone should keep watch a while."

"I could take over for you if you wanted to get some sleep," Desert Rain offered. Seeing as how she was unsettled by the nightmare, she would not mind staying awake for an hour or two.

"Nah, don't worry about it-tkk. I was waiting to see if that fellow followin us-ssck will come over to join us."

Desert Rain thought she had misunderstood him. "Fellow? What fellow?"

"The one that's-ssck been tracking us ever since the elves-ssck went home. He's up the trail that-a way," he said, gesturing off into the shadowed woods.

Desert Rain strained to see into the forest with her nocturnal eye, but could not see anything. "How can you tell?"

Mac snickered. "You don't-tkk grow up being a lizard without knowing when something's after you. Plus, he's-ssck got a small fire going that he's trying to hide by putting his body between it and us-ssck."

The Hijn tried to find this supposed "fellow" again, and caught a faint, muted glow far off—she wouldn't have noticed it at all if Mac had not said anything. The glow wavered, like the light from a campfire, but there was something trying to block its illumination. She was impressed that Mac had picked up on the presence of their follower so easily.

"Who is it, do you think?" she asked the lizard.

"Could be a thief," Mac said, scratching his chin. "Could be a hunter out-tkk for game. Could be some nomad going our way. But I get the suspicion he's-ssck not the aggressive type. We ain't exactly armed to the teeth or nothing. If he wanted to rob or scare us-ssck, he would've done it-tkk by now."

Desert Rain brushed back her hair with her fingers. "He might have seen Chiriku with her hammer. Maybe he's waiting for all of use to fall asleep before risking an assault."

"We were all asleep last night-tkk. He could've jumped us then."

"True. You don't think it's anyone we know, do you?"

Mac shrugged. "If he's-ssck a friend, then he should come on over so we know. Unless he's real shy."

Desert Rain watched the distant glow for a minute, and then she stood up. She started towards the direction of the stranger.

"You be careful, Gila," Mac warned. "You don't know if this-ssck is a trap. He could be waiting for one of us to check him out-tkk, and that's when he'd cause trouble."

"I know, Mac. If he does, I have Silverheart." She took the black pouch out of her pocket and felt inside for the familiar hilt. She drew the sword out a short ways to reassure Mac and herself. Even if she couldn't fight with it the way she had before, maybe the sword itself would be intimidating enough to make the stranger think twice about harassing her. She slipped it back in and started off again.

"Wait," Mac said, as he reached into one of his pockets and took out a small bag of blast powder. He gently tossed it to her, and she made sure to catch it—if it hit the ground, it could blow up at her feet. "Just in case-ssck. Make sure to aim for the face-ssck," he advised.

Desert Rain crept quietly past the trees. These were not the same kind of trees that lived in the rainforest. Here, the trees' limbs sagged, draped in cobweb-like greenery, and the trunks were a bit more bulbous. Compared to the tropical trees of the Basin, these trees looked lazy and out of shape. Mac said that was an indication of them coming into the swamplands, plus that the ground had gotten softer and soggier since they left Juka Basin. Desert Rain had made care to wrap her feet up in strips of cloth to keep her feet a little drier from the soggy earth, but she was so used to feeling the ground beneath her that now she felt unsteady.

She wondered if the stranger was watching her coming, but if he was, he wasn't moving from his spot. As she crept closer, she could clearly see his silhouette against the muffled light of his fire. He was lying down on his side, his head pillowed on his arms. She could hear his slow, steady breathing.

He's asleep. She let out her breath, not aware she had been holding it. *I'll take a quick glance to see who he is.*

She slunk along outside the rim of the firelight. She ducked behind a tree and peered out from behind it. From here, she could get a good view the stranger, barely lit by his dying campfire. He had his traveling hat pulled down over his eyes, and shadows masked the rest of his face. It was this, ironically, that verfied that he was in fact not a stranger at all.

Gabriel! This was getting weird. What was he doing here *this* time? Desert Rain thought back to the ordeal with the Zi'Gax. This man had appeared out of nowhere, with no explanation, in the same way. He could be stealthy when need be — Desert Rain was often caught by surprise back at the sanctuary when he suddenly appeared around a corner. This was too coincidental. Besides, why did he decide to follow her instead of staying with that family that employed him?

I should go. If I give him time, he'll come over to us when he's ready. Then he can explain why he followed us.

She didn't leave, however. She watched him sleeping for a while, and she thought about those penetrating eyes beneath his closed eyelids. She had resolved that this was a regular human, but the question that she couldn't kill was still nagging at her. *The possibility is still there*, the little voice of hope in her head said. *You don't know for sure. Maybe he is who you thought he was.*

No, he's not! I looked into his eyes. He's not Skyhan, her logical side argued.

You convinced *yourself it's not him. You never found Skyhan's body, after all. You never saw his real face underneath his war mask. He might have gotten amnesia, and that's why he doesn't remember you.*

That's ridiculous. It's not the same person!

Look at you! You're arguing with yourself! Obviously, you still wonder about it.

Fine then. I need to show you…I mean, me. A little more proof.

She crouched down onto her hands and toes, creeping around the edge of dim light like a cat. She approached the sleeping man, keeping highly aware if he should jerk out of sleep. She could not see any silver rune markings, since his hands and arms were swathed in cloth wrappings, and she wasn't going to dare try and remove them.

*His hat…I'll take a quick look at his hair. Once I see that it's not silver, that should be enough to convince you…*me, I mean.

She slunk around behind him. She found herself shaking. She shouldn't be so nervous. She shouldn't have to do this at all, but if she didn't, that little voice was going to keep nagging at her, and she wanted to shut it up. She didn't have to pull the hat off the whole way, but enough to see his hairline. No silver hair, no Skyhan.

She reached her hand slowly out, steadying herself. She paused, thinking, *What if it* is *silver hair underneath that hat? What then?*

Well, we'll cross that bridge when we get there.

She lightly pinched her fingers on the wide brim of the hat. She barely pulled up the brim half an inch when Gabriel's hand grabbed her by the wrist. She tried to yank herself free of his grasp, but his strong hand held her firmly. He turned and glared at her, his eyes fierce. Desert Rain's lip trembled; she tried to stammer an explanation, but disjointed jibberish came out. "I…uh…there… you…we…I wasn't…hat…"

He sat up, his hold still on her, and with his other hand he pulled off his hat. Locks of tawny-brown hair spilled out, chopped so it fell barely below his ear line. The strange blotch on the right side of his face was much more disturbing when fully revealed, and the same sort of defacement was on his forehead as well. They looked like inky swirling fingerprints from someone, or something, large. The blotches were blood-red, outlined in charred-black, and embossed deep into the skin, as if it had been branded into him. The skin around these scars was burned, as if the markings had come from a touch of fire.

"Is this what you were so eager to see?" Gabriel seethed, bringing his face within an inch of Desert Rain's. "You think I didn't know that you were always watching me wherever I went? You think I didn't understand what you were thinking when you'd stare into my eyes? You can stop it now. You see what I've been hiding. I'm sure you can tell a lot about me, Hijn, but you don't know everything. It would be a good idea for you to quit trying to find out everything. You should keep your hands to yourself." He released her, harshly pushing her arm away.

Desert Rain rubbed her wrist, not sure what to say at first. "I thought you were someone I knew," she said quietly. "I can see I was wrong."

Gabriel placed the hat back on his head, and turned to face the fire, which was almost out. He was quiet for a moment, and then he let out a deep breath through his nose. "Why did you come over here?" he asked darkly.

"To find out why you're following us," she replied, her voice tense. "Mac and I thought you might be a thief."

Gabriel made a small laugh. "You decided to catch the thief by surprise? What would you have done if I had been a thief, or someone worse? Cut my head off with that—" He made the slightest pause. "—sword of yours?"

"No," Desert Rain retorted. "But I'm glad you're not a thief, if I'm glad about you being here at all. I'd still like to know why you're following us."

The man didn't reply immediately. He picked up a stick at his side and fed it to the fire. "I go where I please," he finally said.

"That doesn't answer my question."

"I go where I feel I'm needed."

Desert Rain cocked an eyebrow at him. "You think I need you? Someone has an awfully high opinion of himself."

Gabriel turned to look at her over his shoulder. "When I heard you were leaving, and all you had with you were that Quetzalin and that blabbering merchant, I figured you might want a bodyguard. Someone who could actually save your skin out here."

That struck Desert Rain as both confusing and creepy. "I don't know if I should say that's sweet of you, but we can take care of ourselves."

"As you were doing with the Zi'Gax before I showed up."

Desert Rain's ears folded back, and her face flushed. "First of all, we would have done fine against the Zi'Gax without your help." Even as she said this, she knew it wasn't true, but she was too mad right now to admit that. "Second, I don't know how I feel about someone who can abandon a family who took him in and gave him a home. What, *they* don't need you anymore? Maybe you don't go where you're needed—you go wherever you might find some excitement."

Gabriel got up to face her. She stood up to match him, although he was quite a bit taller than she was.

"If you are so keen to know everything, Hijn, then I should tell you it was *their* idea for me to go after you," he stated coldly.

Desert Rain's eyes widened. "It was?"

Gabriel was about to retort, but he paused, looking a bit muddled. "It was Alana's idea."

"Oh." She tugged on one of her ears. "What did she say?"

Gabriel sighed. "She told me that you wanted her to tell me goodbye for you. But I guess she must have wanted to repay you for the music you played for her, so she asked me to go with you to make sure you'd be okay. I tried to tell her that my loyalties were to her and her family, but she said that I had already helped them, and now *you* needed my help. Corb and Danal…the famer and his wife, they granted me permission to go. Alana's a… tender-hearted child."

"Yes, she is." Desert Rain smiled at the memory of the little girl. "That's kind of you to carry out a child's request, but if you want to go your own way, I won't tell Alana."

Gabriel narrowed his gaze. "I don't make a promise to break it."

"Then why didn't you ask me if you could come along before we left?"

"Would you have said yes?"

Desert Rain thought about that. She might have, she might not have. Knowing how she felt about Gabriel, about how he made her ache with guilt and confusion every time she looked in his eyes, she probably wouldn't have wanted him to tag along. Chiriku certainly would have put up a stink about it, for no reason. Gabriel seemed to do what he wanted, however, whether he had permission or not. He had not helped fight off the Zi'Gax because he was ordered to, but no one had invited him to join in either. Asking did not appear to be something Gabriel did easily.

"Well, I guess I can't send you back. I wouldn't want to refuse Alana's wish." Desert Rain managed a smile. "But if you're going to be a bodyguard, you can't do much all the way over here by yourself. You better join us at our camp."

Gabriel hesitated, but then he nodded. He picked up what little he had with him—his battlestaff and a handkerchief that had held a small ration of food—and stamped out his fire. They both walked off towards the glow of the campfire where Mac and Chiriku were, Desert Rain's nocturnal eye helping to guide them past the shadowed trees.

"May I ask where you got those scars?" Desert Rain asked.

"You won't get an answer," Gabriel bluntly answered.

Desert Rain tightened her lips, having expected that. "Then may I ask why you helped us fight off the Zi'Gax?"

Gabriel once again paused before replying. "I go where I am needed," he eventually said.

Desert Rain made a nod, knowing that that would be their last discussion for the night.

By late morning the next day, the four travelers had descended into swampier forestland, a veil of mist growing thicker as they went along. Gabriel took up the role of scout, keeping ahead to clear the path for the others. This was problematic at times, since he occasionally vanished in the mist, but he would sooner or later come back into sight, or the others would hear him whack at something with his battlestaff.

Chiriku was not thrilled to find out Gabriel had followed them. Not that she cared too much either way, but she didn't like that Gabriel was trying to take her job as protector of the group. She was the one with the warhammer—all he had was a lousy stick. Desert Rain had told her that he had come to assist them by request, and it was honorable to let him fulfill that request. Pfft, sure. Wait until they got attacked by a wild cat or wolf, then they'd see who was the real warrior.

Mac, on the other hand, seemed glad that their mystery follower was Gabriel. The two hadn't gotten to know each other well yet, but Mac thought him a "nice fellow." When the group stopped to rest, Gabriel and Chiriku went off scouting around — it had evolved into an unspoken competition for who could catch any upcoming trouble first — while Mac and Desert Rain sat on the root of a tree. Mac leaned over to Desert Rain, lowering his voice for discretion.

"Are you thinking what-tkk I'm thinking?" Mac asked, grinning and giving her a wink.

"About what?" she asked.

"About that Gabe fellow following us-ssck. I guess that whole thing with the goblins-ssck gave him an appetite for adventure. Or maybe he's got-ttk other appetites," Mac said slyly, grinning those yellowed teeth.

Desert Rain's face reddened. "Mac! It's nothing like that. I don't know the man, and he knows nothing about me."

"A man ain't got-tkk to know nothing about a lady to fancy her," Mac replied. "Or vice versa. But who knows-ssck? You said that he's-ssck a drifter, so maybe he's drifting our way." The smirk he gave Desert Rain, however, showed that he didn't really believe that.

Desert Rain shook her head with a slight smile. Great, now *Mac* was playing match-maker, as if Clova hadn't been bad enough about that sort of thing. "He's here because the little girl he was taking care of asked him to make sure we'd be all right." She looked up through the mist, at the gray sky above them. "But when we get to the Bayou, he'll have fulfilled his obligation, and he can go on his merry way."

"Sure he will," Mac said, winking at her again.

As the day progressed, the territory grew more and more familiar to Mac, and he was able to identify some wild onions to add to their food supply. Small pools of brown water started popping up all around the landscape, bubbling with a viscous gurgle. Mac advised that they not drink it, although the warning was unnecessary. They came upon one pool of cleaner, drinkable water, where they filled up the flasks that the elves had provided for them before heading on.

The Bayou was one of the eeriest places Desert Rain had ever been. In her days with the artists' company, they had always avoided this place. For one, the soggy, boggy ground would have sucked in the wagons' wheels, and for two, the people who lived in this place were the Bayou Folk, hardly a society worth stopping for to entertain. It was a wonder that anyone could live here, with the perpetual haze that hung over the land, the mud that Desert Rain had to struggle out of more than once, and the odd noises emitting from the stocky trees and the burbling pools. Everything was sopping in grays, browns and dull greens, and even the air felt wet and heavy. There were also strange, unpleasant smells, like rotting meat and swamp gas.

"Nice place you got here, Mac," Chiriku commented dryly. "Between the mud, the view and the smell, it amazes me that you'd ever want to leave this place."

"It gets even better," Mac replied. He was having no problem walking through this scenery—he walked through the mud as casually as if he were on solid ground.

It took about another half hour of walking before they came upon the first sign of an inhabited town. Stretching out over a millpond was a wooden walkway, simple boards tied together with frayed rope. It extended past the pond, off into the brush and fog. The bridge swayed and bobbed up and down uneasily, and Desert Rain feared it would give under their combined weight. Frogs bounded away as they walked by, but other than that and the creaking boards of the walkway, all was quiet.

Mac suddenly stopped, causing Chiriku to bump into him.

"What's the holdup, bottom feeder?" the Quetzalin inquired, placing her fists on her hips.

"If you all could give me a minute, I want-tkk to get comfy in my home surroundings." He smoothed back his red hair, and then jumped off the walkway and into the water, vanishing completely beneath the surface.

"Mac! Be careful, something could be down there," Desert Rain called to him.

"It's not like he can hear you," Chiriku scoffed. She looked at the spot in the pond where Mac had dived in, and she knelt to get a closer look. "What an idiot. Making us wait while he takes a swim in that disease-carrying water. I hope he grows fungus out the sides of his head."

When Mac splashed up through the surface of the water, he had indeed grown something. He no longer had human skin, but bright red scales. His hair had transformed into long, curved spines, which ran from the top of his head down his backside. His fingers now had black hooked claws. The most severe change was his face; although his eyes were the same, his face was fully reptilian, with an iguana snout and striped dewlap under his chin.

"That's more like it!" Mac said as he slithered out of the water, standing up and shaking the algae off his clothes and scales. He puffed out his lime-green chest in pride. "I was starting to miss-ssck my ol' skin."

Desert Rain did her best to hide her shocked expression, for although she knew Mac was a Bayou lizard, she had not expected his transformation to be so severe. Gabriel did not look surprised, but then, surprise was not something he easily showed. Desert Rain wondered if Chiriku had always known what Mac really was—she may have seen his lizard tail peek out from under his waist wrap. The Quetzalin was quiet for a second, but then she laughed.

"That's an improvement," Chiriku sneered. "Certainly easier to look at than your other face."

Before she could continue with any more remarks, Mac whipped his tail at her ankles, tripping her off the walkway and into the pond. She was beneath the water for a mere moment before she popped back up, spurting water and coughing. Mac let out a deep, hearty guffaw at the waterlogged Quetzalin.

"Mac, that wasn't very nice," Desert Rain said, although she hid a small smile.

Gabriel said nothing, but he smirked.

"You stupid four-legged snake!" Chiriku grabbed onto the walkway and lifted herself out. She swatted the algae off her feathers and pants. "I oughta rip those spikes off your head!"

Chiriku then noticed that the others were looking at her peculiarly. She gave them all a glare. "What're you looking at?"

She looked down at her feet, and saw she was standing in a puddle of blue. She looked at her arms, and amidst the royal blue feathers were dingy russet ones. She blushed, putting her arms behind her back and rubbing the back of her right leg with her left foot.

Mac let out a loud, jovial laugh. "You ain't a natur'l blue!"

CHAPTER TWELVE
A Night in the Bayou

Walking through the mist, the four travelers came upon houses that rose out of the swamp, rocking gently on top of the mucky waters. Many of the houses were boats, and others were simple huts floating atop rafts of wood. All the houses were attached to the wooden walkway with rope bridges, which did not look secure. The homes were rustic to say the least, with chipped paint jobs, swollen wet wood, tin or thatch roofs, and moss and mold coating the outer walls. There was not a resident to be seen, nor any lights coming from inside the floating houses. With the gray haze and the echoing noises of the swamp, the place seemed little more than a ghost town.

"Where are we, Mac?" Desert Rain asked in a hushed tone, the spookiness of the dilapidated houses making her cautious.

Mac waved his hand in a nonchalant manner. "Don't-tkk worry, Dez. This is the quiet-tkk side of town. Mostly old folk-kk who don't like the hullabaloo of the young crowd living up the way."

Chiriku scanned the area vigilantly, her hand already reaching back for her hammer. Gabriel, using his battlestaff as a walking stick, seemed more at ease. He brought up the rear, and every now and then he glanced back to see if anyone, or anything, would appear out of the mist behind them. Desert Rain stayed close behind Mac, perking up her ears for any odd noises.

Mac was quite comfortable, and he walked along with his hands behind his head, whistling a little tune. Then, for a moment, he stopped whistling and sped up a little. He broke into a brisk walk, and Desert Rain was wondering what had caused him to move faster.

A floating house appeared on the left, much larger than the other houses. It was probably the nicest one in the lot, made of good water-resistant wood, with a shingled roof and even a little decorated paneling on the top and bottom of the walls. It did not bob on the water, for it was supported by thick legs of wood from underneath. It was a little out of place with the huts and boat homes, although the gray paint job was peeled, and moss appeared between cracks around the windows and doors. The windows, black with shadow, were like foreboding eyes watching all that passed by. Desert Rain wondered if someone was home, for she thought she saw movement in one of the windows. She did not get a chance to find out, because Mac's tail wrapped around her wrist and hurried her along. Chiriku and Gabriel noticed Mac's rush as well and hurried to keep up.

"Does someone live in that big house?" Desert Rain got to ask after Mac had finally slowed down.

"Eh, prob'bly," Mac said, scratching his chin. Mac did not have nervous twitches like Desert Rain, but he did a terrible job hiding the uneasiness in his voice.

The walkway became more complex, branching off into various directions, and was elevated by wooden poles so that it was higher above the water. The haze thinned, so they could see more floating boats and houses ahead, as well as larger structures that may have been taverns, inns or stores. Torches atop the poles burned with a friendly red-orange flame and smelling of charred spice leaves. A faint rhythmic beating pulsated in the Bayou, and as they continued, it evolved into upbeat, brassy music. Mac put a hand to his ear—which, in his lizard form, was really a hole on the side of his head—and let out a contented sigh.

"Ah, now I know I'm back-kk in my home sweet home," he said, smiling broadly. "Can't beat-tkk the good ol' Bayou beat-tkk."

The Bayou became increasingly cluttered with houses as they continued, and a few smaller ones were situated up in the bulky trees due to lack of space on the water. These tree-houses looked like slapped-together nests made from rubbish and planks with slanted tin roofs. It was beginning to look as cramped as Syphurius, or even more so, for there was no even flow or architectural design to it all like the beautiful metropolis. There was about as much thought put into the placement of houses and the pattern of the bridges as one puts thought into sleeping.

Desert Rain had no idea that so many lived in the Bayou, and she saw a wider variety of people than she had ever seen anywhere. None of the species were familiar—no elves, no Falcolin or Quetzalin, no humans, no Stonebreakers—but there was a wide array of furry and scaly humanoids that filled her with awe. Most of them dressed in simple light clothing, particularly those accustomed to moving swiftly through the waters rather than by bridge. Some, on the other hand, had strange, elaborate tastes in clothing styles, which would cause the fashion-sensible Quetzalin of Syphurius to be either repulsed or amazed. There were lizard people, like Mac, as well as frog, possum, otter, snake and rodent kind. The dreary shadowiness of the swamp that had surrounded them earlier was now replaced by the lights and sounds of the downtown Bayou, and the foursome received more than a fair share of curious looks from the locals.

Desert Rain had always felt out of place wherever she went, but it felt particularly odd to be a Noble in a town of Lejenous. She had absolutely nothing against Bayou Folk — after all, Mac was one of her best friends. It was bizarre, however, and a little funny, for the tables to have turned, for the Nobles to be the minority for a change. She kept her eyes downcast, keeping close to Mac so the locals knew she was with him, but she could feel the gazes of reptilians and aquatic mammalians crawling over her, probing her.

A beaver woman bumped into Chiriku, who in predictable fashion, squawked irritably at the furry-faced female. Chiriku cut her squawk short when she looked into the face of the beaver lady, and jerked her head back in disgust. The beaver woman scuttled away from the agitated Quetzalin.

"It would be best to keep a low profile," Gabriel advised Chiriku, and he pulled his hat an inch lower over his brow.

"Oh, like that's possible." Chiriku looked around at the inquisitive faces of the Bayou residents. "A human, a Quetzalin, and a Hijn following a bright red lizard with a big mouth. We'll blend right in."

Mac's home was not what anyone was expecting. The other houses of the Bayou had not been glamorous, but Mac's abode was little more than a giant barrel lying on its side, stranded on a small island of wet sod out on the swamp water. The water here was shallow, ankle-deep, which was probably why Mac had no rope ladder leading out to his barrel-house. A small tin stack poked out from the top, thick iron rings held the barrel together and a red-painted door with a small window welcomed them.

"There's my quaint-tkk and cozy roost-tkk, le Chalet de Mac." Mac took a second to gaze upon his personal abode. "They don't make houses like this-ssck one any more."

"That's because this place is a dump!" Chiriku snorted.

Mac shrugged. "She's not much to look-kk at on the outside, but she's a beaut-tkk on the inside. Come on in."

A large animal loomed outside the barrel, resting in the cool mud. It lazily stood up, and due to its bulk sunk into the mud up to its knees, its belly skimming the bog. It chewed on some swamp grass, glancing at the visitors with shiny black eyes.

"Kurl?" Desert Rain was surprised, remembering that they had left Kurl back in Syphurius weeks ago.

"There you are, my big ol' buddy," Mac said as he strolled up to the strongback, patting him on the nose. "Glad to see you found your way back to the ol' homestead. Kurl always-ssck comes back-kk here whenever we get separated," Mac explained to Desert Rain, answering her question before she asked it.

Kurl grunted happily, still chewing on his grass. He still had most of the merchant sacks strapped to his back, although it looked as if he had been looted once or twice along his way home, so Mac swiftly undid the straps and relieved him of the bags. Kurl plopped down into the mud again, content in knowing that his master was home.

Desert Rain came over and patted Kurl as well, and the strongback nuzzled her hand affectionately. Chiriku wrinkled the nostrils of her beak at the mud-covered beast of burden, and Gabriel did not give any acknowledgment at all. Kurl shimmied a little deeper into the cool mud and grunted to himself.

There was a thick lock on Mac's door, and he couldn't find

the key to it on his person. He found a hairpin in his pocket, which turned out to be useless, so Chiriku removed the lock with one swing of her hammer. The door swung open on its rusty hinges, but the four stood inside the doorway for a moment, since the inside was so cramped with various junk and furniture, there didn't seem to be any other place to stand.

It was one room, but it had the accessories of every room that could be in a house. There was a mattress on the floor in one corner, a tin stove in another, a table with two chairs next to that, a pile of random clothes on the floor next to *that*, a small bookcase full of miscellaneous oddities, a ratty armchair that was really too big for the available space, tacky curtains that trimmed sawed-out holes in the walls, and then various bits and pieces of junk that Mac had been experimenting with to make his next big invention. On a shelf that spanned one whole wall were jugs and bottles labeled "tea."

"Care for a drink-kk?" Mac asked as he took a bottle off the shelf and popped off the cork. "This stuff lasts-ssck a lifetime."

The others shook their heads, detecting a weird odor from the tea bottle.

"Do you have any drinkable water, Mac?" Desert Rain asked. "We emptied the flasks that the Ahshi gave us."

"Hey, there's-ssck no cleaner water than Bayou water. Needs-ssck to be strained a li'l." Mac found amidst the clutter a dented metal bowl and a square piece of wire-screen, and he made his way back outside. "Make-kk yourselves at home," he called over his shoulder.

Chiriku immediately took the armchair and sprawled out in it, since this was the obvious place of comfort in the room. Desert Rain and Gabriel sat down in the wooden, padless chairs at the table. The table was also covered in knick-knacks and do-dads, and some ideas scrawled on pieces of stained paper. Mac must have had quite a lot of free time when he was at home, although the one success to come out of his brain-storming so far was the tea.

Mac reappeared quickly, the bowl full of water, and he shook out the wire screen he had used to strain it. The water looked cloudy and had a few floating particles in it, but it still smelled safer than the tea, however old *that* was. He poured the water into three cups that he found sitting on top of the stove and distributed them to his guests. The others did not have the luxury to be picky. The walk had been long, and any drinkable water was welcome.

Mac found a tinder box and some crumpled paper in the bookcase and used them to start a fire in the pot-bellied stove. The stove fire bathed the room in a warm glow, making it feel homier. He plopped onto the armchair—which meant he also plopped onto Chiriku, who squawked and squirmed out from under him. She moved to sit on the arm of the chair, while Mac shimmied himself into the cushion and sighed.

"As charming as this place is," Chiriku commented, "I'd like to know where we could get something to eat. It doesn't look like you have much here."

"I can whip you all up something," Mac offered, leaning forward. "You ain't tasted nothing like Mac Lizard's patented Super-Spiced Sweet-and-Sour Sizzling—"

"I'd like to eat something that won't kill me," Chiriku cut in.

"We also need to know where the port is, so we can start looking for someone who owns a ship there," Desert Rain added.

"And a place where we can resupply," Gabriel noted.

Mac rubbed his scaly chin thoughtfully and stood up. "Let's-ssck see…we need a nice meal, some seafaring folk-kk, some supplies-ssck…I know where we can get all that in one place-ssck." He started going through the pile of clothing, pulling out some rather gaudy-looking apparel. "We need to visit-tkk my ol' lounge, the Mudpuddle Oasis-ssck."

Chiriku snickered. "Sounds charming."

Mac rummaged a little longer, pulling out some extra clothing. "It's the best-tkk place in all of the Bayou. Good food, good company, and it's the hot spot-tkk for music and dancing."

Desert Rain tapped her fingers on the table. "Mac, I want you to answer me honestly. Do you want to go to that place to party?"

Mac looked at her anxiously. "Dez, I've been away from home for months-ssck. I've spent the last two weeks with elves and sick-kk people, and it was downright-tkk depressing. I—*we*—deserve some fun after all that-tkk. A night out is want we need to chase-ssck the blues away."

"But we're all exhausted. We spent the last three days traveling nonstop. I don't think any of us have the energy for a party."

"Not to mention we're trying to keep a *low profile*," Gabriel repeated. "The last thing we want is for people around here to get too curious about what a bunch of Nobles are doing here. They might get suspicious."

Mac glanced at Chiriku, who did not look too eager to go anywhere. He paused, scratching the back of his head. "Tell you what-tkk—it's still early enough in the day. You all can rest-tkk for a while, and see how you feel tonight. I'll drop into town and pick up a snack-kk for you all." He went over to one of the tea jugs, popped off the cork and turned it upside down, pouring out a few bronze coins that jingled onto the floor. He picked them up and pocketed them, then gave the jug one extra shake to see if he had missed any. Then, humming a little tune, he scurried out the door, shutting it behind him.

"I bet that bum's going to that Mudhole place right now," Chiriku commented. "He'll be back completely drunk."

"Not Mac," Desert Rain said. "He won't forget us. Although I wouldn't mind staying here the rest of the day, whether he goes to that place or not."

"If we are going to find someone with a ship and crew, it sounds like a good place to start," Gabriel suggested. "Better than hunting through every inn and tavern in this town and stirring up the locals. Will that lizard remember to look for a captain and crew on his own?"

Desert Rain sighed. "Mac's reliable, but he might get carried away with the partying."

"Hey, the sooner we get a boat, the sooner we get out of this dump," Chiriku said. "I don't care if we have to steal one. I can figure out how to sail a stinking boat."

"Maybe we should leave the boat hunt to Mac," the Hijn decided. "We might make it harder to get anyone to help us. The Noble Races have treated Bayou dwellers like dirt for who knows how long. They have every right to refuse us. Not to mention we don't have much in the way of payment."

"That lizard may not make it any easier," noted Gabriel. "We don't know how the people around here feel about *him*, being able to make himself look human. Either way, I don't like the idea of staying cooped up in this shack. Someone could get nosy." Gabriel said this as he turned his head towards one of the window-holes in the wall. There was a quick glimpse of some frog faces there, but they quickly vanished, the sound of rapid splashing trailing them.

Chiriku shook her head. "You wanna actually go to that Mudhole place? Donkey Ears is right, they probably hate people like us. And having Mac as an escort won't do any good. He's probably as much a bum here as anywhere else."

"I'm curious, do you do anything other than gripe?" Gabriel asked her.

Chiriku opened her beak to speak, but Desert Rain interrupted. "Hold on a second, I have an idea." She reached into her pocket and took the black pouch.

"You're not seriously going to talk to that moronic goat, are you?" Chiriku asked, sneering at the pouch. "What do you want to bring him into this for?"

"Goat?" Gabriel's eyes narrowed inquisitively.

"He's a Trickster who's tagging along with me. Don't worry, he's really not troublesome…too much. But he might solve our 'staying inconspicuous' problem." She loosened the drawstring and opened the bag. "Gothart? Are you still in here?"

She investigated the bag, seeing nothing but darkness. She shook the bag gently. "Gothart, I need to ask you something."

"Ah, *now* you want my help," she heard Gothart's voice inside the bag, although it sounded distant. "I know I said I wanted to lie low, but you could've been a little more concerned about my well-being than this!"

"Why, are you sick?"

"Sick of being ignored! A goat can play so many rounds of solitaire before it's boring. I've practically eaten all my books. But, because I'm such a nice guy, I'll listen to your silly little question."

Desert Rain considered closing the pouch but decided against it. "I have two questions: one, you must have spellcasting abilities, right?"

"Better and beyond that, my dear. I hope your second question is more interesting than that one."

"All right, second: do you know how to skin mold?"

***

The Mudpuddle Oasis turned out to be a ship—the deck of one, at any rate. Whether the boat was sunk in the swamp, or the underside of the boat was gone, one couldn't say. A walkway led up to the top of the hull, where there were two toad men that stood with sour looks on their faces. On the main deck, it was crowded with people at small, candle-lit tables, or people on a broad dance floor. Past the main deck was the staircase leading up to the quarterdeck, which had been transformed into a stage with a brass-and-drum band, playing the music Mac loved so dearly. There were six rectangular banners, as big as sails, along the railing of the main deck, painted with music-themed murals. On what was visible of the hull of the boat was painted the name of this establishment, in big red, black and yellow letters.

"She's really something," Mac said to his companions. "Some lizards-ssck found the boat sunk-kk here in the Bayou, and we fixed it-tkk up. The old folk-kk don't like it much, but there's always something for the young folk-kk to drink to here." He looked at his friends, observing each of them again, as he had when he came back to his house and found all of them covered in remarkable skin-molds. "By the by, I like-kk what that goat fellow did with you all. If I didn't-tkk know better, I would've taken you for genuine Bayou Folk."

Desert Rain felt odd with the skin-mold on. She could still see, hear, smell and feel the same as always, but when she looked down at herself, she saw turquoise, shiny skin instead of her golden-ochure skin. Gothart had enchanted her bandana to make her appear as a frog nymph, which was a good fit for her, since frog nymphs had modified gills on their heads that looked like hair, so her long dark hair was now greenish in color. Nymphs also had long fingers and toes, so it didn't stunt any of her normal hand movements. Even her face was not so different, except her nose was flatter and her eyes bigger and black, and her moonstone was hidden. Her donkey ears were replaced by fin-like ears, and her attire was sleek and skin-tight, as it was with most water dwellers. It was the sleekness of her outfit that made her nervous, but everything was covered well enough.

Gabriel's hat was enchanted to give the illusion that he was a sort of otter, although it didn't matter much since he was pretty much hidden beneath his clothes anyway. The color and style of his apparel was different, however; it was no longer a muddy brown, but a clean, fine hunter green. His mantle was trimmed in gold, under which was a black shirt and green pants.

Chiriku was not happy with her skin-mold. She was a blue, brown-spotted gecko. Her clothing had not changed from the baggy pants and T-shirt at all, except there was a long-banded tail trailing out behind her. She had to leave her hammer at Mac's house so not to scare any of the locals, but if she had it, she would have beaned that dumb goat. She was tempted to kick off her left shoe that possessed the skin-mold enchantment so to break the spell, but she wanted to get out of this Bayou quickly, and they needed to fine a boat captain to do it.

Then there was one more in their entourage, for Gothart, when he found out they were going to a musical soiree, refused to go back into his pouch. Desert Rain could not do anything to convince him otherwise, and he wanted something in return for his skin-molding services, so all she could do was make him promise to stay on his best behavior. He had not given himself a skin mold, for he would not mar his great goatliness by masking himself in amphibian or reptilian skin. Goat humanoids were not considered Nobles, so there would not be any problems with the locals—providing that Gothart did not choose to cause any trouble. Gabriel was monitoring the Trickster extra-closely, not trusting him any farther than he could fling him with one hand. What had been peculiar was that Gabriel had not looked surprised to meet the white goat that magically popped out of pouches, but as stated before, surprise was not Gabriel's thing.

The music of the Mudpuddle, even from where they stood, was a cacophonous blast of brass, percussion and vocal warbling. It was not like any other music heard in Luuva Gros, and while it was foreign, Desert Rain found herself liking it. It was not the docile, practiced music taught by professional composers and theater artists, but the carefree, improvised, untamed rhythms of the soul. It was what music should be, in Desert Rain's mind, but Chiriku thought otherwise.

"What is this noise?" the Quetzalin cawed, putting her hands on her ears.

"It's the beat-tkk of the Bayou," Mac answered, "and, I should tell you—" he pointed to Chiriku's new face, and said with a smile—"that's an improvement-tkk."

Chiriku scowled at him.

They ascended the wooden walkway to the rail of the

Mudpuddle's deck, where the two toads stared at them warily. Mac, leading the way, puffed out his chest and swished his tail. "Long time no see, gentletoads-ssck! You can strike up the band, 'cause Mac is finally back-kk!"

The toads' eyes widened initially, obviously recognizing the lizard, but then those eyes narrowed, and they crossed their arms. They did not move.

Mac glanced back and forth between the two bouncers. "Come on, you both ain't forgotten about ol' Mac, have you?"

"Not by a long ssssshot," came a hissing voice behind the toads. Out stepped a purple lizard, taller and slinkier than Mac, and not half as friendly-looking. A large circular frill flared up around his head, and his eyes were cold. "You'ssss got sssome nerve coming 'round here."

"Clinktail Bone," Mac addressed the purple lizard, saying that name rigidly. "Nice-ssck to know you never left the Bayou."

"Unlike sssome lizardssss I know."

Desert Rain could sense a bad confrontation coming, but her fears turned out to be unnecessary. After a short stare-down, the two lizards suddenly started laughing, and then Clinktail came down onto the walkway and gave Mac a slap on the back. "Where have you been? The Mudpuddle wasss getting boring without you," Clinktail said.

"Been out and about-tkk, here and there," Mac replied, putting his arm around Clinktail. "Thought I would bring some friends-ssck for a night out-tkk."

"I ssssee," Clinktail said, eyeing the others, in particular Desert Rain. He gave her a crooked smile. "Who'sss the lovely lady?"

Desert Rain knew what Clinktail was seeing was her skin-mold, and not how she really looked. Still, the word "lovely" made her feel patronized.

Mac took his arm off Clinktail to put it around Desert Rain. "This-ssck is my Gila Gul, Rain," he said without hesitation — he had obviously practiced the introduction in his head. "And that-tkk is my cousin Speckle and her groom-to-be Riv. They've come from down the coast-tkk."

Chiriku and Gabriel inwardly fumed at Mac having made them fictionaly fiancés, but they didn't say anything.

Gothart cleared his throat loudly.

Mac glanced over at him. "Oh, and the goat-tkk. He followed me home, so I kept him."

Gothart wrinkled his nose at Mac. "Very cute," he mumbled.

"Any friendsss o' Mac be friendsss o' mine," Clinktail said, taking Desert Rain's hand and kissing it. "I will ssshow you to my perssssonal booth." He gestured for the toads to move aside, which they did, and Clinktail led them through the maze of candle-lit tables and carousing Bayou Folk.

"What was all that about?" Desert Rain whispered to Mac. "The way he first greeted us, I thought he was going to give you trouble."

Mac laughed. "Just-tkk a game we play, Gila. Much more interesting than a simple hello, don't you think-kk?"

Desert Rain nodded, wondering how she was going to pass off as Bayou Folk when they had such strange ways of doing things — even saying hello!

Clinktail's "private booth" was a table for six situated near the rail near the broadside of the ship. It was half-way towards the stage, so the music did not drown out their speaking. The booth was directed beneath one of the mural banners, so at least that was nicer to look at that the swamp water below. The table was covered in a red cloth, and the chairs padded in the same color. Almost as soon as they sat down, a reptilian barmaid came by with an array of wines and ales for them to choose from. Mac and Clinktail chose the "lizard's favorite," a strong ale, and Gothart took a glass of red wine. The others politely refused drinks, which made the barmaid cast confused glances at them.

"They're from down the coast-tkk," Mac explained to her. "It's-ssck dry territory down there."

The barmaid shrugged and walked away.

"Pardon me, gentssss and ladiessss," Clinktail said, "but I have to be on ssstage sssoon. Maybe Mac the Lounge Lizard will join me?"

Mac lifted his mug of ale to him. "Wouldn't miss-ssck it."

As soon as Clinktail was out of ear-shot, Chiriku — or Speckle, as she had been dubbed — got to the point. "So anyway, where do we find any supposed sailors in this place?"

"Relax-ssck, we don't have to get right-tkk down to business right now, do we?" Mac took a gulp of his ale. "We're here to have some fun."

"Finally, someone who speaks my language," Gothart mused, sipping his wine.

Gabriel narrowed his otter eyes at him, and then on Mac. "We're here on business. I don't know how Bayou Folk run things, but we do have some time constraints."

"Oh dear, another boring one." Gothart emptied his glass, and then broke off a piece of the glass and ate it. "I'm going to go schmooze, if that's all right with you."

"No, it's not all right!" Desert Rain grabbed Gothart as he

was standing up, and she pulled him back down. "You are not going anywhere out of sight tonight, got it?"

Gothart half-laughed, half-brayed. "Yes, mother," he joked.

Chiriku sighed irritably. "Let the goat go do whatever he wants. Maybe we'll lose him finally."

"I'm going to go look around and see if I can gather any information," Gabriel said as he stood up and slinked away into the crowd.

"Can we please-ssck have some fun now?" Mac asked as he finished off his ale. "Oh, I like-kk this song. Come on, Gila Gul, let's hit the floor. You too, Eye-pecker."

"You two can go on," Desert Rain said. "I want to sit for a bit."

"Suit-tkk yourself. Join us when you're ready." Mac then grabbed Chiriku and hoisted her to her feet. The Quetzalin did not even get a chance to squawk a protest before Mac pulled her out onto the dance floor. Desert Rain thought they looked cute together, but maybe that was because Chiriku had on a lizard guise.

Gothart watched the dancing and made an annoyed bleat. "Look, you owe me some fun. You've kept me inside that bag for way too long. It was a shame, really, since I heard in on that discussion you had about going on this silly quest and all. If you had bothered to ask me what I thought, I might have been able to give you some valuable insight."

"Like *you* had a plan?"

"A very ingenious one, I must say." Gothart bit off another piece of his glass. "Much more practical than this 'going to find an ancient magical device guarded by xenophobic elves' plan."

Desert Rain curled her fingers. "You know, if you had an

idea, you could have given me a sign!"

"I was, but you were too busy doting on that know-it-all elf's every word," the goat stated. "Oh well, too late now, I suppose. We're here now, might as well forget it."

Desert Rain did her best to stay calm, and not get agitated. She folded her hands together on top of the table. "I suppose I'll regret asking, but what was it?"

"What was what?"

"Your oh-so-ingenious plan!"

"What plan? Oh look, crabcakes!" Before Desert Rain could stop him, he bounded out of his chair and trotted up to a barmaid with a tray of finger food.

Desert Rain rubbed her sinuses. *I think he does that to see the vein in my head pulsate.* She sighed. *Chiriku's right, I can't babysit him all night. I won't get anything done.* She got up and took a walk around, taking in the sights and sounds of the Mudpuddle. She tried to spot anyone who had the appearance of a seafarer, but when she did — a couple of brawny crocodiles hanging out at a side bar — she thought it better not to approach them. She spotted a group of rugged-looking men seated around a table playing cards and wondered if she should ask them if they knew anyone who could help her. As she decided that it would be best to leave them to their game, one of the men, an old possum, looked over at her.

"Hey there, pretty lady," he called, gesturing for her to come over. "Care to join us for a game?"

Desert Rain stood there shyly, but then she saw next to him, leaning against the table, was a staff — a braided greenwood staff. Her initial shyness was erased as she walked up to him, looking deep into his eyes. They were eyes she knew all too well, those of a shaman that had visited her twice before. The possum elder — or so he was *now* a possum—winked at her.

"You again?" she half-whispered.

"Sit for a spell," he said, and his fellow card players nodded enthusiastically. "You know how to play?"

Desert Rain sat down in the empty chair next to him. "Not really, but I was wondering if any of you knew where I could find—"

"A date?" eagerly asked a frog sitting across from her.

"Show some respect," the possum elder said. He turned to Desert Rain, smiling kindly. "You will find what you seek in time. How about a quick round of cards before you move on?"

Desert Rain cocked an eyebrow curiously. Okay, what was this shaman trying to teach her now, and what could he possibly teach her with a card game? "I don't know how to play," she answered.

"There's no trick to it. Here, I'll be your coach." He shuffled the cards, and dealt a new round, five to each player. Desert Rain picked up her cards and looked at them, finding them not to be any sort of playing deck she had ever seen. Instead of numbers, or symbols, or words, there were pictures of various animals. As the game ensued, the players took turns laying out different cards that for one reason or another beat another player's card, and then chose whether or not pick a new card from the deck. Points were tallied according to what card a player played, and Desert Rain did not understand the system at all. The possum took occassionaly glances at her cards, and suggested which ones to keep, and which to throw. Somehow, from the reactions of the other players, Desert Rain thought she must have gotten a good hand.

Then there was one turn left for everyone. This part was called the "top of the food chain," and would determine the winner of the round. Desert Rain looked at her cards: a bluebird, a boar, a lizard, and a spider. She had come to understand a little more of the game by now, but this did not look like a good hand anymore. The elder saw the confused look on her face and leaned over to whisper in her ear.

"We'll work on your game face later," he whispered with a chuckle. "But for now, I recommend you ditch the bird and the lizard."

Desert Rain almost instinctively did as she was told. She put her hands on those two cards, but stopped. She stared at the bluebird and lizard, and then looked up at the elder. She wrinkled her brow and tightened her lips.

"I'd rather not," she said.

"I'm telling you, if you keep those cards, you might lose."

"I'll take that chance."

The elder paused, and then smiled. "Good to know you don't always do as you're told."

Desert Rain blinked, perplexed. So, wait, was she supposed to have learned something from this, or did he? Either way, she lost the round. Fortunately, no one had bet anything, so she stood up, thanked them politely for the game, and started to walk away, when she bumped into Gothart.

"There you are," the goat said, apparently a bit tipsy due to the wine glass he was holding. "You know, for someone who's supposed to be keeping an eye on me, you're not doing a very good job. I mean, this is my…wait, let me think…third, forth…some number glass of wine, and I…"

He saw the possum elder sitting at the card table and instantly sobered up. He dropped his glass, freezing in place. The elder was already shuffling for another game, and he started to look over his shoulder towards Gothart. Instantly, Gothart disappeared, into thin air. Desert Rain looked around in complete confusion, thinking Gothart should have at least poofed into smoke or something, not vanish entirely. She looked down at her feet, and saw a potato lying on the floor.

A white potato.

She felt eyes watching her, and she lifted her gaze back up to see the people at the card table looking at her. She shyly smiled. "I dropped my…potato." She knelt and picked up the tuber, bringing her lips close to it in a harsh whisper. "What in Luuva did you do that for?"

Two tiny eyes and a mouth formed on the potato. "I wasn't thinking clearly! I was nervous!"

"About what?"

"About…never mind. Hide me!"

Desert Rain shook her head and sighed. She took out the black pouch from her pocket and popped the potato inside. "Stay in there, all right?" She realized the card players were still watching her, seeing her talk to a potato. She smiled again and slipped away onto the crowded dance floor.

This turned out to be a bad idea, for she was jostled around by the dancers, bumping back and forth between them. She was rescued when a hand caught her wrist and pulled her into an open spot on the floor. It was Mac.

"Having fun yet-tkk?" he shouted over the noise.

"Sure," she answered, saying it more to reassure Mac. "Where's Chiriku?"

Mac pointed to the side bar, where Chiriku was taking in a few whiskey shots. "Some fellow tried to cut-tkk in on us, and when he made a grab for her, she gave him a good one in the eye."

The crocodiles at the bar that had intimidated Desert Rain so much were not causing Chiriku any trouble—in fact, they were keeping a good distance from her.

"And Gabriel?" Desert Rain asked.

"Eh, he's around. Don't worry about it-tkk. Come on, one dance with your ol' pal Mac?"

Desert Rain hesitated, and then nodded. Now that Gothart was in hiding again, she didn't have to worry about anyone. Gabriel and Chiriku could take care of themselves. She was not used to Mac's style of dancing, however, and found it hard to keep up. Eventually the dancing itself stopped mattering. She *was* having fun, a kind of fun she hadn't had in a long, long time. The beat uplifted her, and for that moment, that single moment, everything else melted away. She could feel it, that artistic passion, deep down inside her again. It must have been that piece of soul she still had, and it was all she needed to take in the music, to feel both energized and peaceful.

The music abruptly came to a dead halt. The movement on the floor ceased. Mac and Desert Rain did not even notice at first that all heads had turned towards the entrance of the Mudpuddle. Trying to see over the crowd, they could not tell what was causing the commotion at first. The crowd on the dance floor parted and they got a solid look at who had come up on deck. There stood a large, shaggy figure, wearing a black overcoat and ratty top hat. He leaned on a cane, and his furry, clawed feet were bare save for some muddy spats. It was the face, however, that was truly daunting, a dark gray-furred face with a bristly muzzle like that of a rat or wolf. A sneer of dirty-brown teeth was set in that muzzle, a sneer that even made the crocodiles quiver. The narrow, beady eyes scanned the room, the pointed ears flattened against his head.

"Who is that, Mac?" Desert Rain whispered. When she didn't receive an answer, she looked at him, and found his face had paled to a pink. His eyes bulged out of his head, and his legs shivered. Desert Rain had never seen Mac this frightened, ever. Katawa himself might as well have entered the room.

Finally, the eyes of the shaggy guest fell on Mac and Desert Rain. He locked on them, his sneer growing into a snarl.

"Macapailius-ssssssck!" he bellowed. "You're in big trouble, boy!"

CHAPTER THIRTEEN
Mr. Rotter

Mac stood there, shaking so badly, he might have shimmied out of his skin. Desert Rain could tell that this was not one of those odd Bayou greetings like the one Mac and Clinktail had shared. This time, the rodent-man addressing Mac was furious.

The rodent-man approached Mac slowly, stalking, his cane thumping the floor. He came so close to Mac, his muzzle was barely brushing the lizard's scaly nose. Mac stared back in frozen terror. The rodent-man's voice was a raspy, vicious whisper. "The back-kk room. *Now.*"

The "back room," as it turned out, was the captain's cabin located behind the quarterdeck, which Mac was tossed into by the two security toads with as much care as throwing away garbage. The rodent-man entered the room next, slamming the door shut behind him. Desert Rain was not even allowed to put an ear to the door to listen, thanks to the toads guarding it. She sought out Clinktail to find out what was going on.

"Mac isssss in deep mud now," Clinktail told her. "That'sssss ol' Missssster Rotter, richessst man in the upper and lower Bayou. He'ssss got a hand in almosssst every busssinesss in the whole ssswampland."

"Why is he angry with Mac?"

Clinktail shrugged. "Alwayssssss been sssome bad vibesss between Mac and Rotter, ever ssssince Mac wasss workin' for him assss a newtling. I'm sssure Mac isssss drowning in debt to Rotter again. Not assss if the ol' coot needsss any more change in hissss fat pocketsssss."

Desert Rain couldn't help but worry about poor Mac. It did not look like this Mr. Rotter would be easily swayed by any of Mac's silver-tongued words. "What is it that Mr. Rotter does for a living?" she asked.

"He'sss runsss the busssinesss in the Bayou that'll never...*die*." Clintail chuckled when he said this, and Desert Rain was not sure why.

"What's so funny?"

Clinktail leaned in close to her, smirking. "He'sss the undertaker."

Mr. Rotter sat at the furnished desk in the captain's cabin, rapping his fingers on the desktop calculatingly. His stare consumed Mac with an icy chill, those white eyes set on the lizard like a predator's. Mac stood on the other side of the desk, trying hard not to sweat, lest his human side start leaking out. He swallowed back his shivers and gave Rotter a flashy smile.

"First of all, it's-ssck a pleasure to see you again, Mr. Rotter sir," Mac began at a rapid-fire pace. "You're looking spiffy, you are. That's-ssck a new hat? New cane? New something, or maybe that's-ssck your dazzling old self—"

"*Shu-ttttk up*," Rotter commanded, accentuating each word with the sharpness of alligator teeth.

Mac instantly quieted.

Rotter folded his hands together on top of the desk, and

gave Mac a pleasant smile, seasoned with spite. "You've been gone from the Bayou a long time, Mac-k-k. You weren't-tttk trying to avoid ol' Rotter, were you?"

Mac shook his head vigorously. "By no means-ssck, my good man. Been doing what merchants do, looking for a good spot-ttk to sell his wares-ssck, that's all."

Rotter's smile dropped. "I hope you're selling well, after all the money I gave you to further those half-brained ideas of yours-ssssck. Which, need I remind you, you haven't-tt-tk returned a single red cent-tt-tk to me yet. But I'm guessing that's-ssssck why you're back in town, to give your old boss Rotter what's-ssssck coming to him."

Mac tugged at his shirt collar, gulping. "Well, nat'rally, my old friend. And, might I add, those banishing dolls-ssck I said would sell, they sold good. Got a good chunk-kk of change for them. But, if I may explain, I was in Syphurius-ssck when this big ol' Nasty started wrecking up the joint-tkk. I lost-tkk a lot of my wares, and I was helping out some good folk-kk, and it's-ssck by Bayou honor that I help folk-kk in need."

"Yes-ssssck, I heard about you hanging out-tt-tk with some 'folk-kk,'" Rotter said, sitting back down. "I heard you were seen walking through town with some strangers-ssssck. Some...*snoots-ssssck*, or so I hear."

Mac's head spines quivered slightly. "Snoots" was a term some Bayou Folk gave to the Noble Races, and, as one could imagine, it was not a term of endearment. Particularly the older residents had grown some deep-down roots of hatred for Nobles, and Rotter might have had the deepest roots of anyone in the Bayou.

"Well, yes, some...snoots-ssck," Mac confessed, the word

tasting bitter in his mouth. "They're lost-tkk, that's all. They were lost in the swamp, and as an honorable lizard, I thought it was the right-tkk thing to do to guide them out-tkk. I took them into town so they could get some food and drink-kk before they go on their way. Just because they're snoots-ssck doesn't mean we have to be all snooty too, right-tkk?"

Rotter squinted his eyes in skepticism. "You consort-tt-tk with some bad company, lizard. And it's that-tt-tk kind o' damned generosity that's-sssck put you in debt, and me losing money! You used to be good at what-tt-tk you do…swindling. Now you're going on about-tt-tk being 'honorable,' and blathering nonsense-sssck." A devious smile spread over Rotter's face. "I still got that-ttk coffin, Mac-k-k. You know which one I'm talking about-tt-tk?"

Mac, with wide, terror-filled eyes, nodded.

"I kept it all these years-sssck. Maybe you'd like to take-kk a walk down to my place, take-kk another look inside—"

Rotter's talk was interrupted by a commotion outside. There was the sound of a scuffle, and the thud of two heavy things dropping on the floor. Then there came a loud pounding on the door, which after about three pounds burst open. Standing in the doorway was a gecko, a blue one with brown spots, and she stood over the two toad guardians, who moaned on the floor, one holding his stomach, the other his face. Behind the gecko was a frog nymph—the one who had been with Mac when Rotter arrived—and an otter dressed in a green cape and hat.

"I don't know who you are," the gecko shouted, "but nobody messes with Mac unless I say it's okay!"

"Chi—Speckle," the frog nymph said bewilderedly, "You didn't have to go kicking down the door!"

"So much for low profile," the otter mumbled.

Rotter stood and curled his lip at the intruders. "Friends of yours-sssck?" he growled to Mac.

"And downright-tkk good ones, even if they're a bit-tkk too loyal," Mac said, looking directly at Chiriku. "You must-tkk forgive them. They're from down the coast-tkk, so they don't know how things work-kk around here."

Rotter raised his bristle-haired nose, sniffing at the intruders. He may have been old, but he was no fool, and his nose was as sharp as ever. He wrinkled his face and stepped out from behind his desk. "They're Bayou Folk-kk as much as I'm a newt-tt-tk!" he snarled. "Bad enough you're hanging out with snoots-ssck, but you've been consorting with bewitched snoots-sssck!" He advanced towards Chiriku, who stood her ground defiantly. "I ain't afraid o' no hexes-sssck, and I ain't fooled by no magic skins-ssck you're wearing. You smell like-kk feathers. You must be a bird snoot-tt-tk." He looked at Gabriel. "And I can smell your human funk-kk all the way from over here! Arrogant, hairless-sssck, flat-faced weasel, is what-tt-tk you are!" He turned to Desert Rain, and his nose wrinkled in puzzlement. He sniffed at her closely—a little too closely, so Desert Rain stepped back a pace. She felt like this scenario was strangely familiar—in fact, Rotter reminded her of somebody, or some*bodies*. Rotter growled and turned back to Mac. "You wanna be a snoot-tt-tk too, Mac-k-k? Is that why you're befriending these…these high-and-mighty turned-up-noses-sssck? Got noses so high in the air, they feel rain coming ten minutes-ssck before the rest o' us—"

"Holy buzzards, will you shut up??" Chiriku blurted. "Who died and made you boss anyway?"

Rotter inhaled a deep breath, as if he were preparing to explode at Chiriku. But his voice came out softly, darkly.

"Interesting you should say 'died'…"

Mac was starting to sweat, and his scales were turning the peach tone of human flesh.

"I'm boss-ssck 'round here because-sssck people die," Rotter continued, advancing on the pretend gecko. "I'm very rich because people die. It's-sssck the one thing you can always-sssck count on…people dying. It's a very profitable thing. You don't get-tt-tk into the Eternal Deep unless you got a few coins-sssck for the man who'll send you there properly." He lowered his face so his nose pressed against Chiriku's. "I've seen so many dead folk-kk, heard so many stories-sssck about how they died, I can even tell how any person I see is-ssck gonna die. Maybe you would like-kk to know?"

Chiriku furrowed her eyebrows, stepping back. "You are one creepy guy," she said.

"Please, Mr. Rotter, we didn't mean to barge on in here and be rude," Desert Rain said. "We were worried about Mac. He's a really kind, warm-hearted lizard, and if you could find it in your heart to go easy on him—"

Rotter barked a boisterous laugh. "I don't-tt-tk know where you're from, missy, but I don't fall for a couple nice words-ssck from a lady. 'Find it in your heart-tt-tk"…I'm too ol' and tired for having a heart-tt-tk!" He stared at her peculiarly, and Desert Rain felt she knew what he was thinking. *What are you really, underneath that magic skin?*

"Surely, we can come to an agreement—" she began.

"I don't make deals with snoots-sssck. And I'm tired of lizards-ssck talking me into loaning them money for stupid ideas-ssck." He looked back at Mac, who was furiously wiping off sweat so that he would remain as red-scaled as possible. "You're gonna work-kk off that debt, lizard, down with the coffins-ssck, and by my count, you've got ten years worth o' work-kk before you even come close to paying me back-kk!"

Mac was shaking terribly now. "Please, I'll get-tkk you the money! I'll go out-tkk and sell double! I'll work-kk my claws to the bone, but-ttk don't make me go down with the coffins-ssck!"

"You're the undertaker, I take it?" Gabriel asked.

Rotter sneered at him. "You're one of the genius snoots-ssck, ain't you? What's it-tt-tk to you if I am?"

"It seems to me that a man of your shrewd intelligence and eye for business wouldn't waste his time on a mangy lizard like Mac. Are you running so short on dead people that you need to scrape money from a lousy merchant? Surely a man of your wealth doesn't need a few extra coins from an unreliable reptile."

Mac was about to protest, but he kept himself quiet, hoping Gabriel was going somewhere with this.

Rotter took another irritated inhale, tightening his fingers on his cane. "Maybe a human like-kk you needs-ssck enough money for himelf, but some o' us folk-kk have families-ssck to take care of. Stupid, free-loading families-sssck." He looked away, his train of thought taking him to a dark place he had been countless times. "Like-kk I would care about collecting debts-ssck if I didn't have to look after those good-for-nothing nitwits-ssck. Always-ssck eating, always-ssck sleeping, and never around when you need them. Supposed to be learning the family business-ssck, but instead they go off and run rampant-tt-tk around the country, and use the money I give them to buy a damned boat-tt-tk so they can go sailing to some damned islands—"

That was the last thing Desert Rain heard before her mind's gears went to work. A boat, owed by some boys who wanted to go north towards the islands of the Coast Keepers? This was too good to be true! Maybe it was that whole "design of destiny" thing again. She had to meet whoever Rotter was talking about—but would he cooperate?

"—and have swamp mud for brains-sssck!" Rotter finished his ramblings. He took a minute to breathe and calmed himself.

"Mr. Rotter, if I may ask—" Desert Rain began again.

"No, you may not ask-kk. And stop calling me Mr. Rotter," he snapped. "That's-ssck my first name, Rotter, and it's unrespectable coming from a snoot-tt-tk. You call me formal-like-kk—Mr. Vermin."

Desert Rain's jawed almost hit the floor. That name—she knew that name! Now she knew who Rotter reminded her of. "Mr. Vermin, you wouldn't happen to be related to three Vermin brothers, would you? One kind of brawny and brown-furred, one skinny and black-furred, and one little and white and can't seem to control how loud his voice is?"

Rotter grimaced, tapping a finger on the head of his cane. "How do you know my nephews-sssck?" he asked.

So they *were* related. What a small Luuva Gros it was!

"Answer me," he barked. "Where do you know my nitwit-tt-tk nephews from?"

"Well," Desert Rain answered, "I was going on a trip to Syphurius, and they sort of ran into me—well, jumped me, is more like it—and they gave me quite a scare, but that was before I realized they were silly boys playing a joke."

Rotter went suddenly rigid. He looked horrified but was keeping himself under control as best he could. His cane rattled on the floor, for his hand was shaking. Finally, he calmed, and his body sunk into itself. He tightened his lips, and cocked an eyebrow, as if he were thinking intensely about something. He looked back up at Desert Rain. "And that was-ssck that? They gave you a fright, and left-tt-tk?"

"Pretty much," the girl replied. "Oh, and I gave them a little food I had, to show no hard feelings, but that was it. No harm done."

This made Rotter go rigid again. This time he looked appalled, and furious. "You…you're coming with me," he hissed, pointing his cane at Desert Rain. "*Now.*"

Rotter Vermin lived in the big scary house in the quiet part of the Bayou, which Desert Rain figured he must have since Mac had been so scared of that house. Now the windows were lit with a faint orange, and it came close to looking cozy from the outside. Rotter was prodding Desert Rain along with his cane, while the others followed behind quietly. Mac would have ventured to say something optimistic, if he weren't terrified of the rodent-man in front of him. Chiriku crossed her arms and scowled, while Gabriel was not either worried or pessimistic about the situation. In his mind, he could see things coming together, and somehow that desert Hijn was making it work.

Desert Rain, meanwhile, could not have been more baffled, but she decided not to ask questions at this time. Hopefully, this meant she was going to get to talk to the three Vermin brothers and convince them to ferry her and her friends up north. What Rotter was up to was not what primarily baffled her, either. What baffled her was the faint sound of piano music coming from inside Rotter's house.

Rotter unlocked the ten locks on his front door from his vast array of keys on a metal hoop, and then entered the house.

The inside was deceptively welcoming, furnished like a modest mansion compared to Mac's hovel. Lanterns lit the rooms, and there was a better flow to the arrangement of furnishings than the entire downtown Bayou. Desert Rain wondered for a moment if Rotter was wealthy enough to have this furniture imported, and if he did, it would have had to been from a Noble City. He disliked "snoots," but not their merchandise.

"Rotter, is that you?" came a gristly female voice from somewhere in the house.

"Of course it's-ssck me, woman!" Rotter roared. "Those three worthless-ssck nephews o' mine around?"

"They're setting the table. We're all ready for dinner. We were waiting for you, but you were out too long for us to keep on starving," was the reply.

"Boys-sssck!" Rotter thundered, stepping into the front room. "Get-tt-tk in here, *now!*"

A rapid scuffling of feet was heard. It grew louder, and finally two of the three Vermin brothers, the black-furred one and the white-furred one, came stumbling into the room, ultimately falling over each other and landing in a pile at Rotter's feet. The third one, the brown one, came lolling in, tearing at a piece of cooked meat. He stood next to his two prone brothers, looking at Rotter carelessly. "What?" he asked smugly.

"Goude, Gimch, Gank-kk," Rotter growled, enunciating each name sharply. "There's-ssck someone who'd like-kk to have a word with you." He stepped aside to reveal Desert Rain, who grinned and waved her fingers at them.

The three of them looked blankly at her for a moment. Gank smiled broadly and looked adoringly at her. Goude gave him a kick to the side of the head, but also smiled eagerly at Desert Rain.

"Aw, Uncle Rot, you old fox. You can pick 'em good."

Desert Rain realized they did not recognize her. It had not been that long since they first met, and she was not exactly forgettable in features—and then she realized her skin-mold was still on. "Silly me," she said, untying her bandana. "No wonder you boys don't remember me."

As soon as the bandana was off and the skin-mold evaporated, the Vermin brothers' eyes went as wide as full moons. They screamed and flew back against the wall, clumped together in terror.

"DRAGON LADY!" Gank squealed. "DRAGON LADY HUNT US DOWN TO PUNISH US!!"

"We said we were sorry!" Gimch whimpered. "We haven't scared anybody since! Honest!"

"Don't turn into a monster and eat us!" Goude pleaded.

Desert Rain sighed. Good gracious, where did they get these bizarre ideas about Hijn?

"Can it, you twits-ssck," Rotter said, thumping his cane as he walked over to a padded chair to sit. He set himself carefully into the chair, and then looked over Desert Rain's true form. "I knew you didn't-tt-tk smell right," he said. "Dragon lady, eh? I'm ever-so honored," he said, bowing his head in mock respect.

Desert Rain was about to say that she was tired of being ridiculed, but she was interrupted by that gristly female voice she heard before.

"Now what's all the commotion in here?" A portly female Vermin, with red-brown fur dappled with light gray, swaggered into the room. She was about as scary-looking as Rotter, or even moreso since she looked big enough to physically take down anyone in the room. She wore a dress made of colorful, multipatterned patches, with a sash of yellow tied around her waist. Her sour demeanor instantly brightened upon seeing the four guests in her house.

"Oh, Rotter, you brought company for dinner. I wish you'd have told me. But I always make more than enough. Mac, you ol' lizard! Give Roeda a hug." Without waiting for a reply from Mac, she went over and gave him a crushing hug, lifting him off the floor. Mac smiled, since he couldn't speak for all the air being squeezed out of him. Roeda set him down abruptly, causing him to wobble on his feet. She then observed her other guests, not having any apparent reaction to Desert Rain's odd looks. If she could smell that Chiriku and Gabriel were Nobles like Rotter had, she did not seem to care. "Why, look at all of you. Aren't you all the nicest-looking strangers I ever saw. Dinner will be done in a few minutes. Why don't you all have a seat in the parlor until I get the food on the table?"

"The boys-ssck and I have something important to discuss-ssck," Rotter started to explain.

"Now Rotter, we don't talk about 'important' things at dinner, you know that. Now don't be a stick in the mud. Take our guests into the parlor, and tell Bee and Lee to come finish setting the table. I will let you know when the meal's on." Before Rotter could protest, Roeda shoved everyone with a shooing motion into the adjoining parlor room.

The parlor was a spacious room of rugs, velvet-padded chairs, polished circular tables, a billowy couch, a brick fireplace, and a honky-tonk style piano. Two little Vermin—girls, for they wore dresses—sat at the piano, plinking out simple tunes together. When Rotter entered the parlor, the girls got up and scuttled over to him, hugging him around his legs and greeting their father excitedly. Then they saw the newcomers with him, and the girls curtsied in mechanic fashion. Rotter patted them on their heads and ordered them to go off to finish getting dinner on the table. As soon as they ran off, he strode over and sat down smack in the middle of the couch, his usual perch. Goude, Gank and Gimch lied down on a rug on the other side of the room, and Mac grabbed a chair farthest from the couch. The others picked random seats around the room, and there were plenty to choose from — it seemed odd to think Rotter had all these chairs, since he did not look like the type to entertain much.

There was a long, ackward silence.

"I don't hear any chatting going on in there," they all heard Roeda call. Rotter sighed irritably.

"Sooooo," Desert Rain ventured to break the silence, "You have a very nice place here."

"It's-ssck the bottom of the Pond of the Beyond," Rotter muttered between his teeth.

"You're telling me," Goude muttered.

"OUR HOME IN LAND ABLAZE BE NICER," Gank blurted out. From the laugh Rotter made at this comment, he obviously disagreed.

"Ah, so you three didn't grow up here. I noticed you don't have the local dialect," Desert Rain observed.

"They talk-kk like snoots-ssck, that's what they do!" Rotter barked. "They come here so they don't-tt-tk have to live like starving rats-ssck no more, but Bayou Folk-kk ain't good enough for them. They're always-ssck sneaking off to run around in snoot-tt-tk territory, as you know," he added, casting a dark glance to Desert Rain. He threw that gaze over to his nephews. "Which is why they're in a crock-kk o' hot water now."

Gank folded back his ears, fear in his eyes, but Goude waved away Rotter's comment carelessly. Gimch shrugged, although he did not look as at ease as Goude.

"Boys-ssck," Rotter continued, standing up, "the lady snoot here tells-ssck me that you went and gave her a scare. That true?"

This was a patronizing question, since Rotter had already seen and heard their reaction when Desert Rain revealed herself. The three of them nodded.

"And you also took-kk food from her, and didn't-tt-tk pay nothing for it?"

They nodded. Even Goude looked more nervous now.

"That's-ssck damn shameful!" Rotter growled, "No Vermin goes and acts-ssck undignified, and no Vermin goes taking something without giving back-kk in equal."

"And you knocked me for talking about-tkk Bayou honor," Mac commented in a low voice.

"Honor has-ssck got nothing to do with it-tt-tk!" Rotter snapped. "But we Vermin got our dignity, and we don't-tt-tk go acting like beggars and ruffians-ssck, not to snoots-ssck, not to anyone!" Rotter stalked towards his nephews, who scooted away from him. "You know what that means, boys-sssck. You better cough up some payback-kk for the girl, I don't-tt-tk care if it's in coin or chore. Or I will tan your hides-ssck so fast—"

"Mr. Vermin, it's not like that *stole* food from me. I offered it to them. They don't owe me anything," Desert Rain insisted.

"We ain't beggars-ssck," Rotter snarled. "We don't need charity. The sooner these idiots-sssck pay you back-kk, the sooner you can be on your merry li'l way."

Desert Rain thought for a moment. The Vermin brothers did not owe her anything, but this did seem to be an opportunity to get on board their ship, possibly for no fee, since she did not have anything on her in the way of payment—nothing she could part with, anyway.

"Well," she replied, "I suppose, since you insist on some form of payback, maybe your nephews could ferry me and my friends on their boat, the one you mentioned before?"

"NO WAY!" Gank instantly whined. But then he remembered it was the dragon lady asking, and he snapped his muzzle shut.

Rotter stroked his chin fur, thinking about this request. "You want-tt-tk a boat ride, eh? With my nitwit nephews-ssck? Heck-kk, maybe they can sink it-tt-tk for good this time." He grinned at the thought, but then he frowned. "How far is it that-tt-tk you want to go, taking my boys-ssck away from home and chores-ssck?"

"Does it matter? I thought this was about regaining your family's dignity," Desert Rain replied. "Besides, they might as well get their, or should I say *your*, money's worth for that boat. You wouldn't want it to go to waste, sitting in the dock, right?"

Rotter tapped his fingers on the head of his cane. Eventually, he made a small nod. "Might-tt-tk as well have them doing something right-tt-tk, rather than running off and besmirching the family name. Fine, you got the boat-tt-tk."

"Hey, don't we get a say in this?" Goude protested. His answer was a rap of Rotter's cane on the top of his head.

"Is this boat big enough to transport all of us?" Gabriel asked so abruptly that it half-startled everyone.

Desert Rain looked at Gabriel peculiarly. All of *us?* "Do you really want to keep going on with us, Gabriel? I think you've upheld your promise more than enough."

Gabriel stared back into her eyes, but there was no hostility in them. "It would not be fulfilling my promise if I let you go on a boat alone with these...*boys*," he replied, glancing over at the Vermin brothers. "All we know is that they bought a boat. That does not mean they know how to sail it properly."

"WE SAIL GOOD!" Gank argued. "WE ONLY CRASHED ONCE!"

"That's more than anyone should crash a boat," Gabriel noted. "I have experience with sailing vessels. I was on the crew of several trading ships for the past few years. I can see you safely to your destination, and then we may part ways, if that's all right with you?" He spoke this last sentence to Desert Rain.

Desert Rain nodded, but somehow she knew, if she was to spend more time with Gabriel, she might not want to part ways when the time came. He had an odd way of growing on people, at least on her.

Gabriel turned back to the Vermin brothers. "I ask again, is your boat big enough for the four of us and you three?"

Goude sat there despondently with crossed arms. Gank wriggled his finger in his ear, digging for earwax. Gimch shook his head at his brothers' indifference. Even though he was often torn between the stubbornness of Goude, and the anxiousness—and stupidity—of Gank, Gimch took it upon himself every now and then to be the sensible one. "It used to be a spice ship. It's big enough for all of us," he replied. "It came stocked with dried food and stuff. Should still be good. The guy who sold it to us said it would last a while."

"Well, that all sounds-ssck good to me," Mac said, clasping his hands together. "When are we setting sail?" He had barely finished his statement when the head of Rotter's cane rammed him under his rib cage, causing him to gasp.

"Trying to run off again?" Rotter growled. "You ain't going nowhere until you work-kk off your debt-tt-tk to me, boy!"

"Leave the poor lizard alone, Rot," Roeda came into the room, with her hands on her hips. "You've got more than enough. Let a few coins slide for once."

Rotter curled his lip. "I let-tt-tk a few coins slide here, a few slide there, and before you know it, ev'ryone in the Bayou thinks-sssck ol' Rotter Vermin is a chump!"

"Mac is a nice boy. And you're always working him too hard." She walked over to Mac and patted him on his spiny head. Mac smiled innocently.

"This-ssck don't concern you, woman—" Rotter seethed.

"The way I see it," Roeda added, "You owe *him* a little leeway for that nasty stunt you pulled on him, shutting him up in that ugly, smelly coffin. Poor thing was scared half to death."

Mac made a puppy-dog face, enjoying the game Roeda was playing with her husband.

Chiriku blurted out a laugh. "You shut Mac in a coffin? You sick creep! I'm sorry I missed that."

"And he wonders why he loses employees so fast," commented Goude.

"There's a one letter difference between 'Rotter' and 'rotten'," said Gimch, to which the other Vermin laughed.

Rotter pounded his cane on the floor. "As I recall, I'm letting you three stay in my house-ssck outta my good will. Maybe I should send you all packing back-kk to those rat holes-ssck you came from!"

"Now now, let's-ssck not lose our temper," Mac said, feeling more confident with Roeda at his side. "I may have a proposition for you that'll even everything out-ttk."

Rotter scoffed at him. "This oughta be good. What'll it be this-ssck time? More ridiculous beverages-ssck?"

"Not at all. You see, you don't-ttk know why my Gila Gul over there wants-ssck a boat. She wants to go up north to see some friends-ssck of hers, ones that are, shall I say, well-to-do. They own some diamond mines-ssck, and they've got so many of the things, they're practically worthless to them. They always let-tkk my Gila take all she pleases-ssck, and she's been so kind as to let me meet some of those folk-kk to fund my latest-tkk idea. But I can use my share to pay off my debt-tkk, if you don't mind the form of payment-tkk."

"You don't think-kk I buy that croc-and-toad story for one second, do you?" Rotter replied.

Mac suddenly produced from his pocket an eye-shaped diamond, to which all the Vermins "oohed" and "awed." Desert Rain recognized the "diamond" right away as an Ahshi crystal, and she clenched her teeth. "Mac…" she started, an edge of anger in her voice.

"It's all right-tkk, Gila. I know you said I shouldn't spread the word about your diamond friends-ssck, but nobody here will snitch." He winked at her.

Desert Rain was not amused. She could not believe Mac had stolen a crystal from the Ahshi, but he probably thought he could get away with it since the Ahshi shared everything.

"Is that for real?" Goude scrambled over, taking the crystal from Mac. He bit it as a test.

"LET ME SEE! LET ME SEE!" Gank squealed.

"Maybe we can meet these diamond people too? We won't tell a soul," Gimch promised.

"That's got to be a fake-kk," Rotter concluded.

"Nope, no fake-kk. And there's plenty more where that-tkk came from. Right-tkk, Gila?" Mac turned to Desert Rain, shining his flashy smile.

Desert Rain felt the heat of all eyes in the room watching her. She grinned half-heartedly, and hesitantly nodded. She did not like to lie, but the "diamond" interested the Vermin brothers so much, it solidified the deal. Plus, she did not want to leave Mac behind, having this Rotter man work him to death. She noticed Gabriel shook his head criticizingly at her, but he didn't say anything. Rotter, however, looked very intrigued.

"Let Mac go with them, Rot," Roeda said. "I always wanted one of those diamond necklaces."

The two little girls appeared from behind their father, tugging at his pant legs. "Us too! Us too!" they bleated.

Rotter huffed, noting the eagerness in his nephews' and daughters' eyes, and the impatience in his wife's. He glared at Mac, who grinned at him. That damned lizard—he always knew he could get Rotter to give in by persuading Roeda and the girls to side with him. Ultimately, knowing he would go insane from his family's persistent nagging, Rotter sighed and nodded. "Fine. Not-tt-tk like that no-good lizard could ever handle a coffin right-tt-tk anyway."

"Now no more of this business stuff," Roeda said, rubbing her hands together. "Who's ready for a good bowl of wormwort stew?"

The music from the Mudpuddle Oasis could still be heard, carried on the night breeze, all the way to Mac's house. Desert Rain was being kept awake because of it, or maybe it was that stew she had eaten at the Vermins' house — it wasn't settling well in her stomach. She looked around the single room of Mac's house, lit by moonlight streaming in through the sawed-out windows. Chiriku snoozed on the armchair, warhammer in hand. She was back in Quetzalin form, having kicked off her shoes the second she came in the door. Mac had given up his mattress so Desert Rain could sleep on it, and now he snored away on top of his pile of laundry. Gabriel had cleared a space on the floor to lie down and slept amidst the random clutter peacefully. Desert Rain had offered to share the mattress with him — nothing implied, of course — but Gabriel had politely declined. She could see that he was back in human form by his chin. He must have taken off his hat long enough to break the skin-mold while no one was looking. According to Gothart, once someone broke the skin-mold, the enchantment came off the charmed article of clothing, so Gabriel was able to wear his hat again and not become the otter-man.

Desert Rain was glad for that fact too. She did not want to become a frog nymph every time she wore her bandana.

She found herself getting up and going over to the front door, opening it slowly so as not to cause creaking. She slipped outside, sitting down outside the door, listening to the throbbing Bayou beat in the distance. Kurl lifted his head out of the mud, glancing over at her. Desert Rain smiled at him, rubbing her arms, a bit chilled by the cool night air. She sat there for some time, her mind as jumbled with thoughts as ever.

"I'm beginning to think-kk you have a sleeping problem," she heard a voice say as the door creaked open behind her.

She turned to look up at Mac. "I've always been a light sleeper."

The lizard had two cups in his hands, and he handed one to

her. "Didn't-tkk have any warm milk, so I made some warm tea. Thought-tkk it'd help you sleep." He sat down next to her. "What's bugging you, Gila?"

She sighed. "You have to ask?" She sipped the tea, which was made from some potent spice that caught her by surprise. "I feel like everything is up in the air right now. I wish I had a better idea of what I was doing."

Mac shrugged. "Hey, we're doing all right-tkk. We got ourselves a boat-tkk pretty darn quick-kk. I gotta say, some coincidence, you knowing old man Rotter's nephews-ssck like that. Glad they ain't as smart as the old rat-tkk." He grinned. "I loved seeing their eyes-ssck pop outta their heads when they saw that crystal. I had a feeling they'd fall for it-tkk."

"Which reminds me," Desert Rain said, her voice getting sharp, "what made you think it was okay to steal a crystal from the Ahshi, after they showed us such hospitality?"

Mac put his hands up in surrendering fashion. "I never stole nothing! They let me have it-tkk, honest! I thought-tkk it might make an extra coin or two around here, so I asked if I could have one, and they said it was-ssck fine. That is frog-honest-tkk truth."

"Still, that doesn't mean you should ask for gifts from them."

Mac shrugged his shoulders. "Forgive a merchant-tkk for doing what he does-ssck best. Besides, it got those Vermin boys-ssck interested, right? Now we know they'll show up at the dock-kk tomorrow instead of leaving us high and dry."

"And what do we tell them when they find out there are no actual diamonds to be gained from this venture?"

Mac smiled his showman smile. "You leave that to me

when the time comes-ssck."

"When the time comes…" Desert Rain clutched her cup tightly. "How is it you'll know what to do when the time comes, Mac? Because I know I won't."

Mac gulped down his tea. "Things have a way of working themselves out-tkk, Gila Gul. I'm always getting into pots-ssck of hot water, but I haven't been cooked yet-tkk. You gotta know how to slip out-tkk of the pot before that lid comes-ssck down on you."

Desert Rain looked over at him, into his warm, kind eyes. She felt the need to ask a question that had been on her mind for a while. "Mac, what exactly is a 'Gila Gul'? To you, I mean?"

"A Gila Gul? It means…it's like a…" He scratched his head in thought. "It's-ssck a good friend, someone a lizard can put his trust-tkk in. And there isn't too many folk-kk like that for a lizard."

"Oh…" She nodded to herself. "Just a friend, then."

Mac's eyes widened, and then he laughed. "Yes, a *friend*, Dez. I wasn't trying to come on to you or nothing. Trust-tkk me, from past experience-ssck, I'm not exactly the dating type."

"Dating? Oh, no!" Desert Rain laughed. "That's not why I was asking. I was curious — about the Gila Gul thing."

"Besides-ssck," Mac nudged her with his elbow, smirking, "I know a fellow who's-ssck got his eye on you, pretty lady. I wouldn't want-tkk to intervene."

Desert Rain set her cup down at her side. She put her arms around her legs, hugging her knees to her chest. "I don't think you realize just how mean of you that is."

Mac was surprised at this. "Who's-ssck being mean? I was saying…"

"Look at me, Mac! I'm not the kind of girl that guys chase after. And I'm fine with that! But I don't need any reminders either. So can we please drop the joke?" She looked away from him.

"Hey, hey now…" Mac put a hand on her shoulder. "I was teasing you. I wanted to see you crack-kk a smile for once. You're always-ssck so troubled all the time. You have a bit-tkk of a low self esteem, don't you?"

"You are the second person to tell me that! And no, I don't. I know what I am." She tugged absentmindedly on her ears.

"I know what you are too. You're the one person to treat-tkk this lizard like more than a bum, even when you knew he's Bayou Folk-kk. You're a good person, Desert Rain. And I don't-tkk find too many of those. That's-ssck why I chose to face that Nasty with you. Lizards-ssck don't let their Gila Guls go fighting Nasties-ssck alone." Mac laughed to himself. "A tad sappy, I know. Chiriku would've belted me for saying that-tkk."

Desert Rain chuckled.

"You see? There's that-tkk smile." Mac put his arm around her. "It'll work-kk itself out, I promise. Cut my heart out in a fit-tkk, drown a beetle in my spit-tkk." He spat on the ground.

Desert Rain thought to herself a moment. "Maybe this is part of that whole 'design of destiny' thing again."

"What?"

"You, me, Chiriku, and Gabriel. Destiny must have decided to bring the four loneliest people in Luuva Gros together."

Mac grinned. "I hope Destiny decides-ssck to let us get some sleep tonight-tkk. We've got a big day tomorrow."

"I don't know if I can sleep right now. My mind's too busy."

Mac took in a deep breath. "Then let me tell you a li'l story from when I was a newt-tkk —"

"Good night, Mac." Desert Rain patted Mac on the shoulder, and then hastily picked up her cup and slipped back into the house.

Mac looked over at Kurl, smiling. "Work's-ssck every time," he said.

CHAPTER FOURTEEN
The S.S. Vermin

The Bayou port was not a busy place, except for a few small
fishing boats bobbing aimlessly in the harbor. The wooden pier
was one of the few structures in the Bayou that looked like
someone had taken time to build it, probably because fishing was a
main source of food in the Bayou. If one took a long walk down
the pier, past the fishing boats, past the floating booth of the
beaver who took care of docking and maintanence fees, past the
children who fished and swam near the shore, one would find a
one-masted trading ship of impressive size in a secluded part of
the port. This cog was the *S.S. Vermin* (it had been the *Merry
Mariner* before it was sold to the impulsive Vermin brothers), and
Chiriku summed up everyone's feelings about it when the
foursome came to see it early the following morning.

"You can't be serious," was her reaction.

The size of the *S.S. Vermin* was all that was impressive
about it. Everything about the ship was about as well-kempt as the
Vermin brothers themselves. The railings of the boat were battered
and splintered, barnacles were visible all along the broadsides, the
sails were ragged around the edges, and there was the haphazard
paint job of the blocky, dripping letters of the new name
bequeathed to it by its new owners. It looked so weather-beaten

and waterlogged, they could imagine it floating ten yards out to sea and then sinking like a rock.

The Vermin brothers were already there, although Gimch was the one doing anything resembling work. He was hauling packs and barrels up onto deck, while Goude lounged on the dock and Gank leaned over the water, swatting aimlessly at guppies swimming by. The two lazy brothers would not even waste their time here if there wasn't the underlying fear that their uncle might show up out of the blue. Gimch, apparently, was used to this behavior from Gank and Goude, for he went about his work, not encouraging his brothers to get off their duffs and help him.

Gabriel, however, took the initiative, grabbing a barrel and lifting it with minor trouble. Once he got it on deck, he lifted the top off, and observed that the barrel was full of semi-clean water.

"This isn't sea water, I hope," Gabriel commented.

"I got it from one of the local pumps," Gimch replied in an impatient tone. "Of course, it wouldn't have taken me so long to pump and drag the barrels here if I had had another pair of hands." He cast a quick glance at his brothers.

Desert Rain, Mac and Chiriku also came up on deck to have a look around. The second that Chiriku came on board, she wobbled and had to lean against the rail. "How long will it take to get to wherever we're going anyway?" she asked, gripping the rail tightly, despite the splinters.

Gimch scratched behind his ear, thinking. "Well, the guy who sold it to us said he could make it from here to Mautaun Island in under a week, given good wind and calm waters. My brothers and I wanted to make this trip for a while, but..." He glanced down over the rail at Goude and Gank below, "Stubborn and Stupid tend to sink more than swim."

"I'M NOT STUBBORN!" Gank shouted up to them.

"For the millionth time, you're Stupid!" Gimch yelled back.

"YOU'RE SMELLY!"

Chiriku took a loud gulp, wrinkling the corners of her beak. "You mean I got to be on this piece of junk for a week? Someone, knock me out and wake me when we get there."

Mac grinned at her. "You don't-tkk come from a line of sea birds-ssck, do you, Chi?"

She grimaced, and then leaned over the rail.

"Who was the person who sold you this ship?" Desert Rain asked Gimch.

"I don't know, some old possum," Gimch replied with a shrug. "Weird guy. He didn't say why he didn't want it anymore. He let us have this boat for real cheap."

Desert Rain decided not to inquire on the previous owner any further. Gimch might say this possum had a green staff and could dissipate into sand, and that would be too bizarre for her.

Gabriel went about checking the supplies on board, including the barrels of dried food that had come with the boat, and some buckets of fresher food the Vermins had provided. It was not a glamourous spread, mostly powdered spices, grains, uncooked rice, some fruit that did not look *too* overripe, a bucket of fish, and some coffee grounds. There was enough rice to feed seven people for a while, but not enough of the other foods. Gabriel could go with one meal a day if need be, but he had the feeling those Vermins could eat their weight in food a day. There also was not enough fresh water; they had but two barrels. If they planned to use it to cook food as well as drink it, it would all be gone in a couple days. Gabriel shook his head. There was serious work to be done before they went anywhere.

"Do you have anyone else who could help crew this ship?" he inquired.

Gimch shrugged. "My brothers and I have sailed a boat by ourselves before."

"And it crashed, didn't it?"

Gimch grinned crookedly. "Kinda."

"I bet you've never sailed as far out to sea as we're going to. This isn't an hour tour. We're going to need everyone to work on this ship. And I mean *everyone*." He marched over to the rail, looking down at Goude and Gank on the dock. "You two, get up here."

Goude opened a lazy eye, and curled his lip. "It's our ship. You're not captain."

Gank laughed hysterically. He immediately stopped laughing when Gabriel strode down the walkway to the dock, took his walking stick and slammed the end of it between Goude's legs, missing his crotch by half an inch. Goude sat up with a start, staring with wide eyes at Gabriel.

"What the—" Goude did not even finish before Gabriel grabbed him by the collar of his tattered shirt and hoisted him up onto his feet.

"I'm going to make this very simple." Gabriel's eyes were dark and intense, boring into Goude. "You either work, or you can take a dive tied to the boat's anchor. Is that clear?"

Goude nodded vigourously. Gabriel released him, and the Vermin hustled up onto deck. The man cast Gank a firm glance, and that's all it took for the rodent-boy to scramble his way up onto the boat. Gabriel followed casually, tapping his walking stick on the ground as he walked. He assembled the others.

"For the next few hours, I'm giving you all a crash-course in manning a ship," he said. "If anyone's planning on giving me trouble, get your carcass off this boat right now."

Chiriku clicked her teeth nervously. "Uh, maybe I can wait on the dock until you need me —"

Gabriel gave her a fierce stare.

Chiriku gulped. "I suggest you get me a bucket then," she said.

After several grueling hours of training and supply gathering, Gabriel's slap-dashed crew awkwardly fumbled with ropes, jerkily raised the sails, and sluggishly hoisted the anchor. The cog, after several close calls in colliding with other boats or the dock, floated lethargically out of the port.

Anthron had been courteous enough to let Desert Rain keep the map, as he apparently had made many copies, so Gabriel took time to look it over and check the compass that the Vermins had with them — although it was the cheapest knick-knack he had ever seen. After steering them into open waters, Gabriel put Desert Rain at the wheel, telling her to keep the wheel straight for now. Then he went about making the three Vermin show that they had learned the proper way to handle the ropes. Mac and Chiriku, not having any immediate tasks to attend to, shared the activity of clinging to the boat's rail. Mac, apparently, was not as ship-savvy as he thought.

Desert Rain kept her hands tight on the wheel and shivered against the chill wind sweeping off the ocean. She could not remember the last time she had been on a boat, and she had certainly never steered one before. She imagined that the endless expanse of water was the same as the endless expanse of desert sand from back home, and it helped calm her a little.

This wasn't so tricky. She could do this. Gabriel knew what he was doing. Why he was so determined to keep his promise to Alana, Desert Rain had no clue, but she was glad he was here. Without him, she would have had to put all her faith in the Vermin boys sailing ability, which it was clear it was not too good. She glanced over at Chiriku and Mac leaning over the rail, and she grinned. *Finally, something they can do together,* she thought.

Night came swiftly, and Gabriel steered while the rest of the crew sat down to dinner. There was an improvised kitchen below deck, with a tin stove that they managed to heat up with Mac's tinderbox. Desert Rain cooked the fish, knowing they would go bad if not eaten soon, and boiled a few cups of rice in a pot that was lying around. She brought some of the food to Gabriel, but he waved a hand at it, saying he would eat when his steering shift was over. The Vermin, on the other hand, were more than delighted to get their hands on the fish and rice, gulping it down as if it were nothing. Chiriku wrinkled her face at their deplorable eating habits, but kept herself quiet. She ate — suffice it to say — like a bird, since her stomach was still adjusting to the unending rocking of the cog.

Mac went about lighting various lanterns that were strewn around the deck. Once he had created a cheery atmosphere, he turned to the others and asked, "All right-tkk, anyone know any sea chanties-ssck? I've always wanted to sing some of those-ssck, but I've never been on a boat-tkk when I want to sing them, and it always seemed wrong to sing them if you're not-tkk on a boat."

"Dear Divine Beasts, please don't sing," Chiriku whined, holding her head in her hands. "I'm already nauseated as it is."

"BONES!" Gank suddenly erupted. "PLAY BONES!" He rummaged through his pockets and pulled out, literally, finger-long bones, painted with different numbers of stripes.

"I'm not playing bones with you anymore," Gimch stated. "You always cheat."

"NO CHEAT! PLAY BONES!"

"I want to hear more about those diamond people," Goude said, coming over to sit by Desert Rain. "So, how many diamonds are we talking about here?"

Gank and Gimch, immediately forgetting their squabble, also scooted over, staring with wondering eyes at the Hijn.

Desert Rain's ears twitched twice, and she hadn't even said anything yet. She gulped and tugged on her fingers. "Well, there are...these people are—"

"Up to their ears-ssck in gems," Mac finished for her. "They own six—no, seven mines-ssck, and they've got the finest-tkk homes you ever did see. Tall spires of iv'ry with diamonds-ssck of all kinds, sparkling in the sun. And they have diamonds-ssck in their clothes, their dishes, even their servants-ssck got diamonds."

The Vermin brothers listened in dreamy fascination, soaking up Mac's every word. Desert Rain felt guilty that she was allowing Mac to go on this way, giving the three boys false hope, but it wouldn't do any good to shatter their good mood now. She hoped Mac really did have an idea about how to break the truth to them gently, whenever he was planning on doing that.

Chiriku shook her head, rolling her eyes. "I bet they sneeze diamonds too," she mumbled. She lied back, closing her eyes and trying to imagine that she was on solid ground. She winced as she heard a musical, resonating tone, a sort of high-pitched wail. She opened her eyes and huffed, "Mac, what did I say about singing?"

"That wasn't-tkk me," the lizard replied.

They all heard the sound again, and it was coming from the

sea. There were no other boats in sight, no lights from any distant towers. Theye were enveloped in the darkness of night, the glow of *la Ternaut* reflecting in silver slivers across the waves. Through that darkness came that unearthly wail, or a cacophony of wails. The wailing reverberated strangely, and no one could be sure what direction it was coming from.

Gank screamed and fell flat to the deck on his belly, putting his arms over his head. "GHOST!" he squeaked.

"Did he say 'ghost'?" asked Desert Rain, since half the time she couldn't understand Gank's loud squealings.

"He means the Banshee," Goude said, making an expression that was somewhere between a wry grin and a snarl. "Plucks sailors right outta their boats and sucks out their souls." He reached over and gave Gank a poke, causing him to jump with a scream. Goude laughed as Gank ran to hide behind Desert Rain.

"It's a rumor we heard," Gimch said. "Word down in the Bayou is that some fishers went out to sea one morning and never came back. All they found were their boat washed up on shore. They say a water spirit got them."

"GHOST THAT SCREAMS!" Gank shrieked, clinging to Desert Rain's tunic.

Theye heard the wailing again. Even Chiriku looked uneasy.

Gabriel took in the sound for a minute, and then chuckled. "What you're hearing are siren fish," he called to the others. "They're noisy but no bigger than a thumb. I used to hear them all the time when I worked on other ships."

"Nah, it's the Banshee," Goude insisted, sneaking over to where Gank was hiding. "And it likes to suck the souls out of scaredy-babies!"

Gank whimpered and clung tighter to Desert Rain. The Hijn patted his head gently. "It's okay. No ghost is going to get you," she said to Gank. She gave Goude a stern look.

Goude snorted. "Eh, you're no fun. Stupid baby, scared of everything." He strolled back to his spot and sat down.

"Not a baby…" Gank whimpered, sniffling.

"It's siren fish," Gabriel reitereated, more strongly this time. He went back to looking out over the ocean, manning the wheel.

The next two days went by without incident. The weather remained calm, although the days were overcast with white-gray clouds. The winds were sometimes unpredictable, being fierce one moment and almost dead the next. It became colder, and Desert Rain spent a good deal of time below deck to stay warm. Mac had been able to coax Roeda Vermin to let them borrow a couple of coats, but they were either too big or too threadbare. The Vermin Brothers, when not being ordered around by Gabriel, passed the time by playing their game of bones. Mac had overcome his queasiness by now, and spent his time jotting down thoughts on scraps of paper he found lying around. Chiriku, however, was still wobbily on her feet, and stayed below deck most of time dreaming that she was back on land. Gabriel was constantly going about one thing or another, and anyone else by now would have been run ragged. He did not show the slightest sign of fatigue, and not once did he complain.

Then came the fog.

Gabriel was on deck at the time. It started to drizzle, so everyone else went down below. Desert Rain offered to take over the steering for him, but he saw how she shivered from the ocean wind and rain, so he gave her the task of untangling some ropes so she could stay below and have something to do. He was tired by now, so his vision was a little blurry, but he remained vigilant and alert, hands firm on the wheel.

He thought, for a second, that he must really be out of it. The ocean was starting to look hazy to him. He could not even make out the individual waves anymore. Then he realized it was not his vision, but a blanket of fog had settled over the waters. The fog spread out for as far as he could see, like a field of gray fuzz. He could not imagine why he had not seen this fog coming. It had suddenly risen around him. He watched as the haze rose higher, coming up to the railing on the broadsides.

"Desert Rain, come up here," he called. He knew that no matter where she was, her sensitive ears would pick up his call.

Desert Rain appeared quickly. She had thrown on a coat, one that was far too large for her, so it dragged behind her. She was startled to see the sudden fog, but she said nothing of it as she went up to Gabriel. "Yes, do you want me to take over now?"

"No, I want you to look over the side of the boat and tell me if you see or hear anything strange."

Desert Rain did as he asked. "I really can't see anything through this fog," she replied. "Did you hear something coming from below?"

"No. But this fog came up from the ocean instead of coming down from above."

"That is odd, isn't it?" Desert Rain reached a hand into the fog, and instantly her arm was soaking, as if she had touched the ocean itself. "I don't think this is fog. It's more like steam, but it's not hot."

"It's mist," Gabriel concluded. "Do you see anything

splashing around below?"

"I don't see or hear anything. Should we keep sailing through this? We might hit a rock or something, don't you think?"

"We're far enough out to sea that we shouldn't be hitting anything that would damage the ship. But I'll lower the sails for now." He left the wheel, which Desert Rain took over instinctively. After he lowered the sails, he came back. "You can go back down below now."

"You've been at the wheel all day. Besides, we won't be going much of anywhere with the sails down. You should go rest."

"It's all right. I can keep going." He began to push her away from the wheel, but she didn't budge.

Desert Rain narrowed her eyes at him. "You train us to be crew on this boat, and then you don't want help from any of us. It won't do any good if you overwork yourself."

"I can handle it," he retorted.

"But we're in this together. Maybe you're used to doing everything yourself, but trust me, okay?"

It was Gabriel who now narrowed his eyes on Desert Rain. "The fact is, I'm the only one on this boat who really knows what he's doing. Let me handle this, and quit being so difficult all the time."

Desert Rain couldn't believe he said that. "*You're* the one being difficult! I thought you trusted me. You showed me your scars, and I thought that meant—"

"It meant nothing. Don't ever mention anything about my scars again." He shoved her away and grasped the wheel in both hands. Then, of course, he remembered the boat really wasn't moving much, so he slackened his grip and leaned wearily on the wheel.

"You don't have to hide from me," he heard Desert Rain say.

He turned to her. Her eyes were full of sympathy, and he didn't like that. "I'm not hiding anything," he argued.

"I know how you feel. I know how easy it is to hide, because you feel like people are staring at you, judging you. I mean, you're talking to the weirdest-looking person in all Luuva Gros. I've spent a lot of time hiding. Sooner or later, you're going to need to trust people who want to help you." She placed a hand on his arm.

He jerked his arm away. "I don't have to trust anyone."

Desert Rain was not hurt by this. She understood, because she had been where Gabriel was. She had not always believed in what she said — she had trusted people who ended up betraying her. She could at least offer Gabriel that chance, and she wouldn't betray him. He had to know that.

She reached up towards his hat. He stepped back from her.

"Do you think because you're a Hijn, you can do whatever you want and I should be fine with it?" he asked.

Desert Rain felt the brunt of that statement. "You no longer have to hide from me, because you know I won't laugh or judge you. If you really do believe in honor, like I think you do, then by *my* honor, I won't do anything to hurt you."

Gabriel was quiet. Desert Rain couldn't tell what he was thinking, but eventually he shook his head. "Why do you treat me this way? Do you think these words of empathy will move me?"

"I'm not trying to move you. I'm being honest. Is that a concept so beyond you?"

Gabriel stared coldly at her. His gaze softened, his rigidness loosened. He looked away. "If you want my trust, you'll have to earn it," he said.

Desert Rain sighed, but acquiesced. "All right. It's nice to know there's a person beneath that mask."

Gabriel gave her a questioning look.

"Hat!" Desert Rain quickly corrected herself. "Beneath that *hat*."

Silence prevailed for a minute, and then Gabriel placed his hands on Desert Rain's shoulders. "Look, Desert Rain, I—"

The ship suddenly lurched wildly. Both Desert Rain and Gabriel lost their balance and fell to the floor, and she landed on top of him. Neither of them had noticed that by now, the thick, blinding mist engulfed the entire ship, and they were drenching wet. Then they heard a wailing, but not like from the night before. This was far horribler, ghastlier, and it was definitely not fish. It was a symphony of very real, very close, moans of pain and despair.

"What in the Eternal Deep is going on?" they heard Chiriku call and the sound of footsteps, but they couldn't see her. "Holy buzzards, what's with the fog?"

"We're over here, Chiriku!" Desert Rain called to her, and she slowly got up and made her way off the quarterdeck and towards the staircase leading to the lower deck. She literally bumped into Chiriku, who had been running her way.

The ship lurched again, tipping dangerously to one side. Gabriel grasped the wheel to keep his balance, but Desert Rain and Chiriku went sliding across the deck. They both caught the side railing before they were pitched overboard. There was the sound of vicious waves slapping against the boat, and that moaning was growing louder. A stampede of footsteps was heard coming up the stairs.

"Now that is the nastiest-tkk sound I've ever heard." Mac's voice was heard over the roar of the ocean. "Good bog, are we under water or something? I can barely breathe up here!"

"GHOSTS!" Gank shrieked.

"Shut up, pipsqueak!" Goude growled.

Gabriel tried to turn the wheel but found it to be stuck tight. "I don't get it. There's no wind, no sign of a storm. There must be something under the boat jamming the—"

The moaning stopped. Silence.

The boat slowed its rocking, and the sea became instantly calm. Yet the mist stayed as blinding, smothering them like levitating rain droplets. Desert Rain could barely see Chiriku standing next to her, yet her blindness sharpened her other senses. There was a faint noise—wood creaking under pressure.

She heard something grasp onto the railing beside her, and thud quietly onto the deck.

"Chiriku…" she whispered almost inaudibly, "someone came on the boat."

"What?" Chiriku asked, rather loudly.

Desert Rain squeezed Chiriku's arm tight to quiet her. "Something…is on…the boat…"

Chiriku was suddenly torn from her grasp, and the Quetzalin made a startled squawk as she vanished in the blanket of mist. Desert Rain heard Gank's squealing, but this time it was blood-curdling urgent. He was accompanied by shouts from his brothers, and several Bayou curses from Mac.

Desert Rain remained utterly frozen. She could hear the pounding footsteps of frantic running, the shouting, and some guttural snarling. Every sound sent bolts of panic throughout her body, and she clung to the railing. She wondered if she should take her chances and jump into the ocean, but she had no clue what was happening to her friends, and she could not leave them.

Then she got to meet the intruders face to face.

Something snagged the back of her coat with its talon-like fingers, and with a sharp tug pulled her off the railing and sent her flat onto her back. Her assailant was over her, its face—if you could even call it a face—hovering over her own. A dark bile seeped from its mouth, and it was so awful in smell, Desert Rain felt the acidic taste of vomit rise in her throat.

There was no way to truly describe that face staring down at her. It was not human, not animal, not anything natural. The skin was gnarled into something other than wrinkles or folds; it was more like bark or twisted tangles of bloody ropes. There were no lips on that face, and the protruding teeth were filed to sharp black points. Patches of muscle showed on the cheeks in bright blood red. What should have been hair was more like a mess of tentacles, and every feature was awash in a purple-green tone.

But the eyes—the creature's sunken eyes were so human, and so full of pain…

The creature fell off her in a blur of movement, and Desert Rain heard the swift snap of bone breaking. A hand reached down and pulled Desert Rain to her feet, and she was now face to face with a more comforting visage—Gabriel's.

"Where's Chiriku?" he asked.

Desert Rain was about to reply that she had no clue as to the whereabouts of anyone, when she heard that bone-chilling snarl again. Three silhouettes came up to them, solidifying in shape and color as they approached. They were as horrid in appearance as the creature that had assaulted Desert Rain, their contorted bodies even worse than their faces. Gabriel jutted his battlestaff at them, but the creatures snapped at them, charged them, forced them to back away. Desert Rain and Gabriel bumped into something behind them—it was the Vermin brothers.

Gank was hysterical by this point, and Goude had to hold him in his arms to keep him from running around like a maniac. "GHOSTS!!" Gank wailed. "THEY WANT TO EAT OUR SOULS!!"

"Get that moron to shut up, will you?" Chiriku's voice penetrated the mist, and soon the Quetzalin and Mac bumped into the group as well.

They were now all together, clumped in a tight bunch. Desert Rain could hear the moaning and snarling all around them. The creatures did not attack but closed in to tighten the group. They were surrounded.

"Now what-tkk?" Mac asked, gulping hard.

"We fight," Gabriel answered.

"But why aren't they attacking us?" Desert Rain asked.

"And where in the Eternal Deep did they come from?" Chiriku inquired. "Did they crawl out of the ocean or something?"

The mist thinned substantially with a whispered word, a word unlike any from the common languages of Luuva Gros. Desert Rain knew that ancient language, and her breath stopped short. She looked towards the direction of that whispering voice, and she could make out a silhouetted figure standing on the deck in front of them.

"Who are you?" Gabriel shouted to the figure. He gripped his battlestaff in both hands. "Whoever you are, you have picked the wrong vessel to board—"

"Gabriel, wait!" Desert Rain steadied herself, waiting as the mist faded away, clearing the stifling air. The features and shades of the figure and the surrounding creatures came into focus. There were seven of those creatures before them — excluding one that was lying dead with a broken neck, thanks to Gabriel — and they became more terrifying as they became clearer to see. They moaned and groaned in agony, like the undead of legend. The other figure, the one who banished the mist, stood silently, his irises wine-red, the whites of his eyes blood-shot. He was tall and lanky, draped in shell-adorned clothing. The foam-white hair was matted and wild, and areas of the sea-blue skin were stained with what looked like purple handprints, the flesh bruised and twisted. Disturbing violet stains bled from the man's nose, ears, lips, and corners of his eyes. His stance was that of a wounded predator ready to pounce.

Desert Rain gasped, "Merros!"

CHAPTER FIFTEEN
Water, Wind and Light

Merros stared silently at Desert Rain. His contorted expression wrinkled his face into a morbid mask, obliterating the composed features the Ocean Rider normally displayed. His flesh spasmed where his skin and joints had been tainted by Distortion, pinched tight or pulled out of shape. His breathing was irregular, his exhales labored and clogged with fluid.

His deformities were nothing compared to the entourage with him. They were the products of the most frightening, macabre, twisted imagination. They all shared the purple-green bruised tones, the gnarled skin, they exposed patches of bloody muscle and bone. They all also had what looked like gills, having been specifically shaped to perform aquatic tasks to suit Merros's needs. From there, they were all bizarrely different, molds of clay shaped into living nightmares that would make any of the Wretched jump out of their skins. Fins, claws, tentacles, muzzles, beaks, spikes, scales, tails, and appendages not yet labeled sprouted from every conceivable place. Their howls were heart-piercing, rendering anyone who listened petrified. They scraped their malformed claws on the wooden deck, and gnashed their horrid, blood-stained teeth.

"What are those things?" Chiriku gasped. Her beak was

turning green in nausea.

Desert Rain knew what they were. She had seen this before, with the elven knights in Syphurius, and, of course, on her own body. The words of the deceased Valdrase echoed in her head.

"His Distorted," she answered. She swallowed back the lump in her throat. "Merros, do you know who I am? Do you remember me?"

Merros did not appear to hear her. He raised his hands, speaking broken words of Dragontongue. His chant was hesitant, pain-filled, but the imprint of the coiling serpent on the palm of his hand glowed nonetheless. From that imprint, tendrils of water flowed, winding like transparent threads towards the captives. It began to entwine them, weaving into an encasing bubble, spreading around them into an egg-shaped barrier.

The rumor the Vermins had heard was true. There was something stealing fishermen off their boats, and it was Merros, bringing them to Katawa to be turned into Distorted. Merros was obviously still under Katawa's mind manipulation. What was Katawa making him do this for? Was Merros even aware who it was he was capturing right now?

"I don't-tkk know what that fellow is up to," Mac said, "but I say we need a plan here."

Chiriku drew forth her Warhammer and swung at the bubble. The enchanted barrier did not give the first time, but the second swing broke the bubble with a loud burst. She beaned one of the Distorted smack in the head, and then made a running charge at Merros.

"Chiriku, stop!" Desert Rain shouted.

It was too late. Chiriku lost her footing on the slippery deck, and Merros turned his hand on her, sending a rock-hard blast of water straight at her. The Quetzalin went flying in the vicious torrent, and it slammed her against the mast of the boat. The water blast lingered on her to the near point of drowning her, but Merros cease his attack right before she passed out. Chiriku sputtered, coughed, gasped for air, but was too shaken to stand. One of the Distorted came over and grabbed her, dragging her limp body across the deck and threw her back into the cluster with the others.

"What do we do?" Goude growled. He was as shaken as his little brother, who whined restlessly.

"We have to take him out," Gabriel whispered in a conspiring tone. "If we could find a way to distract him for a second —"

Desert Rain put a hand on Gabriel's arm. "We can't fight him! That's Merros, a very powerful Hijn. What he did to Chiriku is not even the tip of what he can do to us. Let me try to get through to him."

"Desert Rain, talk isn't going to do any —"

"Let me try. Trust me."

Gabriel's lips tightened, but he reluctantly lowered his battlestaff. Desert Rain moved towards Merros, but the Distorted snapped at her. She stood her ground and spoke in the most authoritative voice she could muster. "Merros, you know me. I'm Desert Rain. You're a Hijn, like I am. You were taken by Katawa, and he's distorting your mind. Please, say something if you understand me."

The Ocean Hijn was silent. He lowered his hands and cocked his head sideways.

"Please, talk to me, Merros! Why are you doing this? What is it that you want?" Desert Rain persisted.

Merros made a sweeping hand gesture, and the Distorted

parted before Desert Rain. He advanced towards her, and for the first time it seemed that he truly saw her. He spoke in an oily voice, trying to speak over the globs of fluid. "De…ser…Rai…"

"Yes, yes, you remember me! Listen to me, Merros, I don't know what Katawa said to you, but it's a lie. He's poisoned your mind. He's not going to relieve you of your pain, no matter what you do for him. You must stop this. Let me help you—"

All of a sudden, Merros clutched his head and emitted an excruciating scream, falling to his knees. Fluid seeped out of his mouth, and his eyes rolled back into his head. His body shuddered, convulsed, and the purple handprints on his skin started to bubble. Desert Rain wanted to go to him, comfort him, but his state of torment was too much for her. The convulsions and screaming stopped as abruptly as it had started. Merros was limp for a moment, but then he raised his head. A funny smirk appeared on his face. He stood up and looked around. It was as if he was taking in these surroundings for the first time. His gaze settled back on Desert Rain. His smirk blossomed into a wicked smile.

"Ah, there's my desert flower," Merros said in a voice not his own. He caressed Desert Rain's cheek, and she stepped back from him quickly.

"Merros…" she started cautiously.

"Oh, come now, Desert Rain. You know who I am. You're such a clever girl."

Desert Rain's jaw dropped, and her whole body shook terribly. "Katawa…"

"Very good," the Merros puppet said, clapping his hands. "I can speak through others by my Distortion. An artist puts a little of himself into everything he creates. Although I wouldn't really call this 'art'," he noted, looking down at Merros's body. "More of a tool, I suppose."

"How…why…" Desert Rain clenched her hands into fists. "Let him go."

"You know I can't. There's so much work to be done, and my Hijn have quite a lot to do. I had the feeling one of them would come across you when I sent them out." He took another moment to look around, and he observed her companions closely. "Although I expected to find you with that green woman, not in the middle of the sea. What are you up to?"

Desert Rain was silent, which she tried to pass off as defiance, although it was truly fear.

Merros, or Katawa, scratched his chin. "It's a shame, actually. I was sort of hoping you'd still have the green one with you. I'm starting to regret giving her up. She could be useful to me—if not as a mage, as something more pleasurable…"

"Dragons damn you!" Desert Rain hollered. "You leave her alone! Leave *us* alone! We have nothing you want."

"Now I wouldn't say that." He cast his gaze among the group. "Hmm, that Quetzalin, and that man, and them—" He gestured to the Vermin brothers, "yes, they could be very useful to me as soldiers."

"Soldiers?" Desert Rain did not understand. "What do you need soldiers for? You already have the Hijn."

Merros chuckled. "Yes, but six Hijn against the entire Darkscale Court is a gamble. I like to have something to fall back on. As you can see, they're quite intimidating, and completely loyal." He petted the head of one of the Distorted creatures.

Desert Rain shuddered, staring into the pain-filled eyes of the Distorted. "How can you do this…they're innocent people…"

"Innocent?" Merros laughed between his gritted teeth. "Let me explain to you the whole illusion of 'innocent.' While you've spent your whole life with your head in the sand, you haven't seen how despicable people truly are. I've seen it. I've lived it! This, my art, is the proof of it. These innocents, as you call them, are as deformed as they already were on the inside. No more, no less."

"Liar!" Desert Rain's green eye flashed. "This is not who they really are. They have been marred by your insane imagination! What good are they to you, other than pets? They have no magic of their own. They'll do you no good fighting the Darkscale!"

The Merros puppet smirked at the flash in her eye. "I would think you would appreciate this, Desert Rain. After all, if the Darkscale are distracted by an army of my Distorted, my Hijn are better protected. Besides, the Darkscale are all cowards, all of them. It's pitiful that the Knighthood defeats them at every turn. Now I can finally put them all to rest, out of their miserable existence."

Chiriku by now had regained her senses, and she pushed her way through to stand by Desert Rain. "You want to mess with us? Then come and get it," she hissed.

"No, Chiriku! We can't fight him! That's still Merros's body. And those creatures were — *are* — people!" Desert Rain pushed Chiriku back. She turned towards Merros. "You tell me all this so openly. Are you so sure you can't be stopped? I'll tell the Knighthood about all of this — "

The Merros puppet snickered, coming over and placing his hands on Desert Rain's stiff shoulders. "Tell them, if you want. You ask, so I answer you. You're my golden girl, after all." He massaged the tips of her ears, and she flinched away from him. He grinned. "It doesn't matter much, anyway. My Hijn have collected many good specimens for me, and they'll continue to collect as many as I like. Sooner or later, they'll find your little green friend and bring her back to me, where she belongs. They'll find the other missing Hijn. And then, of course, there's you…"

Desert Rain felt something slip down her arm and stop around her wrist. She could feel the cool, soothing metal—it was the shaman's bracelet. She shimmied the bracelet off her wrist, catching it with her long fingers and holding it in her hand. It began to feel hot, as if energy was flowing through it.

She remembered the shaman's words. *It will protect you for the time being…*

"What *about* me?" she asked. "Are you going to do to me what you did to Merros and the others?"

"Oh, I don't know about that," he replied. He pulled her close. He could see how uncomfortable she was, especially seeing how it was Merros's body that was holding her. "Although, it was exhilarating to watch you squirm beneath my grasp while you screamed and begged me for mercy. To feel the blood pumping through your body, the heat of your fear…"

"Can you feel me right now? The real you, wherever you are?" she asked.

Merros paused, but then grinned. "Yes, I feel you as much as if it were me standing beside you right now."

"Then feel this!" She slammed the bracelet against Merros's forehead, creating a shock of golden lightning that rippled throughout his body. Merros shrieked in pain, and the electric blast shot him back, sending him sprawling across the deck of the ship. The Distorted howled at the golden light, shrinking away as it burned their eyes. Now that the Distorted were distracted,

Gabriel swung at one of them, knocking it to the floor, and dug the end of his battlestaff into the creature's eye until it drove through with a wet "pop."

"Gabriel, those are people!" Desert Rain reiterated in panic.

"They aren't people anymore. We don't have any choice. That Hijn and these monsters are under the demon's control. We have to fight them," Gabriel said.

"No! It's not Merros's fault Katawa has done this to him! There must be a way to snap him out of it!"

The Distorted broke into a charge. Chiriku beaned one smack in the face with her warhammer, but another caught her by her pant leg and yanked her to the floor. Gabriel thwacked his battlestaff at any Distorted who came his way. Mac and the Vermins made a mad dash for the ropes of the ship, climbing up them towards the mast with the frenzied speed of frightened mice. Three of the Distorted pursued them, struggling as their twisted limbs tried to keep a firm hold on the ropes as they climbed.

Desert Rain was not being attacked by the Distorted, most likely because they were afraid of her now. She watched as Merros staggered to his feet, a burned circle mark on his forehead. His eyes had lost the cunning wickedness of Katawa, but now they were wild, thoughtless, ravenous.

Chiriku bashed the Distorted holding her. She got to her feet, looking over at Merros. "Is that demon still in him?"

"No, Katawa's gone," Desert Rain replied, sliding her bracelet back onto her arm. "But that's the least of our worries."

The coiling serpent mark in Merros' palm shined with a vibrant light, like a blue flame, and he raised his hands above his head as he intoned a sharp, guttural Dragontongue spell. Desert Rain could already feel the immense energy behind that magic, could feel the ripples of power pulsate with each word Merros spoke. She heard the rumble, the increased lapping of the waves, the boat swaying dangerously again.

The waters of the ocean swelled up at the hull of the ship. It began as a tidal wave, rushing higher and higher, roaring in its strength. The wave took on a form — it thickened, swelled, spread its newly grown arms, rose its faceless head. Water ran down the length of its body, as if it was continually bleeding, but it grew larger in size. Everyone, even the Distorted, froze as they saw the water titan, as tall as five ships, loom over them, its shadow casting a blue-green sheen over all below.

The Vermins, clinging to the ship's ropes for their lives, simultaneously screamed in fright at the water titan. Mac's eyes bulged out of his head, and from his panic sweat he turned pink all over. "What in g-g-great g-gurgling swamp muck-kk is th-that?" he stammered.

Desert Rain was petrified. She wished at that moment that she could use the Blueshine on herself, for being instantly shattered into little pieces sounded better than being smashed by a water titan.

The water titan bent down, its body pouring heavy rain down over the boat, and cupped its massive hands around the vessel. It lifted the ship clear out of the water, as if it were a toy boat in the titan's bath tub. The sudden upward rush caused everyone to lose their footing, and they were glued to the deck under the pressure of the lift. When Desert Rain could raise her head again, she looked to find Merros was no longer on the deck.

"Up there!" Gabriel called.

Upon the titan's shoulder, floating on the water, was Merros, his expression blank. No one could guess whether he was preparing to command his titan to smash, crush, throw or tip the ship upside down to spill out its passengers. The titan brought the ship to be level with its head, and Desert Rain could surmise by how tall the titan was that abandoning ship at this height would be a fatal fall.

One idea popped into Desert Rain's head, and it was perhaps the weirdest one she could had thought up. She dug into her pocket for the black pouch, yanking it out and practically tearing it open as she yelled, "Gothart, I'm open to any suggestions you might have right now!!"

Out of the bag poked a little mechanical toy goat's head, blinking tiredly.

"Suggestions for what?" the toy Gothart asked, stretching its little arms and yawning. He looked up and took in the water titan's head, with its three depressions for eye sockets and a gaping mouth. Gothart's eyes sprung out of his head on coiled springs as he bleated at the top of his little lungs, and almost in the same instant, the wind-up key in his back transformed into a little propeller. It twirled rapidly, lifting him out of the bag and into the air.

"What are you doing?!" Desert Rain yelled after him.

"You're on your own, dear," the toy goat answered, flying out of Desert Rain's reach. He propelled himself up and away, zipping off into the sky.

Desert Rain had nothing left. She couldn't even think of the words of Blueshine, even if that could have helped her in this situation. All she could do was squeeze her eyes shut and clasp her hands together tightly. *Great Guerda-Shalyr, or anyone who might hear me, please, please save them — even if it means my life, please save my friends!!*

The wind picked up aggressively. It spun around the ship like an invisible whirlpool, causing everyone on deck to be blown this way and that way. The Distorted that had pursued Mac and the Vermins up the ropes lost their grip and fell to the deck, while the lizard and the three brothers hung on to the rigging with every ounce of strength they had. The titan froze as if it had become ice, and Merros snapped his head around like a startled animal.

"What is he doing now??" Chiriku squawked, trying desperately to keep her balance.

Desert Rain caught onto Chiriku, hoping that they could help keep each other balanced. "Merros can't be doing this. He has power over water, not the wind."

A violent gust of wind drove into the water titan's face, punching a hole clean through it. Then another, and another blast bore into the titan. A wind strike to the shoulder caused Merros to almost fall off, and to lose his concentration. The water titan started to dissolve, and it dropped the ship clean out of the air. Everyone on board screamed as the boat plummeted towards the ocean, sure to be obliterated on the rough, hard waters.

The ship did not smash down into the ocean. In mid-air, its fall slowed, as if sinking into a soft cushion. Desert Rain cautiously opened her eyes, clinging with all her strength to Chiriku, who was clinging onto her as well. She blinked and looked around. She saw a cyclone whooshing around the ship. The cyclone settled the ship down onto the ocean, causing a slight rocking as the boat regained its balance on the water.

From out of the sky dropped a diminutive figure, and it came to hover right in front of Desert Rain. It was a Yopeis-Gichen, with two appendages shaped like gliding fish pectoral fins extending out to the sides of his head just above his small round ears, which allowed him to float on the wind like a kite. He possessed all the typical characteristics of a Yopeis: the ear-fins, the little pearlescent face, the soft scales covering his scalp and backside, and the four-foot height. His buttercream-yellow scale color, however, was a hue no Yopeis possessed naturally – most were green, obsidian, silver or blue-gray. He also wore full attire, which was rare for a Yopeis - he dressed in a leather overcoat with matching boots and gloves that were far too large for his little four-fingered hands, a green vest tied in the front with red ribbon laces, and a pair of bright red trousers that covered his limber legs. Most notable were his long white "whiskers," which were modified illicia like those of anglerfish. Each illicium possessed a pearl-like bulb on the tip. Two of these illicia stemmed from his eyebrows, and two from each side of his nose, and each had the sensitivity to sense each of the four winds. The only Yopeis to have such a trait was the Hijn of the Winds, local protector of the Rings of Springs.

"HiDesertRainhowareyoudoing?" Woasim asked, landing gently on the deck. The Wind Hijn rambled at a pace often too fast to be clearly understood.

"Woasim!" Desert Rain was stunned. "Wh…where did you come from?"

"NiceboatyouhavehereneverthoughtI'dseeyouallthewayout hereoooohwhatarethosethey'renotveryfriendlylookingarethey?" Woasim twitched his long whiskers, wrinkling his nose at the Distorted surrounding him. He didn't seem afraid of them, but curious, even though the Distorted were bearing their jagged teeth at him.

Desert Rain was going to tell Woasim to get off the ship, but before she could say anything, the Wind Hijn inhaled deeply and unleashed a gale-force blow towards the Distorted. For one so small, Woasim's gust of breath was so strong that it sent all the Distorted sliding backwards across the deck like scraps of rice paper. With one final huff, Woasim lifted all the Distorted up into the air, over the ship's rail and dropped them like pebbles into the ocean.

"Ihopeyoudon'tmindthatIgotridofthosethingsbuttheydidn't seemverynice.Let'sseewhat'sgoingonhere." Woasim whisked himself away on his currents of wind, up towards the head of the water titan, where Merros still stood.

"Woasim, wait! Merros is not himself!" Desert Rain's words could not catch up to the quick-flying Wind Hijn.

"What is he doing here?" Gabriel called to her.

"He's the Wind Whisperer. He's another Hijn. He can help us," Desert Rain assured him. *But he has a bad habit of leaping before he looks*, she thought.

Woasim brought himself to hover before Merros, who stared menacingly at him. The Wind Hijn apparently did not notice the ferocity in the Ocean Rider's eyes. "HeyMerrosoldbuddywhatareyoudoing?That'sareallygreatwatergi antyougottheredidyouseeDesertRaindowntherebutanywaydidImis sanythingatthemeetingI'msorryIcouldn'tmakeitbutI — "

Woasim was cut off by a strong gush of water to his face. He rolled through the air head over heels but summoned a cushion of air to keep himself aloft. Before he could finish rubbing the salt water out of his wide, owllike eyes, the titan's hand came down on him, slamming him down onto the ship's deck with bone-crunching force. The hand held him down, entrapping Woasim underwater, the pressure not allowing the Wind Hijn to free himself.

Desert Rain slipped and slided over to try and pull Woasim

out from the titan's hand, but the water poured down the arm like a waterfall, and it was flooding the deck and making the boat start to sink. The rush was too great for her to reach her arm through it.

Gabriel tramped his way through the flooding water and drove his battlestaff through the titan's hand towards the floundering body of Woasim. The battlestaff was long enough to tap Woasim's head, and the Wind Hijn grabbed on as soon as he felt it. With a tremendous pull, with Desert Rain and Chiriku helping, they managed to free Woasim from the deadly water.

"Woasim! Are you all right?" Desert Rain asked breathlessly.

Woasim's ear-fins were wrapped around his face, having created a sort of air pocket while he had been underwater. He retracted his fins and shook his head. "WhydidMerrosdothathe'ssuchaniceguyandIdidn'tdoanythingIjus taskedhowhewasdoingandhetriedtohavethatgiantswishme—"

Chiriku slapped a hand over Woasim's mouth. "Stop talking," she said.

"Merros is under possession of Katawa," Desert Rain explained, knowing Woasim would stay still long enough if she kept it short. "He's not himself, and there's nothing we can do for him. You have to get us all out of here, Woasim, right now!"

Woasim's whiskers shivered as Chiriku removed her hand from his lips. "Merroshasto…" He swallowed, taking a deep breath. He tried his best to slow down. "Merros has to remember who *I* am. We're best friends. I'll jog his memory a little. Be back in a flash." He was up and off again before anyone could stop him.

"He's going to get us all killed!" Gabriel fumed.

The Water Hijn's titan swatted at the zipping Yopeis, who shot gusts of wind at the giant in defense. While the Water Hijn and Wind Hijn dueled, the cog rocked wildly on the plain of battle, staying afloat with a wing and a prayer. The longer the Hijn battled, the more infuriated they both became. The waters became rougher, the wind swirled harder and faster. The overwhelming energy of magic being exerted made the air heavy and hot, making every person on the ship tremble and unable to breathe. The Vermins and Mac, who had made their way to the mast and had been grasping desperately to it, were too caught up in the hurricane, and were ripped from the boat and sent tumbling about in the sky. Desert Rain felt such a crushing weight from the magic that she couldn't even speak, and she dropped to her hands and knees, thinking her body was going to implode.

She saw a glow shining in front of her. Squinting through the wind and water smothering the air, she could see that the shine was coming from the black pouch, lying on the deck. She was not sure how it had got there, as she could not even remember dropping it. She reached for it, looking into the glowing mouth of the pouch. Reaching in, she grasped the hilt of Silverheart, which radiated such a warm, empowering light, it instantly removed the magical pressure from her. She freed the sword from its velvet sheath, its weight no more than if it had been made of straw. She swore she heard voices coming from that sword, voices of authority and power, voices of purity and life, voices of despair and death. It was the chorus of everything and nothing. She felt the sword lighten even more — it was rising out of her hands. She fought to maintain her grasp on Silverheart, entwining the fingers of both her hands around the hilt. She gritted her teeth, and her whole body shook wildly.

Was this Purelight? It couldn't be. Desert Rain did not have the power of Purelight, and Skyhan was not here. It was not as if

Skyhan had passed that power on to her.

Or…had he…?

A force erupted out of Silverheart. The might of it caused Desert Rain's body to jerk back violently, yet she did not let go. She was as rooted and petrified as an oak tree. She watched as the white blaze engulfed all in her sight, radiated up towards the two battling Hijn, who stopped dead at the sight of it. The light pulsated and brightened so that Desert Rain thought she had gone blind. Through that blazing fiery light, she saw it—a shape morphing out of the light, writhing as if it were alive.

Yes, she knew that shape. The equine head, the long neck, the world-encompassing wings. She had seen it the last time Skyhan had used Purelight on Katawa, but now she was standing right under it. She could make out a brawny body, with great arms and legs, and a lashing tail that could smash the boat with a single swat. It was all so brilliant that she was not sure if she was truly seeing it, but she could make out that this great being was covered in shining, white-scaled plating.

The magic was too great. This light, combined with the water and wind magic, was like a dam bursting. Desert Rain could no longer breathe, and she felt all the feeling leaving her body. She closed her eyes, knowing that this power was ripping the life out of her.

*It's too much…*she thought. *It's too much for me…*

A voice, as terrible as thunder but soft as snow, came to her. *Perhaps…but you will learn, bearer of the Moonstone. You will learn…*

She felt her body falling back…

***

Desert Rain slowly opened her eyes.

Everything around her was still, quiet, and dark. Her body was suspended, drifting in an atmosphere of coolness and tranquility. She could see whisps of her hair float around her face, and everything was in slow motion. A light shown above her, far away, and shadows flitted past the light, swimming in graceful form. Desert Rain's brain was fuzzy. She could not think clearly, but she could see that all around her was awash in shades of blues.

So, this is the Eternal Deep, she thought. *It's how I thought it would be, except it's so empty. I thought this place would be crowded with souls, unless I've been sent to some secluded part of the Eternal Deep. The place that people with broken souls go.*

She was not alone. Coming down from the light was a figure, shining with all the radiance of a star. It descended upon her, its arms beckoning to her. It was a man, encased in pearly armor, his face hidden by a metallic mask. His silvery hair floated behind him, and his warm eyes invited her, called to her.

He...he is here! Desert Rain felt peace and happiness wrap around her. She reached up towards the Swordmaster, praying that she would not pass right through him. But they were on the same plane now...she must be able to touch him.

Her hand grasped his, and it was warm to the touch. He drew her up towards him, into the light he shined...

He reached down and threw aside the piece of derbis that was pushing her down.

That was when Desert Rain snapped back into reality and realized she was drowning. The coolness of her surroundings was suddenly ice cold, and everything focused into sharp clarity. Gabriel held her close in his arms and kicked his way back up towards the surface of the water. Before Desert Rain's lungs burst, they broke through the surface, and both gasped for air. Desert Rain floated limply as Gabriel swam with her in one arm. He hoisted her up onto a slat of wood, and she sputtered as Gabriel pulled himself up beside her. Once her sight cleared, she saw that they were floating on a section of the *S.S. Vermin*, and other pieces of the cog were bobbing in the water around them.

"Are you all right?" Gabriel asked, rubbing her arm.

Desert Rain nodded weakly, although she was far from all right. "Wh…what happened?"

Gabriel sighed, shaking his head. "All I remember was an exploding light, and then waking up underwater."

"The others…where are the others?"

"Hey there!" In response to Desert Rain's question, Mac Lizard came bobbing by in a barrel, his rear end stuck inside and his legs dangling over the edge. His hair—yes, hair, for he had once again assumed a human physique—was wet and plastered to his forehead. Yet for his miserable appearance, he smiled over at his friends. "That was something! I would've enjoyed that-tkk more if I had known I would live through it-tkk."

"You crazy reptile!" The familiar gruff voice came from Chiriku, who was clinging to a floating piece of wood. Now her feathers were even more brown, most of her blue dye having been washed away. "We get blown up, and you think it was fun?"

"No sense-ssck in moping about it, since we're alive. Need a hand there?"

Chiriku glowered at Mac. "Find me a bigger piece of wood to grab onto, will ya? This water's freezing!"

Desert Rain breathed a sigh of relief at seeing her friends all right. She looked around at the rest of the remains of the *S.S. Vermin*. She turned to Gabriel. "Did you find the Vermins? And

Woasim? Or Merros?"

Gabriel shook his head.

Desert Rain was too numb to panic. She took a minute to regain her breath and wiped her wet hair out of her face. She looked into Gabriel's eyes, those comforting blue eyes, the ones that had saved her. The ones that had called to her, pulled her out of the depths of darkness. Those eyes—they were hope. Her hope. Even now, in this moment of unknown circumstances, she felt that the others were still alive, that they would be okay. Mac and Chiriku had survived—surely the others did too.

"You...*are* him," she whispered.

Gabriel squinted his eyes, either from confusion or exhaustion. He looked away from her, flipping up the hood of his cloak over his face as he had lost his hat. He reached for a plank drifting nearby. He started paddling with it. "You rest now. We need to get to shore."

Desert Rain clasped him by the arms, turning him to look straight into his eyes. "You are *him*," she insisted.

Gabriel sighed, and shook his head. "You think I'm someone else. I'm not."

Desert Rain's grip slackened. "You have to be him. For me. Then I can get through this. You have to be him...let me believe."

She rested her head on his chest, closing her eyes. He held her, whether for her safety or her comfort, she did not know. Gabriel gently rocked her as they drifted on the calm, open waters, unsure of their course, unsure of their fate. Despite it all, Desert Rain, for the first time, let hope fill her entire being, let it give her renewed strength deep within.

Let me believe...

End of Book Two.

A native of Riverside, Illinois, **A.R. Cook** currently resides in Gainesville, Georgia, and is the author of the YA fantasy series *The Scholar and the Sphinx*. She also has short stories published in the anthology "The Kress Project" from the Georgia Museum of Art, and the fairy-tale collections "Willow Weep No More" and "Shadows of the Oak" from Tenebris Books. From 2009-2013, A.R. was the book review columnist for the *Gainesville Times*, one of the most widely distributed newspapers in northeastern Georgia.

Visit **http://scholarandsphinx.wix.com/arcook** to learn more.

www.ingramcontent.com/pod-product-compliance
Lightning Source LLC
Chambersburg PA
CBHW061017120726
47910CB00006B/1981